SEX, LIES &
SERIOUS MONEY

BOOKS BY STUART WOODS

FICTION

Sex, Lies & Serious Money†
Smooth Operator**
(with Parnell Hall)
Dishonorable Intentions†
Family Jewels†
Scandalous Behavior†
Foreign Affairs†
Naked Greed†
Hot Pursuit†
Insatiable Appetites†
Paris Match†
Cut and Thrust†
Carnal Curiosity†
Standup Guy†
Doing Hard Time†
Unintended Consequences†
Collateral Damage†
Severe Clear†
Unnatural Acts†
D.C. Dead†
Son of Stone†
Bel-Air Dead†
Strategic Moves†

Santa Fe Edge§
Lucid Intervals†
Kisser†
Hothouse Orchid*
Loitering with Intent†
Mounting Fears‡
Hot Mahogany†
Santa Fe Dead§
Beverly Hills Dead
Shoot Him If He Runs†
Fresh Disasters†
Short Straw§
Dark Harbor†
Iron Orchid*
Two-Dollar Bill†
The Prince of Beverly Hills
Reckless Abandon†
Capital Crimes‡
Dirty Work†
Blood Orchid*
The Short Forever†
Orchid Blues*

Cold Paradise†
L.A. Dead†
The Run‡
Worst Fears Realized†
Orchid Beach*
Swimming to Catalina†
Dead in the Water†
Dirt†
Choke
Imperfect Strangers
Heat
Dead Eyes
L.A. Times
Santa Fe Rules§
New York Dead†
Palindrome
Grass Roots‡
White Cargo
Deep Lie‡
Under the Lake
Run Before the Wind‡
Chiefs‡

TRAVEL

A Romantic's Guide to the Country Inns of Britain and Ireland (1979)

MEMOIR

Blue Water, Green Skipper

*A Holly Barker Novel
†A Stone Barrington Novel
‡A Will Lee Novel

§An Ed Eagle Novel
**A Teddy Fay Novel

SEX, LIES & SERIOUS MONEY

STUART WOODS

G. P. PUTNAM'S SONS
Publishers Since 1838
An imprint of Penguin Random House LLC
375 Hudson Street
New York, New York 10014

Library of Congress Cataloging-in-Publication Data

Names: Woods, Stuart, author.
Title: Sex, lies & serious money / Stuart Woods.
Description: New York : G. P. Putnam's Sons, 2016.
Identifiers: LCCN 2016035355 | ISBN 9780399573941
Subjects: LCSH: Barrington, Stone (Fictitious character)—Fiction. | Private
Investigators—Fiction. | BISAC: FICTION / Action & Adventure. | FICTION /
Suspense. | FICTION / Thrillers. | GSAFD: Suspense fiction. | Adventure
fiction.
Classification: LCC PS3573.O642 S49 2016 | DDC 813/.54—dc23
LC record available at https://lccn.loc.gov/2016035355
p.   cm.

Printed in the United States of America
1 3 5 7 9 10 8 6 4 2

BOOK DESIGN BY LUCIA BERNARD

THIS BOOK IS FOR SHAYNE SANGERMAN.

SEX, LIES &
SERIOUS MONEY

STONE BARRINGTON LANDED at Teterboro Airport, having flown nonstop from Santa Fe, with a good tailwind. He and Bob, his Labrador retriever, were met by Fred Flicker, his factotum, at the airport. Bob threw himself at Fred. After a moment's happy reunion, they were transferred to Stone's car.

Stone had spent most of the flight trying to put Gala Wilde out of his mind after their breakup. He had not succeeded.

They arrived at Stone's house in Turtle Bay and Fred pulled into the garage. Stone got out of the car to be greeted by his secretary, Joan Robertson, but Bob got there first and did his happy dance.

"There's somebody waiting to see you," Joan said.

"Anybody I know?"

"Apparently a friend of somebody you know in Palm Beach."

Stone's circle of acquaintances in Palm Beach was not wide. "Dicky Chalmers?"

"Right."

"Give me a minute, then send him in." Stone went into his office, rummaged among the mail and messages on his desk and found a pink message slip.

Stone, I'm sending you somebody you will find interesting.

Dicky

Stone looked up to see a young man standing in his doorway: late twenties or early thirties, unkempt hair, scraggly beard, dressed in a current style Stone thought of as "adolescent lumberjack"—checkered shirt, tail out, greasy jeans, sneakers, hoodie, top down.

"Mr. Barrington?"

"Come in," Stone said, "and have a seat."

"Your friend Richard Chalmers suggested I should see you."

"How are the Chalmerses?"

"Dicky and Vanessa are very well."

"Do you have a name?"

"Sorry. I'm Laurence Hayward." He spelled both names.

"Larry, to your friends?"

"Laurence, if you please." He sounded vaguely English when he said that.

"Laurence, it is. I'm Stone, and this is Bob." Bob came over and sniffed the young man, accepted a scratching of the ears, then went to his bed and lay down. "How can I help you, Laurence?"

"I'm being pursued," Laurence replied.

"Pursued by whom?"

"Everybody."

Oh, God, Stone thought, not one of those. He took a deep breath. "Well, Laurence, why don't we start with your telling me about yourself?"

"What would you like to know?"

"Sixty-second bio."

"All right. I'm thirty years old. I was born in West Palm Beach, Florida. When I was eight, my mother, who was the manager of a small hotel in our community, was swept off her feet by an Englishman, who was an investor in the hotel. She subsequently divorced my father, married the Brit, and he took the two of us to live in England, where, except for summers, when I visited my father, I grew up. In fact, I became, for all practical purposes, English, including my accent."

"I thought I caught a bit of that."

"My American accent comes back when I'm here."

"Go on."

"I was educated at my stepfather's old schools, Eton and Oxford, and after I graduated, I became a tutor at Eton, later an assistant master, teaching English and art history. My stepfather has a successful advertising agency, and I had no interest in a career in his company or any other business."

Fred knocked on the door and stepped in. "Shall I take your bags up, sir?"

"Please, Fred. Oh, and this is Mr. Laurence Hayward."

"How do you do?" Laurence said, becoming English, and they shook hands.

"Fred, what is Laurence's accent?" Stone asked.

"Eton and Oxford, I should think," Fred replied.

"Thank you, Fred. You can take the bags up. I'll be here for a while."

Fred departed.

"That was remarkable, the way Fred picked up on my accent."

"Fred is very good at speaking and recognizing British accents of all sorts," Stone said. "On with your bio."

"I took a leave of absence from Eton and came home to Palm Beach a couple of months ago, after my father fell ill. He had moved to the island from West Palm some years ago as his legal practice grew."

"What sort of legal practice?"

"Real estate. He spent most of his day closing sales and mortgages. Did quite well at it, and used the job to find good investment opportunities in real estate. He died three weeks ago."

"I'm sorry for your loss."

"Thank you. He was good friends with the Chalmerses, who were his neighbors until they bought the big house on the beach, and they visited him often during his illness. I've known them most of my life."

"All right, let's get to the pursuit part."

"A week or so ago, I bought a lottery ticket, then forgot about it. Then I saw the winning number in the local paper, and I remembered I had one. I checked the numbers, and they matched. I called in at the lottery office in West Palm Beach, and this morning, after some days for them to investigate and see that I was who I said I was, I received the check. I also learned that, in Florida, there's a state law against concealing the identity of the winner. I've quickly learned that a great many people have an untoward interest in lottery winners, thus the pursuit. They released my name early this morning, and when I left their office, I was surrounded by media people and others who had come to beg for money. I got out of there as quickly as I could, and when I turned on the car radio, I heard my name on the air. I drove to Palm Beach International Airport, where I had taken flying lessons, and somebody I know there found me a seat on an executive charter flight to Teterboro, for only five thousand dollars."

"What kind of airplane?"

"A Gulfstream 450."

"How did you do in the lottery?"

Laurence reached into a pocket and handed Stone a crumpled envelope. "There were two other winners, in Texas and Washington state, so I got only a third after they took out the taxes."

Stone opened the envelope wide enough to read the sum. "Very nice," he said. "What are you going to do with it?"

"There are some things I'd like to buy, and Dicky thought you might advise me on how to invest the rest of it."

"What do you want to buy?"

"Well, I think I'll need some clothes."

"Good idea," Stone said drily.

"Oh, I know I'm not appropriately dressed for the Upper East Side of New York. My good clothes are all in England and Palm Beach. I'll need some suits and jackets, I think."

"Anything else?"

"Perhaps a car?"

"What sort of car?"

"A Porsche, perhaps."

"Good choice."

"Oh, and I'd like to buy a New York apartment."

"That seems within your means, depending on the neighborhood," Stone observed. "What sort of apartment did you have in mind?"

Laurence produced a folded newspaper page and handed it to Stone. It was half a page from the real estate section of the previous Sunday's *New York Times*. "This one," he said.

"Oh, yes, I saw this. It's the penthouse of an old hotel on Park Avenue that has been remodeled and gone condo. Problem is, Laurence, the asking price for the apartment is twenty-two million dollars, but your check is for six hundred and twelve thousand. Do you have other means I'm not aware of?"

"Perhaps you'd better have another look at the check."

Stone removed the check from the envelope, read it, and gulped. *"Six hundred and twelve million dollars?"*

"You missed a few zeros the first time," Laurence said.

"And this is a third of the prize?"

"It was the biggest Powerball ever."

STONE TOOK ANOTHER deep breath.

"The limo driver from Teterboro this morning recognized me," Laurence said. "I can't go anywhere. It's crazy."

"How long has this been going on?"

"Since this morning—that's when I went to the lottery office."

"I heard it mentioned on TV, but I didn't get the details."

"It seems that a lot of other people did."

"All right," Stone said, "we've covered the clothes, the car, and the apartment. What else do you have in mind?"

"Art and American antique furniture," Laurence replied. "Dicky and Vanessa turned me on to that—their house is full of it. There's a big show on at the Park Avenue Armory."

"Is that it?"

"For the moment. Oh, and I'd like to write a nice check to Habitat for Humanity. I volunteered to help build half a dozen of their houses during my summers in Palm Beach."

"Good. Here are the things I think you should do, starting tomorrow morning. First, we need to get that check into a bank, because every day you wait will cost you considerable income in interest. Then we need to get you introduced to some investment advisors. I want to introduce you to a young partner at my law firm, Woodman & Weld. His name is Herb Fisher, and he will handle all the details of your plans. You will also need an accountant."

"What bank do you recommend?"

"M&T Bank, which has a branch in my firm's building, and which owns an investment company called Wilmington Trust. They were, originally, the DuPont family bank, and they handle the investments of high-end clients. You certainly qualify as that. Also, they have a branch in North Palm Beach, and your accounts should be based there, in order to protect you from being taxed as a resident of New York State. It helps that you were born in Florida. Did your father own a home there?"

"Yes, on Australian Avenue. It was his only home, and he had put it into a trust for me."

"Good. Another thing is, to protect your anonymity, we should set up a Florida corporation in which you can hold large assets, like your apartment. Think of a name for it."

Laurence thought about it. "The LBH Corporation—my initials?"

"Fine." Stone looked at his watch. "We need to get you a disguise, in the form of some barbering, I think."

"Okay."

He buzzed his secretary. "Joan, see if José at Nico's can take a new customer immediately—haircut, shave, mani-pedi, facial. Book him in as Mr. Jones."

"Okay."

"I need all of that?" Laurence asked.

"All of it. I'm going to set up a viewing of your prospective apartment tomorrow, and you need to look as though you can afford it."

Joan buzzed. "They can take Mr. Jones in fifteen minutes."

"Fine. Get Fred to drive him and wait for him. Laurence, do you have any other clothes?"

"I've got a blue blazer and some khakis."

"Where are they?"

"Right here, in my bag."

Stone held up the lottery check. "And I think we should put this in my safe overnight."

"Fine."

"Do you have any cash?"

"About seven thousand dollars. My father kept it in his safe. I used the rest to pay for the airplane ride."

"Let's put six thousand of it in the safe, too. A thousand ought to get you through the next day or two."

Laurence opened his bag, a small duffel, and handed Stone a thick wad of money, secured with a rubber band. "I've got a thousand in my pocket." He went to change, and Stone opened his safe and secured the check and the cash.

Laurence came back looking more presentable. "I think I'm going to need a secretary. And I guess I should ask about your legal fees."

"Oh," Stone said, handing him a printed sheet of paper. "This is a list of my and my firm's legal fees. Please look it over when you have a chance."

Laurence scanned the document, folded it, and put it in his pocket. "I can afford you," he said.

"Good. I'll see what I can do about the secretary. Fred is waiting out front with the car. He'll bring you back when you're done at Nico's. You can leave your bag here."

"I guess I'll need a hotel room, until I have an apartment."

"You can bunk here. I've got a lot of extra room."

"Thank you."

"Get going. I'll start setting up our day for tomorrow."

Laurence left and Stone called Herbie Fisher.

"Herbert Fisher."

"It's Stone. I have a new client for you."

"Okay, who?"

"One Laurence B. Hayward of Palm Beach, Florida."

"What does Mr. Hayward do?"

Stone thought about that. "Let's call him an investor, which he will be, starting tomorrow. And get us a meeting tomorrow morning at nine, nine-thirty, with Conrad Trilling at Wilmington Trust."

"Can I mention Mr. Hayward's net worth?"

"Let's surprise him. Tell him to go ahead and set up a checking account." He gave Herbie Laurence's address in Palm Beach. "The account should be at their North Palm Beach branch. Tell him we'll be making a large deposit, and ask him to call somebody at American Express and get Mr. Hayward a Centurion card instantly. He'll need a Visa card from the bank, too, and an ATM card. He's got a couple of hours before they close."

"Okay, anything else?"

"Mr. Hayward is going to need a secretary. Anybody we can steal from the firm without putting anyone's nose out of joint?"

"Funny you should mention that. You remember that one of our senior partners died about three months ago?"

"Frank Penny?"

"Right. His secretary is Margery Mason. They've kept her on to clean up Penny's affairs, and she's about done."

"Dark hair, going gray, mid-forties, on the plump side?"

"That's the one, and they've been slow to reassign her. The partners seem to go for the more fashionable-looking women."

"She's ideal. Talk to her, will you? Find out what she's making, so we can top it."

"Right."

"Oh, and set up a Florida company for Laurence called the LBH Corporation, to house some assets."

"Right away."

"He wants to buy an apartment in the old Fairleigh Hotel, on Park Avenue, that went condo. Get ahold of their prospectus and have a look at their standard contract. We should be ready for a quick closing, if he likes the place."

"Is he, by any chance, considering the one that was featured in the *Times* real estate section last Sunday?"

"How'd you guess?"

"Magic. I hear the apartments have gone quickly, but they're having trouble moving that penthouse. Most of the apartments are two, three bedrooms and three or four to a floor, but the penthouse takes up the whole fifteenth floor. My advice is, haggle."

"Absolutely. I'll have Mr. Hayward at Wilmington Trust at nine tomorrow morning. Meet us downstairs."

"Will do. Are you going to tell *me* Mr. Hayward's net worth?"

"I'll surprise you, too. And he likes to be called Laurence."

Stone buzzed Joan. "Please call Theresa Crane, a personal shopper at the Ralph Lauren store on Fifth Avenue at, what is it—Fifty-fifth?"

"Close enough."

"And set up an appointment for Laurence Hayward"—he spelled it for her—"at, say, ten-thirty AM tomorrow."

"Right. Anything else?"

"Yes, be prepared for anything, and be prepared to handle it fast."

"What else is new?" she asked.

"Oh, and ask Helene to get the big guest room on three ready. We'll be dining tonight in my study."

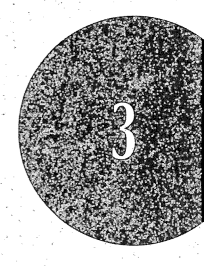

STONE'S PHONE BUZZED.

"Conrad Trilling for you on one," Joan said.

"How are you, Conrad?"

"Very well, Stone. I understand you're bringing us a prospective client tomorrow morning—a Mr. Laurence Hayward of Palm Beach?"

"That is correct."

"I hope you're sitting down, Stone, because I have some bad news for you—you've been had."

"Oh? How?"

"Mr. Laurence Hayward of Australian Avenue, Palm Beach, died three weeks ago. Didn't you think we'd check up on him?"

"That was his father."

"Laurence C. Hayward?"

"The son is Laurence B. Hayward."

"Well, Laurence C. owned a house at that address, which is valued at three million, and he has less than two million in liquid assets, so where is Mr. Laurence B. getting this large deposit he's making to-morrow?" The sound of computer keys clicking could be heard on the phone.

"All will be revealed tomorrow morning, Conrad."

"And I must tell you, Stone, that Mr. Laurence B. Hayward has no credit record to speak of—only a MasterCard, with an okay payment record, and no employer, either."

"That's because he's been living mostly in England since he was eight years old, and he is now thirty. If you'd like to check his credit over there, his employer is Eton College, where he is an assistant master and of which he is an old boy. He came to the States to attend his sick father three or four months ago."

"One moment." More computer keys. "Good news, Stone, the fellow exists! He also has an account at Coutts Bank, which speaks well of him, but it's small potatoes."

"Conrad, would you prefer it if I took him elsewhere?"

"I would prefer it if I knew more about him before I press American Express to deliver a Centurion card instantly."

"Conrad, have I ever brought you a client who didn't meet or exceed your wealth standards?"

"Well, no . . ."

"Then have a little faith, and tell American Express to, as well. See you tomorrow at nine." Stone hung up.

Joan buzzed. "Herb Fisher on two."

"Yes, Herb?"

"Have you done any checking into Mr. Hayward? I mean, Laurence?"

"No, but Wilmington Trust has, and he's real."

"Okay. You have an appointment at three PM tomorrow to view the penthouse at the Fairleigh. It's apartment 15, and the agent is a Ms. Cassandra Gotham—veddy British—and she will meet you there."

"Thank you, Herb. See you tomorrow morning."

IT WAS HALF PAST SIX when Laurence returned from his barbering. He walked into Stone's office and stopped. "Is this any better?"

He looked quite handsome, Stone thought. "I almost didn't recognize you. Let's go upstairs and find you a room, then we'll have some dinner."

Laurence grabbed his bag and followed Stone to the elevator. Stone led him into the large room and showed him where things were. "Do you want to freshen up?" he asked.

"I don't get any fresher than after a couple of hours at Nico's," he replied.

"Then let's go down to my study." They got back on the elevator and got off at the living room.

"This is a very beautiful house," Laurence said. He stopped before a grouping of pictures. "And these are very beautiful, too."

"Thank you. They were painted by my mother, Matilda Stone. She has a few other things hanging in the American collection at the Metropolitan Museum."

"That will be one of my first stops in New York," Laurence said. They went into the study.

"Would you like a drink?"

"Yes, thank you, scotch, a single malt, if you have it."

"I have a Macallan 12, a Talisker, and a Laphroaig."

"I don't know the Talisker."

"Try it, you'll find it spicy and smoky. Ice?"

"A little."

Stone handed him the drink and poured himself a Knob Creek bourbon, and they sat down.

"This is superb whiskey," Laurence said.

"I'm glad you like it."

Laurence sighed. "You must think I'm crazy."

"No crazier than any other thirty-year-old who has just come into more than half a billion dollars."

"Has anything like this ever happened to you?"

"Yes, I inherited a large sum from my late wife—not as large as your sum, but enough."

"And what did you do with it?"

"I invested it, just as you are planning to do."

"You must have bought some nice things."

"Real estate, mostly. I bought a house in Maine, one in Paris, and a country place in England. I also bought the house next door, where my staff live."

"Where is the place in England?"

"On the Beaulieu River, in Hampshire."

"Which side?"

"West."

"I know the area. I've done quite a lot of sailing around there. Do you have a boat?"

"An American motor yacht, a Hinckley 43."

"I've seen Hinckleys—very traditional-looking."

"They are, but under the deck, they're very modern. You said you had taken some flying lessons at Palm Beach Airport?"

"Yes, I got a multiengine rating and a 525, single-pilot jet type rating there. My father flew a Beech Baron, a rather old one. I sold it."

"Where did you do your private and instrument ratings?"

"At Oxford airport, in England, and at Flight Safety, in Vero Beach."

"Are you going to buy an airplane?"

"Yes, I think I am. I didn't mention it because I thought you'd think I was really crazy."

"No, I fly myself. I have a CitationJet 3 Plus."

"I know the airplane. What's the plus?"

"Garmin 3000 avionics, mostly. What kind of airplane do you want?"

"Something I can fly myself—maybe a Citation Mustang."

"My first jet. My son is flying it now."

"Would you recommend it?"

"Yes, but perhaps not to you. You can afford something more capable, and believe me, after a few months in the Mustang, you'd want something more capable, like an M2 or the CJ 3 Plus."

"How much training is involved for the CJ 3?"

"You'll need a 525 type rating, which takes sixteen days but applies to all the CJ line. There's only one simulator, and that's at Flight Safety in Wichita."

"Then I could fly it myself?"

"You'd be legal to fly the airplane, but your insurance company would want you to build some time, before they'd insure you for single-pilot operations. But . . ."

"But I don't need an insurance company, do I? I could self-insure."

"Yes, you could, but you'd want to put in some time with a mentor pilot until you feel comfortable flying alone. How much total time do you have?"

"About twelve hundred hours. Four hundred of that in a King Air. My stepfather owns that, and I began making business trips with him and his pilot, who was an excellent instructor. Eventually, I moved to the left seat, and I guess I've got a little over a hundred hours single pilot."

"If you're comfortable in the King Air, you'll be fine in the CJ 3."

Fred came in and set a table, then brought up dinner. They talked for another couple of hours before Laurence began to look drowsy.

"You'd better get some sleep," Stone said. "You've had a big day, and we've got a busy day tomorrow. Fred will wake you at seven, and we'll leave at eight forty-five. First stop, your new bank."

"Don't forget my check," Laurence said.

"I won't."

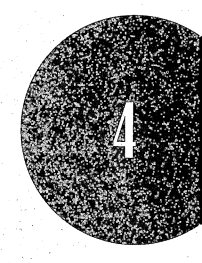

THEY ARRIVED at Woodman & Weld's offices in the Seagram Building at nine, and Herbie was there to meet them. They took an elevator and got off at the bank's offices. The receptionist sent them into Conrad Trilling's office, and introductions were made.

"Now," Trilling said, waving them to seats, "if my information is correct, Mr. Hayward wishes to open both a personal checking account and an investment account."

"That is correct," Laurence said.

Stone took the check from his pocket and handed it to Trilling. "And this is Mr. Hayward's initial deposit."

Trilling looked at the check, then did a double take. "Stone," he said, "are you funning me?"

"I am not, Conrad."

"Will you excuse me for a moment?" he said.

Stone turned to Laurence and Herbie. "Conrad will be telephoning the lottery office in West Palm."

Herbie used the time to grill Laurence about himself. Ten minutes later, Conrad returned and sat down. "Mr. Hayward, the lottery office would like to get your permission to wire-transfer these funds to your new account. I've already given them the account number, you just need to identify yourself and approve the transfer." He handed Laurence the phone and pressed a button.

"Of course," Laurence said.

"I have Mr. Hayward for you."

Laurence gave his name, address, date of birth, and Social Security number, then his driver's license and passport numbers. He was asked and answered personal questions based on information that he had given them when he had picked up their check.

"Mr. Hayward, do you wish us to transfer the entire amount of your prize to the account number Mr. Trilling gave us?"

"I do."

"Very well, the transfer will take place within the hour, and we will cancel the check we gave you."

"Thank you." He handed the phone back to Trilling.

"Now," the banker said, pushing a stack of documents across the desk with a pen, "please fill out the personal information requested on the first document, then sign each of them at the places indicated."

Laurence began signing, handing each completed sheet to Trilling. As he was signing the final page, Trilling's phone rang.

"Conrad Trilling. Yes. I understand. And that amount?" He made a note and hung up. "Mr. Hayward, your funds have been transferred to your new account. I regret that they have deducted thirty dollars from the total for the wire-transfer fee."

"I can handle that," Laurence said.

"Now, it remains only to transfer funds to your investment account. How much do you wish to invest?"

"First," Laurence said, "I want to retain thirty million dollars in my checking account, as I expect to purchase some property quite soon. Second, I wish to purchase thirty million pounds sterling and transfer that amount to my checking account at Coutts & Company in London. Here is a blank check with the account number."

"Laurence," Stone said, "may I ask, how do you intend those funds to be used?"

"I want to make gifts of ten million pounds each to Eton College and Magdalen College, Oxford. The rest is what you might call walking-around money. I may wish to purchase some property in England at a later date."

"We'll discuss this with your new accountant, later, but I should tell you that if you send money directly to your bank account in London, the British Inland Revenue Service will become aware of that almost immediately, and they will regard those sums as income, on which the highest rate of tax will be levied."

"Oops," Laurence said, "how should I handle this?"

"After we have discussed this with your accountant, you may wish to establish a trust, then make those payments directly to the colleges from that trust, without sending them through your London bank account."

"Stone," Laurence said, "you have just earned your legal fee."

"Thank you. Conrad, are we done?"

"Not quite." He reached into a desk drawer, fumbled with something, then came up with an alligator-bound wallet. "Mr. Hayward, this is your checkbook. The cover is a personal gift from the M&T Bank." He handed him an envelope. "And this is your new American Express card."

Laurence removed the card from the envelope. "Why is it black?" he said. "I thought they were green or gold."

"The Centurion card is American Express's highest level." He handed Laurence a thick, leather-bound document. "Here is an outline of the AmEx services to which you are entitled at that level."

"I see."

Trilling handed him two more cards. "And here is our bank's Visa and a separate debit card. Please enter a four-digit PIN and sign this document."

Laurence did so.

"And now," Stone said, "if our business here is concluded, Laurence has another appointment."

"I think Mr. Hayward should come back and see us at his earliest convenience to discuss an investment strategy we will have prepared for him, and meet the team of professionals who will be serving him. Would tomorrow morning be satisfactory? Nine o'clock?"

"May we make it ten o'clock?" Laurence replied.

"Of course."

Everyone shook hands and the meeting ended.

DOWNSTAIRS, Stone said, "You take my car. Fred will drive you. You have an appointment at the Ralph Lauren store at ten-thirty. Your personal shopper's name is on the card." He handed it over. "You may have them send your purchases to my house, if you wish. And we have a meeting with the sales agent at the Fairleigh at three PM."

Laurence thanked him and got into the car.

"Ralph Lauren shop, sir?" Fred asked.

"Please."

THEY REACHED THE store quickly. Fred gave him a card. "Please call me when you're done. I'll be as nearby as I can."

"Thank you, Fred." Laurence went into the store, stopped, and looked around.

A beautiful, dark-haired young woman dressed in a Ralph Lauren suit approached. "Mr. Hayward?"

"Yes."

"I'm Theresa Crane, your personal shopper. What may I show you today?"

"I need a wardrobe," he said. "Not a piece of furniture but clothes. Let's begin with the basics."

"Boxers or briefs?" she said.

He laughed. "I guess that's basic. Two dozen pairs of white boxers, size 34."

23

She made a note. "Shall we start with suits and work our way down?" She led the way to an elevator, and they went upstairs. "Let's see," she said, eyeing him up and down. "I'd say a 42 long?"

"Let's try one on," he said. She led him to a bank of suits and he chose a dark gray pinstripe, then she led him to a dressing room.

Moments later, a tailor was examining him. He bent and marked the trouser bottoms, then stood up. "Mr. Hayward, you are that rare gentleman who is perfectly shaped for a standard size. My only question is, cuffs or plain bottoms?"

"Cuffs, please, and may I wear it out of the store?"

"Ready in half an hour," the tailor said.

"As long as we stick with the Purple Label suits, all you have to do is choose," Theresa said. "The tailor is now superfluous."

Laurence began choosing half a dozen suits and a tuxedo. Next, he chose some tweed jackets, a blue blazer, and two overcoats and a trench coat, then they went downstairs, where he chose a dozen shirts and as many neckties, then on to the shoe department.

"I love alligator," Laurence said. He chose six pairs and some bedroom slippers. The price tags took his breath away, but he steeled himself.

"Jewelry?" Theresa asked.

"I could use a watch," he replied. "Or two." At the jewelry counter he chose an antique Cartier wristwatch and an old Rolex.

"Will you need luggage?" she asked.

"I certainly will."

"Alligator?"

"Oh, yes." He chose three matched cases and a briefcase that were the same chocolate gator as his new checkbook. He avoided looking at the price tags. He bought socks and cuff links and belts and sweaters and two dressing gowns, one cotton, one silk.

In the sportswear department he bought sneakers, boat shoes, running shorts, and a dozen polo shirts. "I can't think of anything else," he said.

"Then let's go and take delivery of your new suit," Theresa said. She delivered him to the tailor and he put on a new shirt, tie, shoes, and belt, then slipped on his Cartier watch, while Theresa disappeared with his new American Express card.

She returned as he was examining himself in the mirror.

"Perfection," she said, handing him the bill to sign. He caught sight of the total as he was signing, and it was a bit over $160,000. "If you'll come with me, American Express would like to speak with you."

She took him to a phone. "Hello?"

"Mr. Hayward," a woman said, "may I ask you some questions?"

"Of course."

She grilled him for a couple of minutes. "I'm sorry to detain you, but it is your first purchase on your new card, and we had to be sure it was you."

"Of course." He hung up.

"And now," Theresa said, "you have just run up the largest sale I have ever made. May I take you to lunch in our new restaurant downstairs?"

"Of course you may."

Shortly, they were seated at a table in the most beautiful room he had ever dined in, outside of Oxford.

When they had ordered, she looked at him questioningly. "Tell me, were all your clothes lost at sea in a shipwreck?"

He laughed. "No, I've just neglected to buy any clothes for a while, and what I have are mostly in England, where I've been living for the past twenty-two years."

"And what do you do, Mr. Hayward?"

"You must call me Laurence, please."

"And what do you do, Laurence?"

"I teach English and art history at a public school."

"Which in England is a private school, is it not?"

"It is."

"Which one?"

"Eton College."

"Even I have heard of Eton," she said. "Did you also attend Eton as a boy?"

"I did."

"It didn't seem to hurt your accent much."

"I'm American born. I assume my American disguise when I'm here."

"Do you live in New York?"

"Palm Beach, but I'm looking at an apartment in about an hour."

"Where?

"Park Avenue."

"Very good. And will you furnish it in an hour?"

"I expect it will take a little longer, though I understand it's already very nicely furnished. Now, you know a lot about me, and I have to catch up. Your sixty-second bio, please."

"All right, born in Delano, a small town in Georgia, twenty-eight years ago, attended local schools, then I won a scholarship to Mount Holyoke College, in Massachusetts."

"One of the Seven Sisters."

"Correct."

"After graduation, I came to New York to make my fortune in finance, but no one would hire me, so I got a job selling neckties at Ralph Lauren, the one at Madison and Seventy-second. Seven years later, I'm still selling neckties, along with everything else in the store. There."

"Seven years? I admire your loyalty."

"They pay me," she said.

"I hope you're on commission."

"I'm not allowed to tell you, but if I'm not, I'll demand a raise after today."

They finished their lunch, and she introduced him to the headwaiter and told him to always take care of Mr. Hayward.

Laurence called Fred, and he appeared almost immediately.

"What a nice car," Theresa said.

"It is, but it's not mine, belongs to my attorney."

"Ah, Stone Barrington. You must be a very good client."

"We'll see. I enjoyed our lunch. Will you have dinner with me?"

"I'm not allowed to," she said. "Against company policy."

"Do you never do what you're not allowed to do?"

She smiled. "Sometimes."

5

STONE STOOD on the sidewalk in front of the Fairleigh and watched his Bentley glide to a halt. He opened the door and held it for Laurence. "I see you've shopped," he said. "That's a beautiful suit."

"Thank you for the recommendation," Laurence said.

"Right this way." Stone led him through the newly renovated, paneled lobby.

"Very handsome," Laurence said.

"When the hotel was built, in the 1920s, they were said to have felled a whole forest of mahogany trees in Honduras."

"Awful."

"Not so much in the 1920s. They've grown back by now."

They entered the elevator, Stone pressed the 15 button and the car rose. "I understand the agent, whose name is Cassandra Gotham, is British. She might like to hear a familiar accent."

"I'll see what I can do."

"Another thing—the apartments in the hotel are pretty much sold out, because there are three or four per floor. The penthouse, being larger and occupying an entire floor, has been harder to sell. Before you make an offer, let's talk."

"Certainly."

The car opened into a large, beautifully furnished foyer, with double doors to the right. A willowy blonde of indeterminate age, wearing a Chanel suit, strode from the apartment to greet them with a broad smile. "Mr. Barrington, Mr. Hayward, which is which?"

Stone handed her a Woodman & Weld card. "I'm Stone Barrington, this is Laurence Hayward."

"How do you do, Ms. Gotham," Laurence said.

"So good to meet you both. Will you come through? I'll try not to talk too much, let the place speak for itself. Just ask, if you have questions."

She led the way into a large living room, with unobstructed light pouring through tall windows on three sides. The room was centered on a carved limestone fireplace, and the ceilings were very high.

"Where did the furniture come from?" Laurence asked.

"All the upholstered pieces and the fabrics are from Ralph Lauren. The wood furniture is from the manufacturer, Baker. The piano, a seven-foot grand, is from Steinway. The pictures are from a number of galleries. All the things are purchasable, not included in the asking price."

"I see. Thank you."

Laurence sat down at the piano and played some chords and scales, then he inspected the interior of the instrument. "Good," he said.

They moved into a dining room, where a table was set for twelve. "The chairs are from Lauren, the table and sideboard from Baker, the china is Wedgwood, from about 1935, the crystal and the chandelier are Baccarat, and the sterling pieces are from a shop down the street that deals in old silver. There is another, more intimate dining room near the kitchen." She led the way through a service door into a large kitchen. "Most of it is original to the apartment," she said, "except, of course, the appliances, which are from Viking. The small dining room is here, with views to the south, and seats six or eight. Again, chairs, Lauren, table, Baker." They went down a hallway. "There is a servant's apartment here, and a second bedroom, here, and an office nearer the living room. The furniture for those is from Blooming-dale's, as are the rugs throughout the apartment, which are among the finest the store has to offer."

"Thank you."

"One other thing—there is a small, two-bedroom, two-bath apartment on the floor below, which is offered separately for three million, and furnished with refinished hotel furniture. It would be ideal for older children or staff. Would you like to see it?"

"Yes, thank you," Laurence said.

She pressed a panel near the elevator, which opened, revealing a staircase, and led them down. Laurence and Stone had a look around.

"Thank you. May we see the bedrooms upstairs now, please?"

They went back to the living room and up a floor in an elevator tucked behind a broad stairway. "Master suite is here," she said, opening double doors. "There are his and her bathrooms and dressing rooms. The woman's is twice the size of the man's." She showed them three guest rooms down the hallway, each with a large bathroom, then led them back down the stairs. "And now, the pièce de résistance, the library."

It was, as was the rest of the apartment, paneled in mahogany, and imposing without being too large. The fireplace was of carved mahogany. "The upholstered furniture is Lauren, the other things, Baker. The books are from the fine-books collection at the Strand, the enormous bookstore downtown. The room is wired for computer use, with a workstation in the corner, there. The entire apartment has high-speed Wi-Fi, and there is a built-in sound system by Sonos that can be operated from an iPhone, plus a four-line office-style telephone system, all of which is housed behind a panel." She showed them the tech closet, went to the mantelpiece and pulled an embroidered cord next to it. The paneling beside the fireplace slid open, and a bar slid nearly silently into the room, with four stools, stocked with bottles and mixers. She led the way to French doors at the west end of the room, which opened onto a large terrace with a swimming pool and views west to Central Park. "The pool is a very rare thing on the East Side," she said, "but the original owner of the hotel built this apartment for himself, and he wanted a pool. It has been inspected and is in excellent condition and well supported by steel beams.

"The monthly maintenance fee on the apartment is twenty-five thousand per month, and that includes daily maid and linen service, room service, concierge service, and parking. The apartment comes with two parking spaces in the underground garage. Have you any other questions?"

"I don't think so," Laurence said. "May we have a moment to talk?"

"Of course." She handed him a leather-bound book. "This is a list of the furnishings with the prices of each piece and phone numbers of the furnishers."

Stone and Laurence sat down in facing, cushioned armchairs. "What do you think?" Stone asked.

"It's perfect, once I sort through the furnishings."

"I suggest you offer eighteen million, with a closing tomorrow."

"Do you think they'll take that?"

"The apartments went on sale nine months ago, and as I said, are sold out. Your position is good. Will you allow me to make the offer? You can be the good cop."

Laurence smiled. "Certainly. I think I'd like the apartment downstairs, too," he said.

"We'll offer two million for that?"

"Good."

"And they're asking twenty-two million for the penthouse. Shall we offer twenty million for the two?"

Stone rang the agent's cell phone, and she reappeared. "Please join us," Stone said, standing and offering her a chair.

"We will be brief, Ms. Gotham. Mr. Hayward would like to offer twenty million for the two apartments, all cash, to close tomorrow before noon. He is not inclined to offer more. He will deal directly with the furnishers."

She appeared speechless for a moment, then recovered. "Please give me a moment." She walked to the edge of the terrace and made a phone call. Her back was to them, but she seemed to be speaking vociferously. She turned and covered her phone. "Twenty-one million," she said.

Stone shook his head and began to stand up. She turned back to the phone, then ended the call. "Done," she said to the men. "They've already begun work on the closing documents."

"They should be sent to Mr. Herbert Fisher at my firm for review," Stone said. "May we meet in his office at, say, eleven AM?"

"Of course," she said. "Mr. Hayward, I hope you will be very happy here."

"I'm sure I shall be," Laurence replied. "Would you mind if we stayed on for a while so that I may review the furnishings?"

"Not at all. This is your home now, pending closing, of course."

"Oh," Stone said, "please tell your people that the apartments will be purchased separately, and the buyer will be the LBH Corporation, of Palm Beach, Florida. A condition of the sales is that no one who does not need to know Mr. Hayward's name will know it, and any requests from anyone for his name will be declined. We expect absolute confidentiality."

"I understand completely."

"Very good," Laurence said. "Although I have not had time to assess all the furnishings, would you do me the favor of calling the owner of the wood furniture and ask them to remove it all tomorrow morning? I shall be replacing those pieces with antiques."

"As you wish."

"Have a wonderful day, Ms. Gotham."

"I already have," she said, and left.

They spent more time there, while Laurence made a list of the pieces of furniture he was replacing.

"You play piano?" Stone asked.

"Since childhood," Laurence replied. "At Oxford I began playing with a jazz trio. We played weddings, bar mitzvahs, college parties— wherever the work took us—and I enjoyed it."

Fred was waiting for them on the street. "Where are you headed?" Stone asked.

"To the Park Avenue Armory," Laurence replied. "I can get a cab."

"Nonsense. Take the car and Fred. It's a nice day, and I could use a little exercise."

"Thank you, Stone." Laurence got into the car and gave Fred the address, then he made a call.

"Theresa Crane."

"It's Laurence. I've bought an apartment."

"Congratulations!"

"Would you please have all my things delivered to apartment 15 at the Fairleigh on Park Avenue after one o'clock tomorrow?"

"Of course."

"And may I ask a personal favor?"

"You may."

"Would you unpack the clothes and put them away in the master dressing room upstairs? I'll be shopping for furniture and art."

"I'd be happy to."

"The concierge will give you the key. One other thing—dinner tomorrow night?"

She paused for a moment. "Yes," she said, finally.

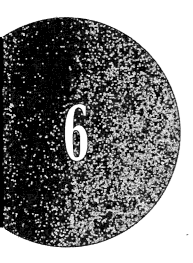

6

L AURENCE GOT OUT of the car in front of the armory and went inside. He picked up a catalog and was told that the sale would
close the following day. It was a show of American art and furniture.

He began at the aisle on his far right and made a quick tour of the
show, making notes on his list along the way, then he backtracked to
the displays that interested him. His first purchase was a federal dining table with a spectacular breakfront in matching wood, the two
pieces offered at $500,000. He haggled and lost, then bought both of
them. He continued, buying end tables and odd pieces, including a
table for the small dining room, plus pieces to be used as side tables
in the bedrooms. He also bought four Milton Avery landscapes and a
number of small sculptures, including a first-century head of Zeus in

alabaster and a larger, Greek head, perfect, except for the all-too-typical broken-off nose. Finally, he found a large coffee table, made by a fine craftsman from antique walnut. He paid for each purchase with either his American Express card or a check, and his total came to a little under $7,000,000. He reckoned he had saved $250,000 because the show was about to close and the dealers didn't want to truck everything home. He arranged for everything to be delivered the following day at the close of the show.

Back in the car, he Googled a London shirtmaker, Turnbull & Asser, used by his stepfather, and discovered that they had a New York shop, just around the corner from his new apartment, on East Fifty-seventh Street. There he was fitted and ordered two dozen shirts to be made, then he bought some pajamas, more neckties, and some pocket squares. That done, he went back to Stone's house and found his new attorney still at his desk.

"How did your shopping go?"

Laurence told him what he had bought.

"Sounds like you now have everything a man needs."

"Not quite. I still have to go car shopping."

"For your Porsche?"

"Yes, and I quite like your Bentley Flying Spur. Today has taught me how nice it is to have a car and driver in the city."

"Good. Herb Fisher has found you a prospective secretary. You'll meet her after the closing tomorrow." He told Laurence what he knew about the woman. "And would you like to join some friends and me for dinner this evening?"

"I'd be delighted."

"We'll leave here a little after seven."

"I'll be ready. I hope you don't mind if I wear the same suit—it's my only one, until tomorrow."

"Of course not."

"I'd better go and freshen up, then."

FARTHER UPTOWN, Theresa Crane came home from work and found, to her alarm, that the door to her apartment was ajar. She was certain she had locked it securely, and it was not the maid's day. Her first instinct was to call 911, but she didn't want to make a fool of herself if there was nothing wrong. She pushed the door open another foot and peeked inside. She could see down the hall and into her living room, and as she watched, she saw a puff of smoke drift across the room. She got out her phone to call the police, and as she did, a man appeared in the hallway.

"Sis?" he said.

She stared at him in shock. "Butch?"

"Give me a hug," he said, his arms spread wide.

She moved into the hallway and hugged him briefly. "I thought you had at least another year to go. How did you get out? My God, you didn't break out, did you?"

Butch shrugged and steered her into the living room and onto the sofa. "Maybe you've read in the papers that there's a move on, nationwide, to rid the prisons of first-time, nonviolent prisoners? Seems they've run out of cell space."

Harold F. Crane, her younger brother, had been doing five to seven years in a minimum-security prison upstate for forgery, money laundering, and theft, and those were just the things he had been caught doing; she suspected there were more crimes in his past. "So," she said, "what are your plans?"

"My parole officer seems to think I might find some work in New York, given my winning nature and handsome mien. Can you put me up for a while?"

"Put out that cigarette," she said. "There's no smoking here, ever." He went to the powder room, flushed it down the toilet, and returned. "Sorry about that. I picked up the habit inside. There was nothing else to do, except read."

"I don't want the smell in here. How did you get in?"

"I knew you always hide a key somewhere, and I found it on the ledge over the door. I didn't want to call you at work. How's it going there?"

"Fine, thanks."

"The apartment is smashing," he said, looking around.

"I get a discount at the store, and I've been buying floor pieces whenever the designs change. I've done a lot of work on the apartment myself."

"I'm impressed."

"Perhaps I'll treat you to a suit tomorrow," she said. "There's a sale starting. God knows, you're not going to get work in that."

He plucked at his lapel. "It's what I was wearing when I went in, and I've lost some weight."

"I noticed that."

"Prison food is lousy, and I worked out a lot, too."

"All you need is some sun on your face, and you'll look like a real person again."

"Do you think there might be something for me at the store? Remember, I worked at a men's store in college."

"I don't know, but I'll ask at the personnel department. Don't get your hopes up, they're very picky about who they hire."

"Groton and Yale aren't good enough?"

"Well, that's not all that's on your résumé, you know, and you can't lie to them. I don't want to lose *my* job."

"Nah, I would never do that."

"Butch, you've been a liar all your life, and I don't expect that to change. Just don't foul my nest."

"I put my stuff in the spare room," he said, changing the subject. "I hope that's all right."

"For one week," she said. "After that, it's the Y."

"So, are you the store manager yet?"

"No, but I had the biggest sale of my life this morning—over a hundred and sixty thousand."

"Wow! How does somebody spend that much in a morning?"

"He buys a complete wardrobe, half a dozen pairs of alligator shoes, and the most expensive luggage in the store. It adds up."

"How about we go out to dinner tonight?"

"I've got some leftover spaghetti sauce in the fridge—how about we eat that?"

"Sure, that would be great. I'll do the dishes. Are you off tomorrow? I'll take you to a movie."

"No, I've got to deliver everything from today's big sale and put it away in the customer's new apartment. If you want to help me, I'll pay you for your time."

"Yeah? How much?"

"Minimum wage, pal, get used to it."

"I guess I'll have to, if I'm going to be an honest working stiff. You want to buy a guy his first drink in three years?"

"It's over there," she said, pointing to a cabinet. "Get me a scotch on the rocks, too."

They settled down to catch up, watched the news, then had dinner. By bedtime, she was feeling more confident about Butch. Maybe she really could get him a job at the store.

7

THEY TOOK ADVANTAGE of the lovely weather and walked down to Patroon, Stone's favorite restaurant since Elaine Kaufman's death and the subsequent closing of Elaine's a few months later.

"With whom are we dining?" Laurence asked.

"With Dino Bacchetti and his wife, Vivian. Dino and I were partners on the NYPD a long time ago. He is now the police commissioner of New York City. Viv is the chief operating officer of Strategic Services, the second-largest security company in the world."

"You were a policeman?"

"I was. Joined right after law school and stayed until they used a gunshot wound to the knee as an excuse to retire me. Dino stayed on and did well. A friend suggested I cram for the bar exam and join his firm, Woodman & Weld, and the rest, as they say, is history."

"Who are your biggest clients there?"

"Strategic Services, the Steele Insurance group, and the Arrington Hotels Group, on the boards of which I sit. And you."

"I'm your fourth biggest client?"

"You're my biggest client—personal not business."

"I'm glad to hear it, Stone."

"So am I. Thank you for calling me. I'll have to send Dicky Chalmers a case of very good wine."

"I'll find him something, too, when I do more shopping."

They reached the restaurant and were greeted by the owner, Ken Aretsky, and introductions were made.

"Take good care of Laurence," Stone said, sotto voce, as he passed. "He'll be a good customer."

"Certainly," Ken said.

Dino and Viv were already seated at the table, and Stone introduced everybody. They ordered drinks, which arrived swiftly.

"Laurence," Stone said, "I have a confession to make."

"Oh?"

"I've broken my promise to guard your anonymity. I've told Dino and Viv all about what's happened, because they can be of future help to you. At some point you may need the help of Strategic Services, and that's Viv, and Dino is just somebody who's good to know."

"I'm fine with that," Laurence said. "You are forgiven." He made the sign of the cross, and everybody laughed.

They looked at menus and ended up ordering a platter of beef chateaubriand for the table. Ken brought complimentary canapés.

"I hear you've bought an apartment, Laurence," Viv said.

"That's correct. Moving in tomorrow. Thank you, Stone, for the shelter, but you won't have to put up with me any longer."

"You're always welcome, Laurence."

"Did you bring any furnishings with you?" Viv asked.

"One small bag of clothes, which I introduced to a dumpster this afternoon. I'm starting from scratch, at least in New York."

"Have you had any problems with being recognized and hounded?" Dino asked.

"Only in West Palm Beach at the lottery office, and then my first New York cabdriver caught me in his mirror. Stone suggested a shave and a haircut, and no one has made me since."

"A clean shave is a good disguise these days," Dino said. "I understand you've spent most of your life in England and that you're a master at Eton."

"An assistant master, though I have hope of a promotion. I'm on a leave of absence right now, but I'm going to have to give a lot of thought to whether I'll stay there after what's happened."

"Do you still have a home there?"

"Yes, I live in a small cottage on a lovely little estate in Berkshire owned by my stepfather. It's a short drive to Eton, where the college offered me only a room. Masters get flats or houses. My parents have a house in London, too, and I have a room there."

"Sounds like you're well stocked with real estate."

"Yes. Also, I inherited my father's house in Palm Beach. I had planned to sell it, but there's no need to now."

"Tell me, Laurence," Dino said, "has Stone given you the lecture yet?"

"You mean, 'don't spend it all in one place'?"

Dino smiled. "No. Let me put it this way—you seem like a bright fellow, but do you have any street smarts?"

"London and Berkshire street smarts, yes, New York City street smarts, no—sadly deficient there."

"New York is a tough town, and I don't mean the muggers, which we keep under control. I mean predators of a different sort."

"What sort?"

"All sorts. For instance, though you're not aware of it yet, there are people around town who are already looking for you."

Laurence looked alarmed. "What sort of people?"

"They like to call themselves journalists these days, but they're the same gossipmongers that have been around since newspapers came along. It goes like this—the cabdriver who recognized you probably has such a connection, and he's made himself fifty or a hundred bucks by telling that connection that the Powerball zillionaire is in town. It would not surprise me if someone offered a reward for news of your whereabouts. You could very well soon be the subject of a manhunt."

"What an awful thought," Laurence said. "The London papers are like that, too."

"In what name did you win the lottery?"

"L. B. Hayward."

"That won't throw them off the scent for long," Dino said. "Is anyone living in your father's house?"

"No, a cleaning lady comes every day."

"Prepare to get a call saying the house has been broken into."

"You think it will be burgled because there's nobody living there?"

"No, I think some private eye, working for a tabloid, will break in and start looking for evidence of your whereabouts."

"What sort of evidence?"

"Anything with your name on it—checkbook, your father's checkbook, family photos, address books—anything. My point is, you're not going to be anonymous in New York for very long."

"There's nothing in the house that would locate me," Laurence said. "When I left I didn't have another residence in this country."

"Might they track you to England with what they find in the house?"

Laurence thought about it. "Yes," he said. "There are letters from me to my father with my return address on them."

"We bought the apartments in a corporate name," Stone said.

Viv spoke up. "That will help. Do you think the real estate agent twigged?"

"No," Stone said, "but if she starts reading about Laurence in the tabloids, her discretion might be taxed."

"There's another kind of predator you have to worry about, too," Dino said. "The financial kind. These people won't need to read about you in the papers, they'll see you going in and out of the Fairleigh, in and out of your car, in and out of restaurants, and, the way you look and dress, you might as well have the word 'mark' tattooed on your forehead."

"What do you suggest I do?" Laurence asked.

"Get out of town."

"Back to Palm Beach?"

"Oh, no, somewhere you're not known, maybe someplace abroad you've always wanted to go."

Laurence said, "A place comes to mind. Stone, I haven't had a chance to tell you about this yet, but I've been talking with the Florida sales director of Cessna, a Mr. Hayes, and he tells me that he's had the cancellation of a sale, due to a death, of a CJ 3 Plus. It's loaded with equipment and has a nice paint scheme."

"When would it be delivered?"

"In three weeks, and I'll need sixteen days of training to get a 525 type rating—in Wichita, Kansas. Is that far enough away, Dino?"

"Wichita is as far as you can get from everywhere," Dino said, smiling.

"And you'll be in the classroom and simulator eight or ten hours a day," Stone pointed out. "You'll be too exhausted to go out at night."

"Then I think I'll kill two birds with one stone," Laurence said.

"Let me negotiate the sale for you. I know David Hayes from past dealings."

"That's his name."

"I'll call him tomorrow. You book your training slot at Flight Safety. You're going to need a mentor pilot for a while, too."

"How long?"

"Thirty to fifty hours, depending on how precocious you are. I have a friend named Pat Frank who started an aircraft management business a couple of years ago. She'll find you just the right mentor. Also, she'll manage the airplane for you. There's quite a lot of paper-work and maintenance records. She can make it painless."

"Does she manage your airplane?"

"Yes."

"Then she's good enough for me." He looked a little embarrassed. "There's something else you'll need to negotiate with David Hayes."

"What's that?"

"I want to buy a Citation Latitude, too."

"That's a big jump up in airplanes from the CJ 3 Plus."

"It is, but I can fly nonstop transatlantic in it."

"Ah, yes. Do you plan to train in that, too?"

"Eventually, but it's going to be nine months before I can take delivery, so I can build time in the CJ 3 Plus while I'm waiting for it, and Hayes said it might be possible to work out a deal where I trade in the CJ for the Latitude."

"That should improve your deal," Stone said. "I'll call him tomorrow. And you should probably schedule time, after delivery, at Flight Safety for the Latitude training. Since the Latitude is not a single-pilot airplane, you're going to need to hire another pilot or two, as well, but Pat Frank can find those people for you."

"Good."

"Laurence," Viv said, "I understand that you can become very English at the drop of a hat."

"Oh, yes."

"Then you have another disguise at your disposal—become English in America for a while."

"Jolly good idea," Laurence said, in his best, broad Eton/Oxford accent.

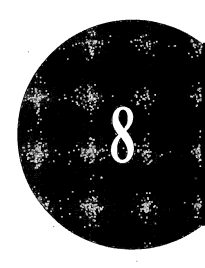

L AURENCE HAD BREAKFAST with Stone the following morning, then he took a cab to the far West Side, where the automobile dealers lived. He found one that had everything he wanted, since they dealt in both Porsche and Bentley.

He found a beautiful Flying Spur on the showroom floor and had lost himself in the window sticker information when a salesman materialized at his side and introduced himself. "I'm Paul Dumont."

"I'm Laurence Hayward," he said.

"Would you like to drive it?"

"Of course, but first, is the equipment list pretty complete?"

"We order our cars loaded," the man said. "It's how our customers like them. We also have one in black, with magnolia upholstery."

"I like these colors. What are they called?"

"Aspen metallic green and the upholstery is saffron."

"Let's drive it."

It took ten minutes to remove the car from the showroom, then Laurence spent ten minutes throwing the car around on the streets.

"Good," he said, as he parked the car in front of the dealership. "Now let's look at Porsches."

"Right this way," the man said, and led him to the showroom adjacent to the Bentley one. "Turbo, perhaps?"

"No, it's a little too splashy-looking, what with the spoiler. I like the Carrera 4S."

"I don't have one in stock, but I can do a dealer search. Let's find a computer." They sat down at a desk. "Color?"

"What's that color there?" Laurence asked.

"Umber—very nice with cognac and espresso upholstery."

"Good."

Dumont typed a few strokes on the keyboard. "No one has that car in stock," he said, "but I see that we have one incoming. It's on a ship right now, and it will be here in about three weeks. It has just about all the options, including ceramic brakes."

"I'm going to need a driver for the Bentley," Laurence said.

Dumont handed him a card. "This is a service that provides chauffeurs," he said, "on an hourly basis. If they send you one you like, steal him."

Laurence laughed. "I like the way you think. How much are we talking about?"

"For the Porsche and the Bentley?"

"For the Porsche and both Bentleys."

"Ah."

Haggling ensued, and shortly they had made a deal, and Laurence got out his checkbook. "Will you call the service for me and get a driver over here right now?"

"That's short notice, but we'll work something out." He made the call, then covered the phone. "They have a man who can be here in forty minutes. He has to take the subway from Brooklyn. If you don't want to wait, I can have him deliver the car to you. Do you have garage space?"

Laurence gave him the address.

"And what would you like to do with the other Bentley?"

"I'd like it to be sent to Mr. and Mrs. Richard Chalmers, Ocean Drive, Palm Beach, and I'd like to include a card."

Dumont produced a card and an envelope, and Laurence wrote: *An expression of my affection and my gratitude for your many kindnesses in a difficult time.* "I'd like the green car registered in Florida, please, but I'll be using it here." He gave the address of his father's house. "Register it at that address."

Dumont repaired to his office to do the paperwork, then returned for Laurence's signature on the documents. "It will take us ten days or so to get Florida plates, but you'll have a dealer plate that will make you legal. I expect you'll want insurance?"

"Only liability—twenty million dollars."

"Let me make a call." He was back in ten minutes and gave Laurence the card of an insurance broker. "You're covered. I've given him your address and other details, and I've told him that you want chauffeurs covered."

"Thank you."

"And I'm having the satellite radio programmed. We'll give you a year's subscription, free."

"With each car," Laurence said.

"Of course."

SHORTLY, a man in a blue suit appeared in the showroom. "Mr. Hayward?" he asked nobody in particular.

Laurence waved him over. "That's me."

"I'm Oliver," the man said, "from Chauffeurs Unlimited."

"Paul, please give Oliver the keys to the car. It's outside, Oliver. I'll be out shortly."

Oliver took the keys and went to the car.

"Is there anything else I can possibly do for you?" Dumont asked.

"Probably," Laurence said. "I'll let you know. By the way, all this must remain entirely confidential. I don't want to see my name mentioned anywhere."

"Of course, and I'll call you with a specific delivery date for the Porsche."

"In three weeks, I'll be out of town," Laurence said. "Hold it for me until I return."

"Of course. Would you like the Porsche sent to your garage?"

"Good idea." He gave Dumont the address. "Just leave the keys with the garage manager."

The two men shook hands, and Laurence went to his new Bentley, where Oliver was waiting with the door open.

"Oliver," he said, "I want you to drive up to Fifty-seventh Street and Madison Avenue, then drive very slowly up Madison."

"Yes, Mr. Hayward," Oliver said, closing the door and getting behind the wheel. "Beautiful car, a pleasure to drive."

"And, Oliver, please turn on the satellite radio to the Light Classical channel."

"Yes, sir."

DRIVING SLOWLY up Madison Avenue, with a Chopin étude wafting around the interior of the car, Laurence did some window-shopping for galleries and made notes on which ones he wanted to visit. At Seventy-ninth Street, he put away his notebook. "All right," he said, "let's go home."

"Yes, sir," Oliver replied, "and where would that be?"

"The Fairleigh, on Park Avenue. The garage entrance is on the side street."

"Yes, sir."

Laurence took the elevator to 15 and let himself into the apartment. A strange young man walked out of his bedroom.

"Laurence Hayward?"

"Yes, and who are you?"

"I'm Butch Crane. My sister, Theresa, is putting your clothes in your dressing room. She asked me to help."

"I hope there wasn't too much heavy lifting," Laurence said. He walked into his bedroom and found Theresa fussing with the final location of everything. "Good afternoon."

"Oh, hello, Mr. Hayward."

"It's Laurence, please."

"Hello, Laurence," she said.

"You're fired," he replied.

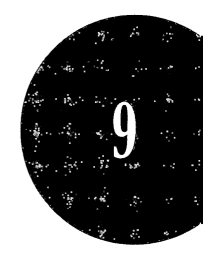

THERESA BLINKED, and her jaw dropped. "Fired?"

"I am mindful of your company's prohibition against your having personal relationships with your clients, so I am no longer your client. Will you stay for lunch?"

She smiled. "I'd love to."

"Do something with your brother," he said. "No witnesses."

"I'll speak to him."

He heard momentary sounds of an argument, then the door slammed.

She returned. "Where are we having lunch?"

"Here," he replied, leading her into the study and the bar. "What would you like?"

"You decide."

Laurence picked up the phone and pressed a button. "Good afternoon. I'd like a lobster salad for two, hold the celery, and a bottle of well-chilled Puligny-Montrachet. Thank you." He hung up. "May I get you a drink while we're waiting for delivery?"

"A Campari and soda, please."

He poured the drink and himself some mineral water.

"And how did you spend your morning?" she asked.

"I went car shopping, then cruised Madison Avenue in search of promising galleries for later visits."

"You're fond of art?"

"Very."

"What will you be shopping for?"

"Young painters with promise, occasionally older or deader artists."

"Auctions?"

"I don't like the idea of bidding against people with more money than I. I'd rather bargain with a dealer."

"Did you buy a car?"

"A Bentley Flying Spur. That's the smaller model."

"Nice choice."

"Thank you. Tell me about your brother."

"Butch? He's just moved to New York and is job hunting. I've gotten him an interview with our personnel people for a sales position."

"Is that all he's qualified for? He looks old enough to have some job experience at something."

"Oh, Butch has knocked around for years, since college. I think he's finally decided to settle down and start a career."

"Good for him."

"The apartment is gorgeous. Didn't I see a piece about it in the *Times* recently?"

"You did, as did I. I fell in love with it immediately, and again at first sight. I've bought some new pieces of furniture and some pictures, which will be delivered this afternoon."

"I noticed you were missing a dining table."

"Among other things. The place was furnished, but I didn't like everything. Ralph Lauren is well represented, though, and I didn't send back any of his pieces."

"I'll tell him you said so."

The doorbell rang, and Laurence admitted a waiter with a cart and pointed him to the study. He served lunch, poured the wine, and left them.

"Thank you for arranging my dressing room," he said.

"I was happy to fill it for you. I noticed that you didn't glance at a menu when you ordered."

"If they couldn't make a lobster salad and come up with a good Puligny-Montrachet, I'd move out."

"I've also noticed that your accent has become very British."

"I have dual citizenship, but I've spent most of my life in Blighty. Somehow, the accent is more natural to me."

"What are your plans for the afternoon?"

"After ravishing you? I have to see my lawyer, interview a woman for a job as my secretary, and sign my new will."

"Your first one?"

"Yes. I never felt I needed one before, but since my father's death . . ."

"I see. And by the way, you're not ravishing me this afternoon. I still have a job."

"We can talk about that at dinner," he said. "Name a restaurant."

"I like the Monkey Bar," she said. "It's not far from here, in the Hotel Elysée."

"Done. I'll call for you at seven."

"Sounds good."

They spent a pleasant hour together, then she left.

LAURENCE ARRIVED at the offices of Woodman & Weld on time, and was taken in to see Herb Fisher.

"How's it going?" Herb asked.

"Very well, thanks."

Herb placed a thick sheaf of papers on his desk. "Here's your will and a trust document, which you may take as long as you like to read."

"Tell me the short version."

"All right. Fifty million each to Eton and Magdalen College, Oxford, a hundred million to your mother, and the rest to a charitable trust, with Stone Barrington and I as administrators."

"Perfect," Laurence said. "Have you a pen?"

Herb handed him a silver Montblanc, and he signed the will and the trust document. "Beautiful pen," he said.

"The pen is a gift," Herb said, "from the firm."

"Thank you, I'm grateful to the firm."

Herb glanced at his watch. "Are you ready for the job interview?"

"Of course."

Herb made a call, and shortly a woman entered his office and offered Laurence her hand. "I'm Marjorie Mason," she said. "Everybody calls me Marge."

"I'm Laurence—no mister, please."

"As you wish."

They offered her a chair. "Tell me what you've been doing recently," he said.

"I joined Woodman & Weld after college, and for the last eleven of those years I've worked for a partner, who recently died."

"And what did you do for him?"

"As he used to put it, 'Everything a wife does, except for sex.' In short, I managed his life, dealt with his banking and investment people, found him domestic staff, arranged his social life, and anything else he could think of."

"That sounds like what I'd have you do for me. I'll be traveling a lot, and you'd be on your own. Are you all right with that?"

"I'm the best company I know," she said.

"Then I'll offer you a hundred and twenty-five thousand dollars a year, health insurance, and a 401k, I believe it's called. Your office will be in my New York residence, at the Fairleigh. Four weeks of vacation a year, but not more than two at a time, and a clothing allowance. Is there anything else you need?"

"I'll let you know. In the meantime, I accept."

"When can you start?"

"My late boss's affairs are now in perfect order. I'll take the rest of the day to clean out my office, sign my pension documents, and be at the Fairleigh at nine tomorrow morning."

He gave her a key to the apartment. "Let yourself in and find your office. It's on the south side, not far from the kitchen. Order whatever you need for office supplies and get yourself set up with a computer and printer and anything else necessary." He stood up and offered her his hand. "Thank you, Marge. See you tomorrow."

She shook his hand, thanked him, and left.

"Now, Herb, if you'll excuse me, I have furniture being delivered, and I need to place it."

"Of course. Good move with Marge," Herb said. "She's a great person."

"I could tell," Laurence replied.

WHEN HE ARRIVED back at the Fairleigh, men with the dining table were waiting near the concierge's desk. He waved them toward the freight elevator, then went upstairs to his apartment.

For the next two hours, people arrived with furniture and paintings. He placed everything exactly where he wanted, then stood back to admire the results. With the fresh flowers he had ordered, the place was starting to look as though someone lived there.

10

THERESA ARRIVED HOME a little after six and at a run. As she closed the door behind her, she caught sight of a man in her living room. He was short, clipped bald, and had a flat nose: much like Curly of the Three Stooges, but with a more sinister mien. She stalked into the living room and found him pouring Butch a drink.

"Hey, sis," he said, waving his glass. "This is my pal Curly. You can see where he gets the name. We shared a cell for the last year. I thought that, since there are twin beds in my room, he could stay a couple of nights with us while he gets reoriented."

"You thought wrong," she said. "I want you both out of the apartment NOW, and when I get home, about ten, you'd better be here alone. Got it?"

Curly raised both hands in submission. "Hey, I don't wanna be where I ain't wanted."

"I'm glad you understand. Butch, get him out of here."

Butch tossed off the Macallan 12. "We're gone," he said.

Theresa saw them out and bolted and chained the door behind her. She ran into her bedroom, threw her dress at a closet, stripped and dove into the shower. When she came out and went to her dresser for some things, she noticed that her underwear drawer had been disturbed. Someone had been searching for something. She did her hair, got into a dress, grabbed a jacket, and let herself out of the apartment. As she came out the front door, a green Bentley glided to a halt, and Laurence got out and held the door for her.

"I would have come up for you," he said.

"Not necessary. My apartment is a mess, anyway. Butch brought home a friend, and they got into my scotch and God knows what else."

"Butch is staying with you?"

"He's moving to the Y tomorrow, but he doesn't know it yet."

"Oliver, the Monkey Bar," Laurence said, then turned back to Theresa. "I would not deny you shelter, should you need it."

"Would you like to shelter Butch and his friend Curly?"

"Thank you, no."

"I didn't think so."

"Who's Curly?"

"You remember the character from the Three Stooges?"

"I do."

"Him, but not in the least funny."

They arrived at the Hotel Elysée, and Oliver had the door open in a flash.

"Hover, please, Oliver," Laurence said.

"Yes, sir." He handed him a card. "My cell number, sir."

"Get something to eat," Laurence said. "We'll be a couple of hours."

The Monkey Bar was crowded with handsome young people, some of them waiting for their tables. They checked in, were inspected and shown to a good table. The walls were hung with period paintings, and good jazz played in the background. They ordered drinks.

BUTCH LET HIMSELF and Curly back into Theresa's apartment. "I'll get packed," he said. "You get your stuff together."

"Where we going?"

"The Y, unless you have a more affordable idea."

"Why?"

"Did you get the impression that my sis didn't like you?"

"Sorta."

"That's why. I'd be thrown out tomorrow anyway, so we may as well go now." He went into the kitchen, opened a tea canister and shook out two hundred dollars, leaving an IOU.

"So tell me about this mark you got," Curly said.

"Nothing to tell yet, except he's well heeled. I'll need to do some research."

"When?"

"I've got a job interview tomorrow morning. I'll know more after that. You might look around for a way to make a reasonably honest buck. I can't support you, Curly."

"I still know how to pick a pocket. I've been practicing."

"I don't understand how someone who looks like you could get close enough to anybody to pick his pocket."

"All I need is a crowd. I'll go over to the theater district about curtain time and case the bunch leaving the theaters. They're always in a hurry."

"You're going to get busted, and there goes your parole."

"I told you, I didn't get paroled. I served my time. I'm free as a bird."

"Until you get caught picking a pocket. And remember, I don't have bail money for you."

THEY DINED on excellent beef and a very fine wine. Laurence had decided that his newest regular indulgence would be never to drink plonk again; he had had enough of cheap wine at Oxford to last him a lifetime.

"Is your mother still alive?" she asked.

"Very much so, and married to the man she married when I was eight."

"Who is he and what's he like?"

"His name is Derek Fallowfield. He's a very nice guy, who I think of as more of an uncle than a stepfather. He has his own successful ad agency in London and knows everybody."

"I had a stepfather, too, but not nearly so nice a guy. I hated him."

"No longer with us?"

"No, thank God. When he died he left my mother with enough to get by on, but not much more."

"Where does she live?"

"In Greenwich, Connecticut, but not on the best side of town. At least she's got the house, but it's mortgaged. He was a traveling salesman—hale fellow, well met, you know?"

"I know. Derek is a bit that way himself, but in a charming and sophisticated way. He took me to his tailor when I left Oxford and had some clothes made for me. It was his way of sending me off into the world. He gave me my first car, too—his ten-year-old Mercedes Roadster, which I drove into its grave in a few years."

"Were you a hell-raiser at Oxford?"

"I wasn't exactly a Hooray Henry, but I partied my share. I was very busy—I played in a jazz trio, and we worked two or three nights a week, then I had to get up early and be greeted by the shining faces of Eton boys, not all of them eager to learn."

"Were you eager to learn?"

"Not terribly, except music and art history. I got a first, but just barely."

"A first-class degree?"

"Right."

"Something like the dean's list?"

"I guess." They finished dining, and Laurence asked for the bill. Theresa looked at her watch.

"Early day tomorrow?" he asked.

"No, it's my day off."

"Then you must let me show you my new apartment."

"I believe I've seen it."

"Yes, but not with the new furniture and pictures. It's much better now."

"All right, but no ravishing."

"We can always ravish each other at a later date."

"Maybe," she said.

"I'll take that as an expression of affirmation."

BACK AT THE FAIRLEIGH, he took her around and showed her the fruit of his shopping.

"It looks very different now," she said.

"Like somebody lives here?"

"Like that."

He took her in his arms and kissed her.

She kissed him back, then said, "Remember, no ravishing."

"But I'm off to war," he said.

"War?"

"War with a flight simulator. I have to go to Kansas for a couple of weeks of flight training."

"You're learning to fly?"

"I'm already licensed, but I have to get a type rating for my new airplane."

"And you consider that war?"

"Those simulators are dangerous. You can crash and burn."

She laughed. "And it takes two whole weeks?"

"Sixteen days, to be more precise, and then I have to get some hours with a mentor in the new airplane before I can fly it alone."

"It's beginning to sound like a long time before I'll see you."

"Tell you what, take some off time, and I'll come back and get you, and we'll fly around the country."

"Well, I do have some vacation time built up."

"Then it's a date, in sixteen days, starting day after tomorrow."

"You're on," she said.

"You won't need a nightgown, you'll be too busy to use it."

"Promises, promises," she said.

"No, vows." He took a key from his pocket, one with a Fairleigh fob and the number 15 embossed on it. "In case you need shelter from the storm," he said.

"I won't, but thank you." She tucked the key into her handbag.

11

STONE BARRINGTON picked up the phone and called Laurence Hayward. "Good morning."

"Good morning," Laurence said. "What time is it?"

"Nearly eleven. Did you sleep in?"

"I guess I did."

"I just got off the phone with Cessna. You are the proud contractor of two jet airplanes, one to be delivered the day you finish your training, the other in eight and a half months." He read the terms.

"That's wonderful," Laurence said, sounding fully awake now.

"They're e-mailing me the contracts for both airplanes. Why don't you stop by late this afternoon and sign them."

"Five o'clock?"

"Perfect. Did you confirm your training dates?"

"I did. I fly out tomorrow in a Cessna jet and start at eight AM the following day."

"I spoke to Pat Frank. Your new mentor will meet you in Wichita on graduation day, having picked up the airplane at the factory that morning. He'll also have spent the three previous days doing acceptance flights, which is when he looks for defects and gets them corrected."

"Great. I'm going to do some flying with him after that, to put some hours in my logbook."

"Good idea. How's the apartment?"

"Looks like I've always lived here."

"Good. See you this afternoon."

"Certainly." They hung up.

THERESA WOKE UP LATE and went into the kitchen to make her breakfast. She opened the tea canister and found more than tea: an IOU from Butch for $200 and nothing else. She stormed into his room and found the bed unslept in and what clothes he owned, gone. She decided it was worth the $200 to get rid of him. She sat down and called a neighborhood locksmith and arranged to have her front door lock changed. He promised to come the following day.

Later, as she was washing her breakfast dishes, the phone rang.

"Hello?"

"Theresa, it's Carl Winger, in Personnel."

"Good morning, Carl."

"I thought you'd like to know, I just hired your brother, Harold—or Butch, as he prefers to be known."

"My goodness." She wanted to tell Carl to keep Butch away from cash registers.

"We're going to give him a few weeks of switching departments, starting in shoes, and then, if I'm any judge of material, he'll be ready to work in any department at any store. He's on his way now to the shoe shop at the Seventy-second Street store."

"Well, I'm glad it worked out, Carl."

"Thank you for sending us such a good candidate."

"You're welcome." She hung up feeling guilty. Butch was going to screw this up; she just knew it, and it would be her fault.

LAURENCE KNOCKED on Stone's office door at five sharp. "Is this the airplane store?"

"You're in the right place. By the way, did you bring your checkbook?"

"Always in my pocket."

Stone sat him down and placed two stacks of documents before him. "You have a pen?"

Laurence held up his silver Montblanc. "Courtesy of Woodman & Weld."

"Then start signing. Joan has marked the places with green tabs."

Laurence finished the first stack and handed them to Stone for checking, then started on the second stack. Stone gave the lot to Joan to make copies and pack for FedExing. "Now, two checks," Stone said, "one for the entire price of the CJ 3 Plus, and another for the deposit on the Latitude. You'll make progressive payments on that."

Laurence wrote and signed the checks. "Whew," he said, mopping his brow, "I think I now own everything I want to own."

"Trust me, you'll think of something else."

"I expect so, but nothing with that many zeros attached."

"Where are you planning to fly with your mentor?"

"Well, first, I'll pick up my girl at Teterboro, then maybe to San Francisco, L.A., and other points west."

"I keep a house at the Arrington Hotel in L.A.," Stone said. "You're welcome to the use of it while you're out there. You could spend a few days in L.A. and make training flights every day, flying the local instrument approaches."

"Great idea!"

"Your girl will like the house and the shopping on Rodeo Drive."

"I expect she will."

"Call me when you get back," Stone said.

BUTCH LET HIMSELF into his sister's apartment. "Sis?" he yelled. "I forgot something." No answer so he beckoned Curly to follow him in. He went to the liquor cabinet and retrieved an unopened bottle of the Macallan 12 whiskey. "Okay, let's make tracks." As he walked past the coffee table he saw a familiar key lying there and picked it up.

"What's that for?" Curly asked.

"It's the key to our mark's apartment," Butch said. "Pity we don't have time to get it copied."

"You can't get a locksmith to copy a hotel key," Curly said. "I know because I used to work for one. But I know how to duplicate it. Has your sis got any candles?"

They went into the kitchen and found one.

"First," Curly said, "we melt the candle, then I can make an impression of the key in the warm wax and make the copy myself with a couple of tools available in any hardware store."

Butch found a saucepan, and soon they were able to pour the melted wax into an empty kitchen matchbox. They waited a while for the wax to cool a bit, then Curly pressed each side of the key and the tip into the wax and closed the matchbox. "Now," he said, "let's find a hardware store."

"There's one called Gracious Homes over on Third Avenue," Butch said.

"Pretty fancy name for a hardware store."

"Pretty fancy neighborhood," Butch replied. "Let's get out of here before Sis gets home." He carefully replaced the key on the coffee table, cleaned up the kitchen, grabbed the bottle of scotch, and they departed the premises. They hoofed it over to Third Avenue and found Gracious Homes. Curly located two files and a small vise, then he saw the key department. A clerk waited on them, and Curly selected two blank keys from their collection. "I think that'll do it," he said.

"Is this going to work?" Butch asked.

"You bet your sweet ass," Curly replied. "All we have to do is find out when our mark won't be there."

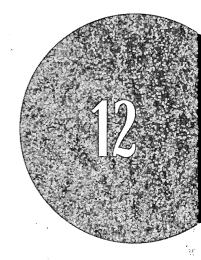

B UTCH CALLED THERESA. "Hello, sis."

"Hello, Butch. I hear you got the job. For God's sake, please don't screw it up. You'll ruin my reputation with the company."

"Don't worry about it. I guess you've noticed that Curly and I cleared out of your place. We found a furnished studio in the far East Eighties, and we'll bunk here for a while. What have you been up to? Seeing your new client?"

"My new client has buggered off to Wichita for a couple of weeks."

"Oh, well."

"Don't worry about it. Okay, maybe I'll see you around the store," she said.

"Good luck, baby." They hung up.

"Curly," Butch said, "there's good news—our mark is leaving town for two weeks. We're in."

"Oh, yes!" Curly exclaimed.

LAURENCE MET the Cessna pilot at Teterboro. The aircraft was a CJ 3 Plus demo, and for having ordered two airplanes, he rated a free ride to Wichita. He was allowed to fly left seat for the nonstop flight, and he flew an instrument approach into Eisenhower Field. He was in his hotel suite half an hour later and looking forward to a good night's sleep.

CURLY AFFIXED the small vise to the kitchen tabletop in their new apartment and went to work on one of the key blanks. Since he didn't have an emery wheel, he did all the work by hand, filing the blank until it dropped easily into the wax form, fitting perfectly. "Okay," he said an hour later, "we're ready."

IN THE LATE EVENING, Butch and Curly took a cab south, got out a block short of the Fairleigh, and walked from there. "We'll go in through the garage," Butch said, "and avoid the gaze of the concierge and hotel staff." They found the garage entrance on the side street and waited across the way until the drop-off area was clear of workers, then hurried in and took the elevator straight to the fifteenth floor. They emerged in the entrance hall.

"What if there's an alarm system?" Butch asked.

"Hotels don't have alarm systems on individual units," Curly said. He produced the key. "Now watch." He inserted the key, and with a little jockeying, it worked smoothly. Curly pushed open the door. "After you, sir."

Butch walked in and felt for a light switch; he found one that turned on all the living room lights.

"Jesus Christ!" Curly said, looking around. "I thought this was going to be a regular hotel suite! It looks more like the inside of a mansion!"

"Yes, it does."

"What are we going to do, clean out the place?"

"Absolutely not," Butch replied. "Don't you take so much as a pair of cuff links. We're looking for documents."

"What kind of documents?"

"Bank correspondence, brokerage statements, anything that leads to money."

"Where do we start?"

"In the study." Butch got the lights on, and they searched the room. "The only thing here of value to us is the booze," he said. "You want a drink?"

"Don't mind if I do," Curly said.

Butch poured them a couple of large single-malt scotches, and they eased into leather chairs and sipped.

"I could get used to this life," Curly said.

"Don't. Remember, we're transients here." Butch washed the glasses and wiped them dry, then returned the scotch to the bar. "Let's try the master suite." He led the way into the big bedroom, then into the dressing room. "My sis sold him all this stuff in a single morning," Butch said, showing him the suits, shirts, and shoes.

Curly began opening drawers. "What's this?" he asked, pointing to the contents of one.

"English pounds sterling," Butch replied. "We'll take some, but not all. We can change it at a bank later." He fished out three hundred pounds from the stack of notes. "I think what we need is to find his office."

They went through the rest of the place and found an office off the kitchen, neat as a pin, everything in its place. Butch started opening drawers, but they were nearly bare; only the usual office tools and stationery. He tried some file drawers and found a file with the name of a trust company on it. The folder held some documents.

"Holy shit," Butch said. "If I'm reading this thing right, it acknowledges the deposit of six hundred and twelve million, less than a week ago."

"You must be reading it wrong," Curly said. "There isn't that much money."

"What kind of a forger are you?"

"Prison-trained," Curly replied. "What do you want forged?"

Butch handed him a document. "This signature," he replied, "Laurence B. Hayward." He handed Curly a blank sheet of paper and a pen.

Curly looked at the signature. "Make a copy of the document," he said, pointing at a machine.

Butch did so.

Curly sat down at the desk, put the copy near his sheet and slowly drew the signature, copying every loop and twist.

"Too neat," Butch said.

"Relax, okay? I'm just getting started." Curly drew the signature again and again, a little faster each time.

"Looking good," Butch said.

Curly continued until he got half a dozen signatures he liked, each a little different from the others. "Got it," he said. "You see a check-book anywhere?"

Butch went through the drawers and came up with a large one. "Here you go."

"How much do you want to steal?"

"Well, we can't cash a check for all of it."

"Any bank statements?"

Butch looked. "Not yet. He's new in town and probably hasn't been sent one yet. And we can't just walk into his bank and cash it. We'll have to open an account somewhere and deposit the check and wait for it to clear."

"We need a company name to open the account," Curly said. "The bank is unlikely to just pay a check to some John Doe."

Butch thought about it. "I know, we'll create a corporation, using an online legal service. It'll cost a few hundred bucks, but we'll have incorporation papers to use to open the account."

"We'll need a credit card to do that," Curly said. "I've got a better idea. I know a disbarred lawyer from prison who's out now. We'll track him down and get him to do the legal stuff."

"Then you'd better forge some checks now."

"Nah," Curly said. He flipped to the back of the checkbook and tore out two pages of three checks each, then found an envelope and tucked them inside, along with the copy of the financial document.

"We'll just hang on to these until we have our ducks in a row." He picked up a small metal box. "Look, it's a check-writing machine." He ran a sheet of paper through it and printed out an amount. "We'll pick up one at an office supply store." He wrote down the name and model number.

They shut off the lights and went into the living room. "Hey," Butch said, "those paintings on that wall weren't here the first time I came. The guy's buying art. We'll create an art gallery, and he'll buy pictures from us—expensive ones. We ought to be able to grab a few hundred grand, if we do it right."

"I like the way you think, Butch. You keep doing that."

They turned off the lights, locked up, and took the elevator to the garage. Soon they were looking for a cab uptown.

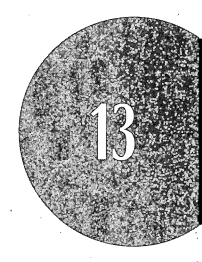

STONE AND DINO were having dinner at P.J. Clarke's, Viv being out of town on business, as she frequently was.

"How's your new client the rich kid doing?" Dino asked.

"Pretty good, by his own account. He's actually enjoying himself at Flight Safety, which I always find to be a grind. He even likes the flight simulator, which I detest."

"Can you really learn to fly in a simulator?"

"You can learn to fly the simulator," Stone said. "It doesn't handle exactly like an airplane, but the cockpit layout and the avionics are identical, and the view out the windows is cities, fields, and airports, which are pretty realistic. It's good for testing your judgment and learning to make quick decisions."

"Better you than me."

"He's got less than a week to go, and he's not in the least discouraged. I was tearing my hair out at that point. And when he finishes there, he's going to start flying his airplane with a mentor pilot aboard. Pat Frank arranged that for him."

"How about you? I haven't seen you with a woman for a while. That's unlike you."

Stone laughed. "Sometimes you're lucky, sometimes you're not."

LAURENCE HAYWARD FINISHED his last simulator session and went back to the instructor's office, where he filled out some paperwork.

"You did well," the man said. "Better than most owner-pilots. Don't try to do too much in the new airplane, until you're feeling confident in it, and don't start feeling confident too soon. And listen to your mentor pilot."

Laurence glanced at his watch. "He should be waiting downstairs for me. Are we about done?"

"About," the man said, signing a document and handing it to him. They shook hands, and Laurence went downstairs and found a tall, thin man of at least sixty to be the only person in the waiting room.

"Laurence Hayward?" he asked.

"I am."

"I'm Don McEvoy," he said. "Pat Frank sent me to mentor you. Sit down for a minute, and let's talk."

Laurence sat down.

"Where do you envision flying the next couple of weeks?"

"To Teterboro this afternoon, overnight there, pick up my girl-friend, then to San Francisco tomorrow morning. After that we'll improvise."

"Okay."

Laurence's iPhone went off. "Excuse me. Hello?"

"Laurence, it's Mom." She sounded funny.

"Mom, are you all right?"

"Not really. Derek had a heart attack this morning—it was too early your time to call you—and he's having an emergency triple bypass as we speak. His doctors are very optimistic about the outcome."

Laurence knew that bypass surgery was routine these days, but he was immediately worried about his mother. "I'm so sorry. What can I do to help? Do you need anything?"

"I need you," she said. "Can you fly over tomorrow?"

"Hold on a moment, please." He turned to Don. "Change of plans. I'd like to fly to London tomorrow. My stepfather has had a heart attack and surgery."

McEvoy shrugged. "We can do that. I'll set up flight handling with Pat Frank. We'll just go east instead of west, via Newfoundland."

"Mom? I'll be there tomorrow night. Are you at the London house?"

"Yes. I'll have Wanda get your room ready."

"Have her get the adjoining room ready, too. I'm bringing a girl—her name is Theresa Crane."

"All right. Hold on, here's the doctor." She covered the phone and spoke to someone for a couple of minutes, then came back. "Derek came through the surgery just fine. He should be able to go home in three or four days. I'll take him to the country for his recovery."

"That's wonderful. I'll see you late tomorrow night. Don't wait up, I'll use my key." He said goodbye and hung up. "Where will we land?" he asked Don.

"Did you fly the London City approaches in the sim?"

"Yes, I took the international course."

"We'll land there, but if you're staying a few days, I'll find somewhere else to park the airplane, and I'll make my own living arrangements."

"Good, west of London would be best."

"Got it."

Laurence called Theresa.

"Hello, there. What time are you getting in?"

"Not until tonight sometime. Do you have a passport?"

"Yes."

"Bring it. We're flying to London tomorrow. Bye-bye." He hung up.

THERESA STARED at the telephone. "Hello?" She hung up. "Well," she said to herself, "that was abrupt, but exciting."

"LET'S GO LOOK at the new airplane," he said. The two men got into Don's rental car and drove to the Citation Service Center. The airplane was there, gleaming in the afternoon sun.

"Let's do a quick walk-around, and we'll get out of here. I'm already filed for Teterboro."

"Okay." Laurence stowed his bags in the forward luggage compartment and followed Don as he walked around the airplane, checking gauges and the levels of fuel, oxygen, and hydraulic fluid. He showed him how to connect the airplane's main battery, then they got into the cabin and closed the door. Laurence took the left seat and looked around him. All was familiar from his first flight on the Cessna airplane and from the simulator. He worked his way through the checklist, with Don making helpful comments, then started an engine and cranked up the air-conditioning. Then, with both engines running, he got clearance from the tower and permission to taxi.

Ten minutes later, they lifted off the runway and headed east, with the setting sun behind them.

A little after nine PM, Laurence set down the airplane gently on runway 19 at Teterboro, and taxied to Jet Aviation, where his newly rented hangar space awaited them.

At the terminal he ran through the shutdown checklist and flipped off the battery switch. Silence greeted them for the first time in nearly four hours.

"My car is waiting for us," Laurence said. "I'll put you up for the night."

"What time do you want wheels-up tomorrow?"

"Nine AM?"

"Sounds good."

AT THE FAIRLEIGH, Laurence found a note from Marge on his pillow: everything was fine—she'd see him in the morning.

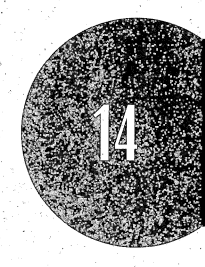

THEY WERE AT TETERBORO by seven-thirty, where they stowed their luggage and went through the emergency gear Don had ordered: three dry suits, GPS locator, handheld aviation radio, food, and water. Laurence had already ordered a life raft as part of the airplane's original equipment. Don showed them how the suits worked and how to handle an emergency ditching in the North Atlantic. To Laurence's surprise, Theresa took it in stride.

At nine AM sharp, Laurence began his takeoff roll, then rotated, got the landing gear and flaps up, and set a course in the flight management system for St. John's, Newfoundland. They climbed to flight level 410—41,000 feet—and Don checked the range ring on the GPS.

"Good tailwinds today," he said. "We might be able to make London after St. John's without stopping in Ireland for fuel."

THEY REFUELED in St. John's, then climbed to altitude. Don pointed at the range ring. "Unless that changes, we're nonstop to London." He pulled the power back a little, and the range ring moved outward. "Just in case we want to go to Norway," Don explained. "It doesn't hurt to have some extra fuel in reserve. I'm going to stretch my legs." He got out of the cockpit.

A moment later, Theresa took the right seat. "I'm still alive," she said. "I can't believe it."

"We're in good hands with Don," Laurence said. "He has a world of experience."

"I feel I'm in good hands with you."

THEY WOULD BE landing in the dark. Don, back in the right seat, talked Laurence through the setup for the approach. The weather was uncharacteristically clear, and Laurence saw the runway as they turned final.

"The autopilot knows the way," Don said. "Stand by for a steeper-than-usual final leg—it's a characteristic of this particular approach."

Laurence devoted himself to slowing the airplane for the steep descent, with flaps, landing gear, and, as necessary, speed brakes. They touched down exactly where he had aimed the airplane and taxied to the ramp, where there was a car waiting.

"You go ahead," Don said. "I'll find a hotel and move the airplane to Oxford tomorrow. I've reserved hangar space there."

"That's perfect—half an hour from my folks' place in the country."

"You can always reach me on my cell phone," Don said. "Let me know when you have a departure time, and I'll make the arrangements and get the paperwork filed."

They shook hands, and Laurence and Theresa got into the hired Jaguar. "Wilton Crescent, Belgravia," he said to the driver.

"I know it well, sir."

Three-quarters of an hour later, Laurence was letting them into the house. He put their luggage on the elevator and they rode up two stories. "You'll have your own room," he said.

"That's very considerate," she said, "but unnecessary."

They turned in together and fell quickly asleep. She woke him in the morning, and the ravishing was accomplished.

LAURENCE'S MOTHER had breakfast waiting for them, and he made the introductions. "Theresa, this is my mother, Dorothy, who likes to be called Dot." The two women got on well immediately.

"Derek had a good night and will be walking around today," she said. "I've hired a private nurse to help him in the country. His private insurance pays for part of it."

"Don't worry about the money," Laurence said. "Dad left me well fixed." Somehow, he didn't feel ready to tell them about the lottery. He hadn't told anyone, so far, and he wasn't sure how to handle it.

"I didn't know he was all that well off."

"He made some very good property investments in Palm Beach."

"Good for him, and good for you. I'm relieved that you can help. Derek has always made a lot of money in advertising, but he's spent most of it in living well. I expect he'll sell out to his junior partners, and that should see us right. We might have to part with some property, though."

"Don't worry your head about it."

"Why don't you and Theresa drive down to the country today or tomorrow and settle into the cottage? You can take Derek's car and have some time together."

"Tomorrow, perhaps. I want to make sure you're all right here."

LAURENCE TOOK THERESA shopping at Harvey Nichols and bought her some clothes and a new suitcase to hold them, then, the following morning they set out for Berkshire in Derek's Aston Martin Rapide, a four-door sedan with just room enough for their luggage. After an hour's drive, Laurence drove through the gates to the property, which was called Westward Ho!, past the handsome main house and to his cottage. Theresa found it completely charming.

TWO DAYS LATER, his mother arrived, driving her Jaguar XJ with Derek in the passenger seat.

"You look very good," Laurence said, giving him a hug.

"Just a little tired," Derek replied. "One more good night's sleep, and I'll be fit."

"Don't rush it."

They dined at home, on a dinner prepared by a local cook who served them most weekends at the country house. Derek excused himself before dessert, and Laurence helped him to his bed.

"It's good to see you, kiddo," Derek said, as Laurence tucked him in.

"You too."

"All this happened a little before I was ready for it, you know."

"I guess it's always that way."

"The boys at the shop are taking care of things. I'll make an appearance as soon as I feel up to it, to calm the clients, but I think I'm going to pack it in as soon as we can work out a price and a smooth transition. I hear they're already looking for financing."

"You can spend more time out here, then."

Derek shook his head. "I won't be able to afford it without a big salary coming in, so I think it will have to go. We might be able to manage the London house, but if not, then we'll sell that, too, and take a flat."

"Derek, don't trouble yourself about all that, just rest and get well. I can help you."

"You, help me?"

"Dad left me well fixed. Trust me, I can help."

"And I thought you'd be playing piano in some dive for the rest of your life, while teaching pubescent schoolboys in the daytime."

"Maybe not." He kissed him on the forehead and went back downstairs.

"Was he talking about selling everything?" his mother asked.

"Yes, but don't worry, you won't be moving house."

"We won't? That's not what Derek was saying."

"Please trust me, Mom. Derek and I will sort it all out together."

"If you say so, darling."

"I do say so, and it will be so."

They had a cognac together, then everyone went to bed.

Laurence and Theresa walked back to the cottage in the moon-light. "They're such nice people," she said.

"They are, and I'm glad to have them as my family."

"I envy you that," she said. "My family has always been such a mess."

"Butch, too?"

"Especially Butch. I worry about him."

"You'll have to tell me all about it when I'm sober," he said.

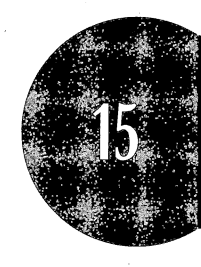

MARGE MASON let herself into apartment 15 and went directly to her new office. She had spent the day before arranging the room and making file tabs and ordering office supplies. As she sat down the morning light struck the little check-writing machine on her desk. It wasn't where she had left it, and the angle of the light revealed a fingerprint on the metal surface. She held her own fingers near it and compared: it was larger than any of her prints.

She remembered something she had once seen on television; she found a roll of cellophane tape in her desk drawer, applied a length of it to the print on the check writer, then peeled it off, taking the print with it. She took an index card from the drawer and applied the tape to it, then noted the date, time, and circumstances on the card and signed it. Her phone rang.

"Good morning, Mr. Hayward's office."

"Good morning, Marge, it's Laurence."

"Are you up? I didn't hear you when I came in."

·"I'm up, and I'm in England."

"*England?* I thought you were coming back to New York from Wichita."

"I did, but my stepfather has had a heart attack and surgery, so I came to be with my mother." He gave her the telephone number. "Best to reach me on my cell, though."

"Of course. How long will you be gone?"

"I don't know—a week or ten days, I suppose. I have some business to take care of here. Everything all right there?"

"I think so, but when I came in this morning I noticed that my office wasn't quite the way I left it."

"It's the hotel maids," he said. "They come in every day, and they move things around."

"Ah, I should have thought of that. Is there anything I can do for you here?"

"I don't think so. You can pay the bills as they come in. E-mail me anything you're uncertain about for approval."

"Certainly."

"I'll let you know when I have a return date. Oh, I hired the driver from the chauffeur service I've been using. His name is Oliver Mann. Please put him on the payroll at seventy-five thousand a year, with effect from yesterday."

"Will do."

He gave her Oliver's phone number. "You can call him for his Social Security number and address, et cetera. If you need to run any errands, Oliver will drive you. He'll be at the apartment every day to help you, should you need him."

"Grand."

"I have to go now. Call me, if you have any questions."

"I will. Goodbye." They both hung up.

BUTCH WAS HAVING an idle moment in the shoe department when his cell rang.

"It's me," Curly said.

"What's up?"

"My ex-lawyer friend is here, and I need some information for the incorporation papers. What do you want to call it?"

"How about Internet Arts?"

"Sounds good."

"Rent a post office box in that name, and have some stationery printed. I've already arranged for a website, internetarts-dot-com, but there's nothing on it yet. Put that on the stationery, and have some cards printed for both of us. Change the pounds we took to dollars and use that for expenses. Oh, and put this motto on the stationery— 'Fine art at your fingertips.'"

"How much should I have printed?"

"Not much, we have only one client—customer. Gotta run." He hung up.

LAURENCE SAT DOWN for lunch on the terrace with his stepfather; his mother and Theresa had gone to the village to shop for dinner.

"I've accepted an offer from my partners for the agency," Derek said.

"Was it what you wanted?"

"Nearly. I also spoke with a friend in real estate who's familiar with our properties. He says I should ask eight million and take seven for this place."

"How about Wilton Crescent?"

"Ask and get ten million. Unless it's a Russian or an Arab, in which case I should ask fifty percent more. Trouble is, that market isn't what it used to be."

"Let me make you a different sort of offer."

"All right."

"I'll give you twelve million pounds sterling for both properties, with a guaranteed lifetime tenancy for both of you. That way, you get a pile of cash, but you don't ever have to move."

Derek looked at him narrowly. "You can come up with that kind of money?"

"I can. What's more, you should have a chat with your accountant. You might be able to shelter much of it from the tax man by taking payment in the States. I can arrange for the people who handle my investments to handle yours, too."

"I don't think I want to have that particular chat with my own accountant, but my chief financial officer at the agency would know exactly how to handle that."

"Perhaps that's best."

"Laurence, I accept your offer with pleasure."

"Nothing need change for you. I don't expect to be spending that much time here. I'd love for you two to visit me in New York, though.

I have lots of room, and if you want more privacy, I own a second flat in my building."

"Give me a few weeks to get hale and hearty, and we'll take you up on that."

"When you've got things sorted out, have your solicitor draw up a contract, and I'll sign it and put the cash anywhere you want it."

Derek smiled broadly and shook his hand.

THERESA CAME BACK from her shopping trip with Dot, and the two of them had a drink in the cottage before going over to the main house for dinner.

"You like this estate, do you?"

"I think it's superb," she said.

"I'm glad, because I just bought it—and the London house—from Derek, with a lifetime tenancy for him and Mom."

"Congratulations!"

"Something else."

"What's that?"

"You have interior designers at your store, don't you?"

"Yes, in the home department."

"I own a second flat at the Fairleigh, number 14A, one floor down from my apartment. It's furnished with hotel things, and I'd like it redone. Can you call somebody there and have them put their best person on it?"

"Certainly. I'll call the department head."

"It's a two-bedroom apartment. Do you think a million dollars would handle everything?"

"I'll give them that budget."

"Good. I'd like it done in, say, six weeks, please. They can have samples and drawings for me when we get back."

Theresa looked at her watch. "She should be back from lunch now. I'll call her."

"There's a phone in the study."

She went there.

Laurence took a sip of his drink and sat back in his chair. He felt very good about this; it was much more rewarding to do something for the people he loved than just to spend the money on himself.

THAT NIGHT at dinner with his very happy parents, his mother turned to Laurence. "You know," she said, "we'd been thinking about doing over the Wilton Crescent house. A friend of mine, Susan Blackburn, is one of London's top designers, and I was going to speak to her about it. Now, though, I'm going to have her redo it for you, Laurence, and that will be our gift. You've made us so happy."

Laurence had to fight back the tears.

BUTCH AND CURLY had been busy; they had downloaded dozens of paintings from other websites to their own and had made purchases possible only with a password, which nobody else possessed. Finally, they sat down, and Butch watched while Curly inserted a check into the check writer and printed out one for $75,000. Curly signed it, forging Laurence Hayward's signature, then Butch put everything in an envelope and walked down the street to a new bank branch that had just opened and approached the manager's office.

"Good morning," he said. "I'm Harold Bremmer, and I'd like to open an account." He handed over the fake driver's license that Curly had had made.

The man invited him in and took his application. "Do you have your paperwork and a corporate resolution?"

"Right here." Butch handed him the documents and the check. "And the proceeds from our first sale as our opening deposit," he said.

"What are you selling?"

"Art. We've started with things from my own collection, but we're buying other things to sell."

"An expensive picture," he said.

"Mr. Hayward is a wealthy collector," Butch said, "and we expect him to make other purchases, perhaps even larger ones."

"I wish you luck."

"Thank you. How long will it take the check to clear? We have bills to pay."

"I'll put a rush on it," the manager said. "The funds should be available tomorrow afternoon."

Butch shook his hand and left with a checkbook tucked under his arm and arrived back at his studio apartment. "We're in business," he said. "You know, there's a better apartment available on the top floor. I think we should take it."

"Good idea," Curly said. "It's getting a little tight around here."

"Or you can keep this one, and I'll move upstairs. We can pay the rent from our new bank account. And we'll make another deposit tomorrow, this one for a hundred and twenty-five grand."

"An even better idea," Curly said. "Who needs a cell mate?"

A FEW DAYS LATER, Derek Fallowfield's solicitor appeared at his country house with the documents for the property purchase. Laurence signed them and phoned his bank with instructions for transferring the funds.

The following day Laurence and Theresa said goodbye to his parents, then they met Don McEvoy at Oxford Airport and flew back to the States, via Iceland and Labrador. Oliver met them at Teterboro, where they cleared customs, and Laurence took Don aside. "How am I doing in the airplane?"

"Very well. Your experience in the King Air has been of value, and your technique is very good. I'm impressed with your knowledge of the avionics. Frankly, you're better at that than I am. If you're feeling good about flying the airplane, I don't think you need me anymore."

"I'll call you when I need to brush up on things."

"All you need to do now is fly," Don said.

IN THE CAR, Laurence said to Theresa, "I've grown accustomed to your company. Why don't you move into my place, and we'll get your things tomorrow?"

"All right," Theresa said, "we can experiment with that, but I'm keeping my apartment, just in case."

BACK AT THE FAIRLEIGH, Laurence found a thick envelope from the Ralph Lauren designer with fabrics, wallpapers, pictures of furniture, and drawings waiting for him.

"This looks wonderful," he said. "I particularly like the way they've enlarged the master bath by using the closet next door. Tell your colleague it's a go, I won't change a thing."

"First thing tomorrow," she said, "right after I see how Butch is doing in the shoe department."

BUTCH, as it turned out, was doing very well in the shoe department. "My specialty has become moving customers up from leather shoes to alligator," he told her over lunch. "It's easy to spot the ones who can afford it. They're moving me to the Purple Label suit department at the end of the week."

"That's good news. Once you've worked in a few more departments, you should aim for a personal shopper's job. You've clearly got the personality for it."

Butch beamed at her. "Thanks, sis, that's high praise, coming from you."

"I see you're expanding your wardrobe," she said, fingering a lapel. "Don't overdo it—even with your employee discount, it's expensive."

"I'll be very careful, I promise you. Oh, I moved into a slightly nicer apartment yesterday. You'll have to come over."

"Is Curly still with you?"

"Nah, he's got his own place and a job doing legal research for a lawyer acquaintance of his. He got a lot of experience in the prison law library—he was even writing appeals for other prisoners."

"I'm glad you're both doing so well," she said. "Your parole officer must be pleased."

"I'm off parole," he said. "What with all the guys getting released early, the parole officers are overworked, and I've got a job and an apartment, so they cut me loose. I'm a regular citizen again."

"Welcome back to the world," Theresa said.

Butch bought lunch.

THAT NIGHT, Butch went to see Curly. "We've got one check left, right?"

"Right."

"We'll deposit this one, and next week I'll close the account. Hayward's back in town and, sooner rather than later, he'll twig to what's going on. By that time, there will be no trace of us, and we'll have a tidy grubstake to take care of us."

"What we need is another scam," Curly said.

"I think I'm going to cool it," Butch said. "I'm pretty well set up now, and I'm liking my job."

"Tell me again, what is it you're doing?"

"My sister got me a trainee's job at her store."

"Ah, I would have figured it was something to do with money."

"Everything is something to do with money, Curly."

LAURENCE HAD JUST finished breakfast when Marge came to see him.

"Something's wrong," she said.

"What do you mean?"

"Have you written six checks totaling three hundred thousand dollars to a gallery called Internet Arts?"

"I've written a number of checks to galleries, but I don't remember that one."

She showed him the canceled checks. "The signatures match yours very closely, but I suppose they could be forgeries. Shall I call the police?"

"Let me take care of that," Laurence said. "I know somebody who knows somebody."

LAURENCE CALLED Dino Bacchetti and was put through. "Good morning, Dino, how are you?"

"Not bad, Laurence, and you?"

"I'm afraid your advice about bad people in New York has proved to be accurate."

"I hope you're not hurt."

"Nothing like that, only my checking account is damaged. Someone appears to have forged six checks for a total of three hundred thousand dollars."

Dino excused himself for a moment and covered the phone, then came back. "I'm sending Detectives Kehoe and Grappa of our financial fraud squad over to your place. They'll be there in half an hour."

"I can't thank you enough, Dino."

"Don't worry about it. I'll personally keep track of the investigation." They hung up.

HALF AN HOUR LATER, the front desk announced the officers and they were sent up. Laurence met them at the door and escorted them back to Marge's office. "Marge, these are Detectives Kehoe and Grappa," he said. "Please walk them through what's happened."

Marge did so. "Something else—I've just noticed the check numbers, which are higher than the checks I've written." She opened the checkbook. "I discovered that two sheets of three checks each have been ripped out and were used for the forgeries. The bastards are even using the same check-writing machine I use." She showed them the machine, then she remembered. She dug an index card out of her desk drawer. "I noticed a thumbprint clearly visible on my machine, and I did my best to preserve it." She handed Kehoe the card.

"Ms. Mason," Kehoe said, "you're a very smart lady. If you ever get tired of working for Mr. Hayward, I wish you'd join the NYPD."

"I watch way too many cop shows on TV," Marge said.

"We'll run this print today. Tell me, Mr. Hayward, who has a key to this apartment?"

"Marge, my girlfriend, Theresa Crane, and me. And, of course, the hotel has pass keys. Theresa and I were out of the country when this happened, and she certainly would have had nothing to do with this."

"Does your girlfriend live here?"

"Yes."

"Is she here now?"

"No, she's at work."

"And who is her employer?"

"Ralph Lauren, at the store on Fifth Avenue and Fifty-fifth, but perhaps you'd better call her before you show up."

They took charge of the canceled checks, asked a lot of questions, then left. Grappa drove over to Fifth Avenue, and Kehoe found Theresa Crane and introduced himself. "Ms. Crane, Mr. Hayward tells us that you have a key to his apartment, and that you were recently out of the country together."

"That's correct," she replied.

"Can you tell us where your key was when you were traveling?"

"In my purse," she replied, "which was with me the whole time we were gone."

"Is there anyone else of your acquaintance who might have had access to the key at some point?"

She shook her head. "No one at all."

"Thank you, Ms. Crane. I'm sorry to have bothered you."

"No bother," she replied.

"If you think of anything else we should know, here's my card."

She tucked it into her bra. "Thank you. I'll call, if I do."

The detectives returned to the 19th Precinct and processed their evidence. They ran the fingerprint, but there was a computer glitch and a delay for the results. They phoned the manager at the bank that cashed the checks, Harmon Wills.

"Yes, I remember some of those checks," the man said. "The company, an art gallery, opened the account a couple of weeks ago and deposited a check for seventy-five thousand."

"Who opened the account?"

"A man named Harold Bremmer. He had all the required documents and ID. He gave me a PO box number for an address, and a cell phone number."

"Can you describe him?"

"I'd say, mid-thirties, about six feet, brown hair, medium build, dressed in a business suit and tie."

"Any distinguishing marks?"

"None that I can recall."

Kehoe called the cell number and found it not in use.

Grappa phoned the post office and learned that the box number did not exist. He went back to Kehoe. "We've got a dead end here," he said. "Anything on the print yet?"

"Yep, we've got a match." He handed his partner a rap sheet with a photograph. "Name of Marvin Beemer Jones. Looks like that guy in the Three Stooges. Currently in a cell upstate."

"Mr. Jones has a pretty long reach, if he can leave a thumbprint on Park Avenue."

"We better do some checking." Half an hour later they had determined that Jones had been released, and they had the name of his parole officer.

"We cut him loose last week, on orders from above," the PO said. "We've been overworked and understaffed since the big prisoner release that's going on right now, statewide. We discharged the ones with nonviolent records from parole, and Jones was one of them. My record has him staying at the Y in Chelsea." A call to the Y revealed that Jones had stayed one night, then checked out and left no forwarding address.

"Well," Kehoe said, "we can list him as wanted, but unless he gets busted for something, we're at a dead end."

"You'd better call the commissioner," Grappa said.

"Me?"

"You're the one he called to give us this case."

"Oh, all right." Kehoe called the commissioner and told him the results of their investigation.

"Congratulations on identifying the suspect so quickly," the commissioner said. "Now find him."

"His name will be on the list of wanted felons tomorrow morning," Kehoe said. "But unless he gets himself picked up, we've got nothing to go on."

"Friends and relatives in the city?"

"None. Jones is from New Jersey and has no next of kin listed. He had no visitors in prison."

"Keep me posted," he said.

DINO CALLED LAURENCE. "My detectives have identified a suspect," he said.

"That was fast."

"He left a thumbprint at the scene. His name is Marvin Beemer Jones, an ex-convict, recently released from prison, where he was serving a sentence for possession of drugs with intent to sell. We've listed him as a wanted suspect in a felony, but since we have no other record of him or his whereabouts, we'll have to wait until he's arrested for something else before we can lay hands on him."

"Any idea of how long that might be?"

"No idea at all. Since he appears to have plenty of money—yours—he may not feel moved to commit another crime anytime soon."

"Thank you for trying, Dino," Laurence said.

"You can probably get your household insurance company to reimburse you for some of the cash."

"I'm self-insured."

"Then it's unlikely that you'll ever see that again. I'd suggest keeping your checkbook in your safe."

"Good advice, Dino, and thank you again." They hung up, and Laurence buzzed Marge.

"Yes, Laurence?"

"Do we have a safe?"

"No."

"Please order one for your office—no, better make it two, I'd like one in my dressing room, as well."

"Right away."

Laurence hung up and dismissed the incident from his mind. After all, he could afford the loss.

LAURENCE AND THERESA took the elevator down to the garage. "I've something to show you," he said, taking her hand and walking her around a corner. "You like it?"

Theresa put a hand on the Porsche and walked around it.

"The dealer delivered it this afternoon."

"It's gorgeous," she said.

Oliver was waiting beside the Bentley.

"Theresa, something popped into my mind after the police left. Your brother, Butch, was in the apartment that day when you put away my clothes."

"That's right, he was."

"Would he have had access to a key to the place?"

Theresa thought about it. "No, someone from the front desk walked us upstairs and let us in. Neither of us had a key. The door locked itself when we left. I hope you don't suspect Butch of anything."

"Oh, no, I was just trying to think of who else might have a key."

"And my key was in my purse the whole time we were in England."

"That's right."

Oliver drove them to a restaurant farther uptown, Caravaggio, where Stone and the Bacchettis awaited them, at Laurence's invitation. He introduced them to Theresa.

"I hear you've had a problem," Stone said.

"Yes, someone got into my apartment and stole some checks from my checkbook. They got three hundred thousand while we were in England."

"I didn't know you were in England."

"Yes, my stepfather had a heart attack and bypass surgery. I went to be with my mother while he recovers, and he's doing well. We had planned just to fly around the country, but we went across the Atlantic."

"Did the airplane do well?"

"It did very well indeed."

"How about you?"

"My mentor pilot said that he could be of no further use, so I'm on my own now."

"Laurence," Dino said, "did you have any further ideas about how someone could have gotten a key to your place?"

"The only thing I can figure is that some member of the hotel staff used a pass key."

"My people ran a check on everybody who might have had access," Dino said. "Nobody with a criminal record, and most of them are longtime employees."

"Well, I'm just going to have to let it go," Laurence said. "Let's order." They did so.

"Are you going to do any more flying soon?" Stone asked.

"I thought, if Theresa can take some more time off, I'd run down to Palm Beach and make sure the house is in order. It's being painted in my absence."

"I had a month of vacation time built up," Theresa said, "but we've used ten days of it. How about I take another week?"

"We can get a lot of miles under our belt in a week," Laurence said. "Stone has kindly offered us his house at the Arrington, in Los Angeles. We could start there, then maybe pop up to Napa and stock up on wines."

"Sounds good," Theresa said.

THEY LANDED at Palm Beach International and took a cab to Laurence's father's house. When they turned into the driveway, they found a police car parked there.

Laurence opened the door and put their bags in the hallway; he could hear voices. Hilda, the housekeeper, came out of the study. "Oh, Mr. Laurence, I'm so glad you're here."

"Why the police, Hilda?"

"Someone's been in the house. I found your father's desk ransacked."

Laurence went into the study and found two detectives waiting. "Was anything taken?"

"I don't think so," Hilda said.

"It appears they were looking for something," a cop offered.

"They were looking for me," Laurence said. "A policeman friend warned me this might happen."

"Why were they looking for you?"

"I came into some money, and it made the papers."

"Ah," the detective said, "you're the Powerball guy."

"Powerball?" Theresa asked.

"I'll explain later."

"What could they have found here?" a cop asked.

"Perhaps my address in England, but that's about it."

"You think the press is hunting you down?"

"That's what I think." He turned to Hilda. "Are the painters done?"

"Yes, yesterday, and they did a beautiful job, cleaned up after themselves, too. And by the way, I want to thank you for giving me your father's car. I just love it."

"I think that's what he would have wanted," he said.

Laurence thanked the cops for coming, and he and Hilda took their bags upstairs.

"Powerball?" Theresa said, when she had gone.

"That's where the money came from," he replied. "I hadn't gotten around to telling you."

"No reason why you should have," she said.

"Dino warned me this might happen. I think we should go on to L.A. tomorrow. I don't want to be seen here."

"That's fine with me."

THEY LEFT the house early in the morning for the airport and took off half an hour later. They made Santa Fe, where they stopped for fuel, then continued to Los Angeles, landing at Santa Monica Airport, where Stone had sent an Arrington Bentley for them. Soon they were ensconced in a guest room in the handsome house.

Shortly afterward, Laurence's cell phone rang. "Hello?"

"Laurence, it's Mom. Something very odd is going on here."

"What is it?"

"We've had two newspaper reporters on the property today, and the phone has not stopped ringing."

"Uh-oh."

"We're baffled. They're saying you won some sort of lottery?"

"I'm sorry, Mom, I should have explained while I was there. The story is true, but you don't need to confirm or deny it to anyone, just hang up if they call again, and call the police if they come onto the property."

"What sort of lottery?"

"It's called Powerball, and I won several hundred million dollars."

"That's astonishing!"

"Yes, it is. Theresa and I are traveling right now, so I'm hoping all this will blow over before we return to New York."

"How did they get our names and number?"

"They broke into Dad's house in Palm Beach, and they must have found his address book or some other paper with my English address. I was told this might happen, but I didn't believe it."

"All right, we'll follow your instructions. Give our love to Theresa."

"I certainly will. Goodbye, Mom." He hung up.

"They're harassing your parents?"

"Yes, I'm afraid so."

"Are they likely to track you to New York?"

"Perhaps. Dino warned me this might happen. At least no one knows where we are now."

"Thank God for that."

THEY WERE HAVING breakfast in bed, when Laurence's cell phone rang. "Hello?"

"Laurence? It's Marge."

"Good morning, Marge. What's up?"

"I've had a call from the hotel manager this morning. He says the front desk has been besieged by press and media people, looking for you."

"Oh, shit."

"Exactly. What do they want?"

"They've discovered that I won Powerball, that's all. They'll go away when they can't find me."

"The manager has refused to give them any information about you, or even to acknowledge that you live here."

"That's exactly what he should do. Please thank him for me."

"Is there anything you want me to do?"

"The telephone there is not listed in my name, so you shouldn't be harassed. If any of them get upstairs, call hotel security."

"All right."

"Call me if anything of importance happens."

"I will."

Laurence hung up. "They've already traced me to New York and shown up at the Fairleigh," he said to Theresa.

"We're sheltered here," she said.

Laurence picked up the house phone and rang the concierge.

"Yes, Mr. Hayward?"

"If anyone inquires if I'm staying here, please deny it."

"We would never divulge such a thing to anyone, sir."

"Good. When the New York papers arrive, will you send them all to me?"

"A *Times* was sent with your breakfast, sir. The tabloids will be in this afternoon sometime. I'll send them to you."

"Thank you." He hung up and turned to Theresa. "Shall we hit Rodeo Drive this morning?"

"All right. I'll need an hour to get myself together."

Laurence ordered a car and asked the concierge to get them a table at Spago Beverly Hills for lunch. He had a thought. "Please book the table in the name of Beresford," he said.

"As you wish, sir."

"Where did you come up with that name?" Theresa asked.

"It's my mother's maiden name and my middle name."

"Nice to have an alias, in the circumstances."

THEY WERE DRIVEN to Beverly Hills and strolled Rodeo Drive, looking in windows and doing some light shopping. When he started into the Ralph Lauren shop she tugged at his sleeve. "I'd rather do that at home and get my discount."

They visited Cartier, and Laurence bought her a tank wristwatch and an extra-large one for himself. When they pulled up to Spago for lunch and got out of the Bentley, someone with a camera ran up and took their photograph.

"Can they know?" Theresa asked.

"Unlikely. They probably shoot everyone who gets out of a Bentley." Inside he gave the name Beresford to the woman at the lectern.

"Oh, yes, Mr. Hayward, right this way." She led them to a table at the center of the garden.

"How did you know my name?" he asked the woman as they were seated.

"Just a moment." She disappeared and came back with a newspaper. "See the entertainment section," she said.

Laurence found it, and his photograph was on the first page, with the headline "English Schoolmaster Wins Powerball Big." Full details followed.

"You had a beard?" Theresa asked, looking at the photograph.

"Yes, and as you can see, a lot more hair. Dino said a shave and a haircut were a good disguise for me, and he was right. At least they don't have a more recent photograph."

THEY WERE IN the middle of lunch when the woman approached. "Mr. Hayward, I'm afraid that there is a knot of paparazzi at the front door. When you're ready to leave the restaurant we can get you out the rear door. You might let your driver know."

"Thank you so much," he said, and called the car. "Park somewhere near the rear of the restaurant, not at the door, but within sight of it. I'll call back when we're ready to leave." He hung up. "Relax, let's finish our lunch."

After he had paid the check, he called the driver. "Right now at the rear door, and have the car door open when we emerge." He hung up. "Shall we make our escape?"

The head waitress escorted them to a rear door and peeped outside. "Your car is there and ready," she said.

They ran from the door to the waiting car and dove into the rear seat, then they were off.

"If we're followed, try to lose them," Laurence said to the driver.

"If it's the paparazzi, they'll know the car is from the Arrington. They have all our license plate numbers. They may meet us at the hotel."

"Let's drive out to Malibu, then."

"Yes, sir."

It was a beautiful day, and they enjoyed the drive out Sunset Boulevard and up the coast, then they headed back to the hotel.

"Is there another entrance besides the main one?" Laurence asked the driver.

"Yes, sir, there's a more discreet one that we use for heads of state and the like, who are staying in one of the two presidential cottages, which are next door to Mr. Barrington's house. I'll phone ahead for access."

"Good man."

They made it onto the property, apparently undetected, and were driven to the house. The New York tabloids were waiting for them.

LIMEY POWERBALL WINNER LANDS
IN BIG APPLE, LIVES LARGE.

"My God, they've got photographs of the apartment from the *Times* piece," Laurence said.

The butler greeted them. "Good afternoon, Mr. Hayward, Ms. Crane. Security called and warned of paparazzi near the hotel." He handed them two small devices with wristbands attached. "It might be a good idea to wear these, should you leave the house. They will summon Security instantly."

"Thank you," Laurence said, and they both put them on. He looked at Theresa. "I was thinking of a skinny-dip in the pool," he said, "but now, not so much."

"Let's curl up in bed and watch a movie," she suggested.

"I need to make a call first." He pressed the button for the concierge.

"Yes, Mr. Hayward?"

"What time does the sun come up in the morning?"

"One moment. Five forty-six AM," he replied.

"I'd like a car to depart at five-thirty," he said.

"Of course, sir."

"Two other things—see if you can get us a nice suite at . . . just a moment." He found a copy of *Sunset* magazine and looked up an ad he had seen. "At Auberge du Soleil," he said.

"Certainly, sir."

"And please call Atlantic Aviation at Santa Monica Airport and have my airplane fueled and ready for departure at five-thirty AM."

"I'll confirm shortly," the man said. "How many nights?"

"Ah, three. And please arrange hangar space and a luxury rental car at Napa Airport." He hung up.

Ten minutes later, the concierge confirmed all his bookings.

Shortly before dawn the following morning, their car left the hotel and headed for the airport.

STONE BARRINGTON put down the newspaper and called Laurence's cell phone.

"Hello, Stone, how are you?"

"Very well, thanks, but I'm concerned about you."

"We're just fine. We saw the New York papers yesterday, and we flew up to Napa this morning. We're at Auberge du Soleil, in Rutherford."

"Very nice place. Are you being bothered?"

"Not while they don't know where we are. I checked in under my middle name, Beresford. I don't know how they could trace us here, we're out in the country."

"Just be ready for it."

"Everything Dino had predicted has happened," he said, "right up to their breaking into my father's house in Palm Beach. We walked in to find the police there."

"I'm sorry to hear it. How long are you staying in Rutherford?"

"Maybe three nights. I want to buy some wine while we're here."

"And what's your itinerary after that?"

"Wherever the wind blows us."

"All right, keep in touch."

Laurence hung up. "Stone is concerned about us."

"Sooner or later we'll be right in the middle of it," Theresa said.

"Maybe they'll be tired of us by the time we get back."

"I had a thought," she said. "An old girlfriend of mine from college lives in Santa Fe. She's always asking me to visit. Have you ever been there?"

"No, I haven't seen a lot of the West. Sure, let's go there from here."

"I'll give her a call."

THEY SPENT the next two days touring the vineyards, and Laurence bought a dozen cases of wine for his cooler in New York. After the third night, they flew to Santa Fe, rented a car, and found Theresa's friend's house. "Her name is Becky Gardner. Her husband is Ted. He's a writer."

The house was off Tano Road, on the north side of the town, and it was roomy, comfortable, and had wonderful views of the Jemez Mountains. The Gardners were cordial, and their room was delightful.

"I've invited some people over for dinner tonight," Becky said. "I hope that's all right."

"Of course," Laurence said.

ONE OF THE DINNER GUESTS had brought a copy of *People* magazine and handed it to Laurence. "I don't know if you've seen this yet."

The magazine fell open to a spread of pictures, of himself and the New York apartment. "No, I haven't seen this, but I've been expecting something like it." He handed the magazine to Theresa. "Now I'm a national item, I guess." The others passed it around.

"You look better without the beard," a woman said.

"And harder to recognize," her husband pointed out.

"What's it like to become rich overnight?" someone asked.

"Extremely weird," Laurence replied. "I managed to avoid the media, until they broke into my father's house in Palm Beach and found my address in England, and from there, they traced me to New York, and so on. I don't suppose they've followed me to Santa Fe yet. We'll try to be gone before they do," he said to his hostess.

"Don't worry about it. Stay as long as you can. We're off the beaten track out here."

BACK IN NEW YORK, Butch Crane and Curly were reading *People*. "I guess I didn't really understand who my sis had gotten involved with," Butch said.

"We need to figure out a way to hit him again," Curly said.

"Listen, we both did very well out of our little caper. Let's cool it now. Anyway, the guy is getting to be family, and I don't want to foul my own nest."

"Don't worry, I'll foul it for you, and you won't need to lift a hand," Curly said.

"Listen to me, Curly," Butch said, closing the magazine. "We're going to leave the guy alone. In fact, there is no more 'we.' I don't want to hear from you again."

"You don't want me for an enemy, Butch."

"Curly, I don't want you for anything. We each made a hundred and fifty grand, and that had better keep you out of my hair."

"Don't threaten me."

"Don't make it necessary." Butch got up and left Curly's apartment and went back to his own. He was liking his new life, but he knew Curly would eventually find a way to screw it up for him; the guy was like that.

LAURENCE AND THERESA were walking up Canyon Road, where most of Santa Fe's art galleries were housed.

"I like it here," Laurence said. "It's a beautiful town in a beautiful part of the country. Would you like to live here?"

"Well, sure," she said, "but please remember, I still have a job, and I'm going to have to get back to it soon."

"Why don't you leave the job and just hang with me?"

"Because I don't know you well enough, nor you me, to make a long-term commitment."

"Think of it as an experiment, not a commitment—that can come later, if it's what we want."

"Look, I've got more than a job, I've got a career, and I've invested a fair number of years building it. What would I do if you tired of me and just took off?"

"More likely, the other way around, but I'll tell you what. If I should do that—or if you want to leave—I'll give you a million dollars to tide you over while you're thinking about a new career."

"A pre-breakup agreement?"

"Even better, I'll give you the million right now, and you can take off anytime you get tired of life with me."

"I'd feel like a whore."

"That's nonsense. Have you felt that way at any time since we met?"

"Well, no, but I haven't been paid."

He turned her around and used her back for a desk, then tore out the check and handed it to her. "Here. Cash it, if and when you need it. Think of it as insurance."

She looked at the check. "All right, I'll think of it that way, and I'll quit my job, but you have to quit your job, too. I'm not going to be an English schoolmaster's lady friend."

He laughed. "I'll write to the headmaster today. I'm sure he's heard all about me by now, anyway, and he probably wouldn't want me back—too much notoriety for Eton."

"Then you've got a deal," she said, tucking the check into her bra. "And if you want to look at some houses, it's okay with me."

He stopped her in front of a real estate office and looked at the pictures in the window. "Pick something," he said, "and we'll make a start."

21

THEY HAD HARDLY sat down in the realtor's office when Laurence's cell phone rang. He excused himself and walked outside to answer it. "Hello?"

"It's Marge," she said.

He didn't like the sound of her voice. "Yes, what is it?"

"Someone has been in the apartment again," she said, "and it's not the hotel maids."

"Did they steal anything?"

"Not that I can tell, but there are little traces around the place that tell me someone was here. I checked, and the maids haven't been inside since I left work yesterday."

"We haven't been using the security system, have we?"

"No, we've been waiting for the company to come in and activate it."

"All right, activate it, and have cameras installed—the best and least conspicuous available, at least two in each room. I want wall-to-wall coverage everywhere."

"Right away," she said. "Any idea when you're coming home?"

"Not yet—at least a few days. I'd like the cameras operating by the time I get there, and I want to be able to check them on my iPhone. I've read that can be done."

"I'm on it," Marge said.

Laurence hung up and went back inside. "I'm sorry," he said. "Where were we?"

"Theresa has been giving me a list of what she wants in a house. Now tell me what you want," the agent, whose name was Diana, said.

"A view, new enough not to require remodeling, a study where I can read and work, enough room to swing a cat."

Theresa laughed. "That's Britspeak for pretty roomy."

"Let's start at the top," Diana said. "Something very good has just come on the market. It's a new house built by a woman who is widely regarded as the best builder in town, named Sharon Woods. She bought the property, designed the house, built it, had the landscaping done, and furnished it. It's a large, two-bedroom house with a two-bedroom guesthouse and a sitting room. It has every modern convenience, and it's in one of the best neighborhoods. Would you like to see it?"

He looked askance at Theresa, who nodded. "Now would be a good time," he said.

"Then let's go." She drove them to a spot overlooking the city, with views for a hundred miles. The house was beautifully designed, finely crafted, and handsomely, completely furnished, including linens and kitchen and dining things. The study was lined with bookcases, and there was a second, smaller one. The guesthouse was cozy, and the landscaping was wonderful. There was a pool, a hot tub, and a three-car garage. Diana gave them the price.

"Any wiggle room there?" Laurence asked.

"No, because you're the first to see it. If you want to avoid a bidding war, you should consider committing now."

He took Theresa aside. "What do you think?"

"I don't think 'ideal' is too strong a word."

He went back to Diana and took out his checkbook. "To whom would you like the check made?"

"To Woods Design and Construction."

He wrote out the check and handed it to her, but he kept hold of a corner. "The owner will be Theresa Crane, and everything about the sale will be held in the strictest confidence, especially my name."

"Of course, Mr. Beresford."

"Oh, and we'd like to move in today."

"Let me make a call," she said. She walked out onto a terrace and spent a minute on the phone, then returned. "Done, if your check is good."

"Have your bank call my bank now. My name isn't Beresford. The real one is on the check."

"Let's go back to my office and sign a contract," Diana said.

———

LESS THAN AN HOUR LATER, they had a completed sales contract, with closing to come a few days later. Diana handed Theresa the keys. "Congratulations on your new home," she said. She took a map from a drawer and made some marks on it with a highlighter. "This is how to get back to it. I'll have the utilities and phone put in your name immediately. Is there anything else I can do for you?"

"We have only to do some grocery shopping and pick up our luggage at a friend's," Laurence said. "Oh, and I suppose we'll need a car. What kind would you like, Theresa?"

"Is there a Mercedes dealer here?"

"Yes," Diana said. She made more marks on the map. "A ten-minute drive, and if you'll give me a grocery list, I'll take care of that."

THEY ARRIVED BACK at the house later in a new Mercedes station wagon, to find the refrigerator stocked and a bottle of Dom Pérignon on ice, with a note from Sharon Woods, welcoming them and saying that she would visit them to see if they wanted any alterations to the house.

They took the champagne and glasses onto the terrace and sipped as they watched the day laten and the sunset wax and wane.

"That was breathtaking," Theresa said. "I think I'm going to like living with you."

"I'm going to like it, too," he said.

22

S TONE WAS AT HIS DESK the following morning when Joan buzzed. "Laurence Hayward on line one."

Stone pressed the button. "Good morning, Laurence. I understand you've approved the recommendation of Strategic Services."

"I have, Stone, and thank you for your help. They should be working on the installation now. I called to tell you that I've bought another house."

Stone chuckled. "And where is the new one?"

"In Santa Fe, New Mexico. It's brand-new and completely furnished. We spent our first night in it last night."

"Congratulations. When is your closing?"

"Next week."

"I'll let Herb Fisher know. By the way, I'm coming to Santa Fe tomorrow to spend a few days with friends, on the way to L.A. I'd like very much for you to meet them."

"Wonderful! And you must come for dinner here during your stay."

"I accept. I'll be landing tomorrow afternoon, and I'll call you to make arrangements."

"How about dinner here the night after? Bring your friends."

"Sounds good. Their names are Ed and Susannah Eagle."

"Theresa and I look forward to seeing you." They hung up.

"STONE IS ARRIVING in Santa Fe tomorrow to stay with some friends," Laurence said to Theresa. "I think it's time for our first dinner party. Perhaps Diana will recommend a caterer?"

"I'll call Becky Gardner, she'll know someone. May I invite her and Ted?"

"Of course." Laurence became absorbed in his laptop.

"What are you doing?"

"I'm looking for a piano dealer in Santa Fe."

She handed him a newspaper, the *Santa Fe New Mexican*. "This arrived on the doorstep this morning. Check the classifieds."

"Good idea. I guess I'd better stock the bar, too, if we're having guests."

STONE LANDED at mid-afternoon in Santa Fe, and as he taxied to the ramp, he saw a familiar Range Rover waiting there, one belonging to

Gala Wilde, Ed Eagle's sister-in-law, with whom he had parted company a few weeks ago. He felt an unexpected pang.

Gala greeted him as he descended the boarding steps. "Ed and Susannah asked me to meet you and bring you to them. I hope you don't mind."

Stone kissed her on the cheek. "You're the most attractive taxi driver I could have wished for."

He loaded his luggage into the car and buckled in.

"They've also asked me to dinner tonight," Gala said.

"What a good idea!"

"Am I forgiven, then?"

"I think I'll wait for a more opportune moment to forgive you."

She laughed. "Just name it."

AT DINNER THAT evening, Stone said, "I've a friend and client who's just moved into a new house in Santa Fe, and he and his girlfriend have invited us all to dinner tomorrow evening. Is that convenient for you?"

"That means I won't have to assemble dinner tomorrow night," Susannah said, "so it's convenient."

"Who are these folks?" Ed asked.

"He's a very wealthy young Brit with a beautiful girlfriend. He's recently bought a spectacular New York apartment, and now a house here, new and furnished."

"I'll bet I know the house," Susannah said. "It's got to be Sharon Woods's new place. She's a local builder and she also builds spec houses, and she has a new one just finished."

"That would explain how he bought the house and occupied it in the same day," Stone said.

"He's a fast mover," Ed said.

"He certainly is. He bought the New York apartment after seeing photographs of it in the *Times*. He also flies the same airplane I do. Just got his type rating in Wichita."

"What does he do in England?"

"He is employed as a schoolmaster at Eton College."

"They must pay very well."

"I'm afraid that's all I can tell you—attorney/client privilege. However, if you have a copy of *People* magazine . . ."

"As a matter of fact, we do," Susannah said. "There's an article in it about my new picture." They moved into the library for drinks, and Susannah found the magazine. "Goodness, that is a spectacular apartment! And he won the lottery! How brilliant of him!" The magazine was handed around. "And he teaches at Eton," she said. "That makes him sound stuffy."

"Not in the least," Stone said. "He's bright and charming, and so is his girl. I introduced them, sort of. She's a personal shopper at Ralph Lauren, and he needed a wardrobe compatible with his new status."

"So she dressed him, then undressed him," Susannah said. "How romantic!"

LAURENCE RETURNED to the house to find Theresa at work arranging flowers.

"What, you came back without a piano strapped to your back?"

"I found a Steinway Model A at a church, advertised in the paper.

It was their rehearsal piano for the choir, and they've bought a concert grand to replace it. It's being delivered and tuned tomorrow morning."

"And the booze?"

"Should be here before sundown. The flowers look lovely."

"Thank you. I like a lot of flowers in a house."

"So do I, but I don't expect you're going to be able to grow a lot of them here."

"It's all right, there's a flower shop."

The doorbell rang, and a man with a hand truck brought in a dozen boxes.

"So much booze?"

"Most of it is wine. We have a wine cooler in the kitchen, you know."

"I hadn't spotted that. I guess we'll be discovering things in the house all the time. I spoke with the caterers and ordered our dinner for tomorrow night."

"Stone rang and said there'd be four of them."

"So with Becky and Ted, that's eight. Perfect."

"You like giving dinner parties, do you?"

"I do."

"Good, since I prefer that to restaurants, though I've nothing against restaurants."

"Then we'll have to make more friends, if we're going to give dinner parties."

"That suits me just fine."

"When do you think we'll be able to go back to New York?"

"Are you in a hurry to get back?"

"I'd hate to resign over the phone."

"I wrote the headmaster today."

"Then I guess I can resign over the phone."

STONE WAS RIDING SHOTGUN in Ed Eagle's car, as they turned off Tano Road onto Tano Norte. They were almost to Hayward's front gate when he saw a car parked in a road opposite with its head-lights off. "Ed, can you stop for a minute?"

"Sure," Ed replied, braking.

"Do you have a flashlight in the car?"

"Glove compartment."

Stone found a small SureFire light there; he got out of the car and approached the parked vehicle, switching on the flashlight. The bright beam revealed a man behind the wheel, looking startled. "Good evening," Stone said, loudly enough to be heard.

The car started and sped past him, turning toward Tano Road and disappearing in a cloud of dust. Stone went back to the Eagles' car and got in.

"What was that about?" Ed asked, continuing toward the gate.

"I'm not sure, but my best guess is that somebody from some newspaper or magazine has sniffed out Laurence Hayward in his new home."

"Either that, or somebody is casing it for a burglary."

Stone laughed. "Trust a criminal attorney to think of criminal intent."

Ed parked the car; they rang the front bell, were admitted by Laurence and Theresa, and introductions were made.

"What a beautiful place," Gala said.

"I'm afraid we can't take any credit for that," Theresa replied. "Only the flowers were added by us."

"Sharon Woods always does a beautiful job. Have you met her yet?"

"She's dropping by tomorrow."

They went into the living room, and a waiter took their drink orders. Laurence sat down next to Stone. "Herb Fisher called, and our closing is set for next week."

"You certainly found a great place. How much land is there?"

"About twelve acres—enough to keep the neighbors at bay."

Stone lowered his voice. "Someone is already paying attention to you."

"How do you mean?"

"There was a car parked across the road from the house as we drove in, with a man behind the wheel, lights off. I approached him, and he started up and accelerated in a hurry."

"Have they found me already?"

"Ed suspects a more criminal intent, maybe a burglary. I'd be careful while you're here."

"What are the gun laws like in New Mexico?"

"Lenient, I would guess. We're in the West, after all."

"Perhaps I'd better do some shopping."

"Laurence, have you any experience with firearms?"

"Quite a lot with shotguns and birds."

"If you buy a handgun, you're putting yourself and your fortune at risk."

"How's that?"

"In the past I've known two men who shot intruders in their homes, one of them fatally."

"Didn't they have that right?"

"They did, legally, but the civil lawsuits went on for years. One had to sell his house to pay the legal fees and settlement costs. The other, stuck with the huge medical bills of the intruder, has paid out nearly a million dollars, only some of it covered by his household insurance."

"I don't have any insurance."

"Get some liability, at least twenty million. It's fairly cheap. When complainants spot somebody wealthy, you become a target, no matter how right you are. I can arrange the insurance, if you like."

"Please."

"On the New York apartment and the Palm Beach house, as well?"

"Yes."

"But don't buy a gun," Stone said emphatically.

"If that's your best advice."

"It is."

THEY WERE CALLED to dinner, and Stone was seated between Susannah and Theresa, so he and Laurence didn't pursue their conversation.

"Laurence, I see we both have had the attention of *People* magazine this week," Susannah said.

"Of course, you're Susannah Wilde. Your new picture looks interesting."

"The difference between us is that I pursued the publicity, but you didn't."

"Tell me, does the reach of these magazines and tabloids extend to a place as remote as Santa Fe?"

"It doesn't matter where you are," Susannah replied. "Everybody with a cell phone camera is a stringer."

"What's a stringer?"

"A part-time reporter."

"Ah."

"I should think you'd be acquainted with that sort of journalism, coming from a place where tabloids have such a huge circulation."

"Certainly that's true of England, but somehow I've never come to their attention until now. Any advice?"

"Be courteously rude to them when they approach, and tell them nothing. People in my business have to be polite to them, because the public do read those papers—they're available at every supermarket checkout. But you're a private citizen, and if you communicate it to them that you expect to be treated as such, they'll eventually get the idea. Above all, don't smash any cameras or throw any punches. They love that sort of thing, and you'll end up in court, as so many celebrities have."

"And make no mistake about it," Ed said, "you are now, officially, a celebrity."

"That's an alarming idea. I had thought Santa Fe would be out of that particular loop."

"Alaska might be out of that loop, but hardly anywhere else in the United States or Europe," Ed replied. "Just ignore them and be uncommunicative, as best you can."

"Thank you, I'm grateful for the advice." He turned to Theresa. "See what you've gotten yourself into?"

"I'm not complaining," she said.

"Did you have any problems in Los Angeles?" Stone asked.

"We were spotted getting out of an Arrington Bentley at Spago, but we escaped out the back way after lunch. Our driver and the hotel staff seemed to handle it all very well, and we didn't have any problems on departure. Mind you, we left the hotel before dawn and took off very early. And we didn't have any problems in Napa."

"Perhaps they haven't figured out yet that you have an airplane, so they didn't cover Santa Monica or Burbank."

"I hope they never figure it out," Laurence said.

A **COUPLE OF DAYS LATER** Laurence got a call. "Hello?"

"Mr. Hayward, this is Chris, from Strategic Services."

"Good morning, Chris."

"I wanted you to know that we've completed your installation, and when you return, I'd be happy to come back and take you through it."

"That may be a while."

"In that case, let me e-mail you a short video that you can watch on your cell phone, then I'll call you back and walk you through installing the app to operate it."

"All right."

"Just hang up, and when you get it, tap on the arrow."

Laurence did so, and a moment later he was watching a tour of his apartment, featuring close-ups of nearly invisible cameras and a voice-over by Chris, showing how to operate the system. He hung up and waited, and Chris called back.

"I hope that gave you an idea of the system's capabilities."

"It certainly did."

"If you'll give me a four-digit code, I'll program the system to allow you to operate it."

Laurence gave him a code.

"Now let me walk you through downloading the app to your iPhone."

Five minutes later, Laurence was in full control of the system. He switched from one room to another, zoomed in and out, and watched Marge at her desk. Theresa looked over his shoulder.

"That's amazing," she said.

He called Chris back. "It worked beautifully," he said. "Now, I have two other houses, one in Palm Beach and one in Santa Fe. Can you install the same system in both?"

"We certainly can," Chris replied. He wrote down the addresses.

"We're in Santa Fe now, so you might do that one first."

"We'll be there the day after tomorrow," Chris said.

Laurence hung up. "There, I feel better now."

EXCEPT HE DIDN'T feel all that much better. That afternoon, he drove into Santa Fe to a gun shop he had passed before. After a few minutes of looking, he chose a small 9mm pistol and filled out the form for a background check. While he waited for a response, the salesman took him to the shop's indoor firing range and taught him the basics of using the weapon.

"Any other advice?" Laurence asked.

"Yes. Don't shoot anybody. Even if you're right, and if you remain safe, you'll be in for a lot of bother, and it's not worth it. That's unless the other guy shoots you first, then you don't have a choice."

Half an hour later, Laurence left with his gun in a hip holster and a box of cartridges, an extra magazine, and a cleaning kit in a bag.

Once home, he put the pistol and cartridges in the back of a bedside drawer, where Theresa would be unlikely to see it.

ALMOST SIMULTANEOUSLY, an editor at a tabloid, the *National Inquisitor*, took a phone call in his Miami, Florida, office. "This is Pat Bolton," he said.

"Hi, this is Chip, in Santa Fe. Do you remember me?"

"Yeah, Chip, you helped us out on that junkie actress last year."

"That's me. I've got something else for you."

"Tell me about it."

"You know the guy who won the Powerball a few weeks back?"

"L. B. Hayward? Right. We haven't been able to pin him down."

"I got him in Santa Fe."

"Are you sure?"

"Absolutely."

Bolton was skeptical. "Tell me exactly how you tracked him down."

"My mother is friends with a lady who sells real estate, Diana Zill.

She came over the other night for a drink, all excited. She had just sold this big spec house out on the north side of town."

"And you think Hayward bought it?"

"Well, it's like this—the guy wrote a check on the spot for the full amount and moved in the same day, so he had no shortage of ready cash."

"And that was Hayward?"

"Diana showed my mom the contract, and I got a look at it. The name of the buyer was Theresa Crane."

"Not Hayward?"

"Haven't you seen the spread in *People?*"

"Not yet, I guess."

"Hayward's got a girlfriend."

"Ahhh," Bolton said, "now *that's* good work, Chip. Did you get any photographs?"

"Not yet. I was out there, but I got rousted by a guy with a flashlight, so I guess he must have some security around the place."

"Well, I'm going to need at least one good photograph, Chip. You got the balls to get that for me? There's a grand in it for you, if you do."

"Oh, I got the balls, and a camera with a long lens, too."

"That's the boy! E-mail it to me." He gave him the address. "How soon can you get it for me?"

"Maybe tomorrow."

"Go get him, Chip!" Bolton hung up. "Sheri, bring me the new *People.*" She did and he flipped through the magazine and found the article. He read it twice, and there was no mention of a Theresa Crane. "Shit!!!" he screamed.

"What's the matter, Pat?" Sheri asked.

"I'm on the hook for a grand, and the girl's name isn't in the piece."

"What name?"

"Theresa Crane."

"Who's that?"

"You know the Powerball guy we can't find?"

"Hayward?"

"Yeah, Hayward. This Crane is supposed to be his girlfriend, but she's not in the *People* piece."

"Well, that doesn't mean she's not his girlfriend, does it?"

"I guess not."

"And if I know you, you're not on the hook for a grand, unless she is."

"Right. And until I get a photograph of Hayward, too."

"So relax, either you get it or you don't."

"'I don't' is not an option. We're short of really good stuff this week, and Hayward is really good stuff. If he's in Santa Fe, that would be a solid gold scoop for us. This guy won over six hundred million bucks!"

"Wow," Sheri said. "That's big cabbage!"

"No, it's big bucks. That's what our readers go nuts over."

25

CHRIS, FROM STRATEGIC SERVICES, had already been through the house with Laurence and had pointed out where his cameras should go. Now he was looking at a plat of the twelve acres the house sat on. "We've got something new that will be particularly good outside," he said.

"Tell me about it."

"It's basically a motion-detector camera, but it has an important new feature. If it sees motion, it rotates or pans up and down to zero in on the intruder, then it fires a very powerful strobe light for a fraction of a second. It's like ten old-fashioned flashbulbs going off all at once and concentrated on one spot. It does two things very well—it blinds the intruder, temporarily, and it scares the shit out of him."

"I like it," Laurence said. "Install it."

"I'll order it, then work on the interior stuff today. The new stuff will be here tomorrow."

"Great, Chris, I'll leave you to it. Let me know if you need anything."

Laurence went into his new study and busied himself learning to operate the house's built-in sound system from his iPhone. That done, he chose a classical music station from New York and turned on all the speakers in the house.

Theresa came into the study. "Can you turn that down a bit, please?" she shouted.

Laurence obliged. "Sorry about that. I was learning the system."

"The books you ordered from the Strand bookstore in New York have arrived. Shall I have them bring the boxes in here?"

"Yes, thanks."

Two men with handcarts wheeled in fifty or so boxes and followed Theresa's instructions to set them on the floor near the bookcases. Laurence tipped them. "Shall we put them away?" he asked.

"Sure. How would you like to do it?"

"You tell me what the books are, and I'll put them where they should go."

She opened the first carton. "Winston Churchill, history of the Second World War." She began handing him the books, two at a time, and he put them on a shelf.

"Gibbon, *Decline and Fall of the Roman Empire.*"

They repeated the process and continued until he had a well-organized library of more than five hundred volumes in the book-cases, with plenty of room left for new books.

Laurence surveyed their work and mopped his brow. "I think we deserve a drink."

"Just as soon as we break down all these cardboard boxes and put them out for the trash collector."

THEY SAT ON the deck facing the Jemez Mountains and let the late-afternoon breeze wash over them.. Then Chris came out.

"I'm pretty much finished with the indoor fixtures," he said, "and they're up and running. Would you like me to set up your iPhones to run the system?"

"Sure, Chris. Would you like a drink?"

"A beer would be nice," he said, accepting Laurence's phone and starting to work. Theresa brought him a cold beer, and he set up her phone and showed her how to run the system. One of the cameras captured them on the deck and the setting sun.

"Wow!" Theresa said. "We're on live TV."

"Zoom in," Chris said.

"Wow again!"

"My guys have done the trenching and laid cable for the outdoor fixtures," he said. "All we'll have to do is connect them and set them up. We'll be on our way to Palm Beach by mid-afternoon."

"How do the plane connections work for that flight?"

"No problem there. We have a Citation that will take us there, nonstop, with a decent tailwind. Equipment has already been shipped there, and we'll be at work the following morning."

"My turn to say wow," Laurence said. "That's very good service."

"That's what you get from Strategic Services," Chris said. "Oh, and Viv Bacchetti sends her regards. She's our boss."

"Please give Viv our best," Laurence said.

Chis polished off his beer and said good night, leaving them to the sunset.

"Nice guy," Theresa said.

"Everybody Stone Barrington has introduced me to has been a nice guy," Laurence said, "starting with you."

"I talked to my boss today and made my resignation official. I'll use up my accrued vacation time, then I'm off their books. He was sweet enough to let me keep my employee discount."

"Do they have a ready replacement for you?"

"I recommended Butch. He needs a couple more weeks of training, but I think he'll be good at it."

"Good for him."

"I also rented Butch my apartment, with an option to buy it eventually. He'll box up my things and send them to the Fairleigh."

Laurence grinned and squeezed her hand. "A step in the right direction. By the way, the Eagles have invited us to dinner tomorrow evening, and I accepted."

"Oh, good, I like them. Would you play something for me on the piano?"

"Of course. What would you like to hear?"

"Some Gershwin?"

"Coming right up." He played Gershwin while she got dinner together, then they sat down together.

"I have an idea," she said.

"Shoot."

"Why don't you record a whole lot of things on the piano, then we can listen together at dinner?"

"I like it. There must be a recording studio in town, I'll see if I can find it."

THE FOLLOWING MORNING, Chris turned up with the newly arrived outside cameras with their flash warning. While his people were setting them up, he marked the plat of the property with their locations. "I've set this up in a way that you won't blind passing motorists on the road, and, also, I've made sure they aren't pointed at any of your neighbors' houses. I'm sure you wouldn't want complaints from them."

"Good thinking," Laurence said.

"By the way," Chris said, "these things will detect coyotes, too. I understand you have them around here."

"I haven't seen any, but I've heard them at night."

"You don't have any pets, do you?"

"No—not yet, anyway."

"If you get a dog or a cat, it would be a good idea to keep them indoors at night. Remember, coyotes are carnivores."

"I'll keep that in mind."

Chris finished up his work and added the outdoor cameras to the iPhone app. "That's it," he said.

Laurence handed him a key. "This is for the Palm Beach house. There's no security system to get past."

"I'll call you from there if I have any questions," Chris said, then departed.

"I wish I had done the Palm Beach house weeks ago," Laurence said to Theresa. "Then the tabloids wouldn't have found us so easily."

CHIP ARNOLD PARKED his car a couple of hundred yards up the road from the house, then he slung his camera around his neck and started down the hill. The sun was already behind the mountains, leaving a red sky, slowly darkening, and as he left the road it seemed to get dark all at once. He used a penlight to find his way through the piñon trees; he wanted to be about a hundred feet from the house. The 300mm lens would do the rest.

He had no more than a few paces to go when everything turned white for a moment, followed quickly by black, stopping him in his tracks. He blinked rapidly, trying to regain his normal vision, but all he could see was a red dot. He sat down on the ground and waited for his sight to return.

———

LAURENCE WAS UNDRESSING for bed when, simultaneously, a flash momentarily filled the bedroom window and his iPhone chimed. It took him a moment to realize what had happened. He slipped back into his loafers, opened the bedside drawer and extracted the new pistol, then ran for the door. He could hear Theresa, still in the shower.

He came out of the house at a dead run, heading into the piñons, then he was overcome by darkness and stopped, waiting for his eyes to become accustomed. Fortunately, there was enough backlighting from the house to make it possible to move through the trees. He worked the action of the pistol, pumping a round into the chamber, and thumbed up the safety to the on position.

CHIP HEARD a rustling noise from down the hill, then he heard the metallic snap of the pistol's slide closing. He stood up and looked around. He could see the lights of the house, but that way was a man with a gun. He turned and ran blindly through the trees, holding up his arms to keep piñon boughs from slapping him in the face.

LAURENCE COULD HEAR the running footsteps ahead; then, for the first time, it occurred to him that whoever was out there might be armed, just as he was. He thumbed off the safety and moved slowly up the hill, his trigger finger laid along the weapon's slide, as he had been taught at the range.

———

CHIP MADE THE ROAD and now he could see well enough to run flat out. He made the car in record time, started it, and reversed up the road and around a bend, before he felt it was safe to turn around. He expected gunfire through his rear window at any moment, but it didn't come.

LAURENCE MADE THE ROAD and saw the dim shape of the car ahead, then it disappeared around a curve, and he saw the lights flicker on behind the piñons and heard the engine accelerate. He eased the hammer down on the pistol and took some deep breaths, his heart pounding. He knew he would have fired if he had seen a target, and that gave him pause. He walked down the hill in the road, to avoid setting off another flash, and a moment later he was back inside the house. He was in the bedroom when Theresa came out of the bath, naked, and he was able to get the pistol back into the drawer before she could see it.

"I was hoping you'd already be undressed," she said.

"That won't take long," he replied, shedding clothes and climbing into bed beside her.

CHIP'S PHONE WOKE him shortly after dawn. "Hello?"

"It's Pat Bolton at the *Inquisitor.* You got my photographs?"

"I was there last night, and I got blinded by a flash of light, then I heard somebody approaching, and a gun being racked. I got the hell out of there in a hurry."

"What do you mean, a flash of light?"

"Like the flash on a camera, but brighter. I couldn't see a thing for a couple of minutes."

"Well, shit, kid, you're going to have to do better than that."

"What, you mean I should get shot taking your fucking pictures?"

"Life is full of risk."

"I'll get your photographs, but I'm not going to get killed doing it."

Bolton slammed down the receiver.

CHIP LAY THERE for a moment thinking about it, then he got up, got dressed, and grabbed his camera bag. It was before six in the morning, and he had a shot at getting photographs in daylight. This time he drove past the house, then walked back toward it. He turned into the trees and made his way slowly toward the house. The sun was up now, and while he could see, he knew he could be seen. He made his way past the pool and stopped with a view of a terrace. Then he heard a noise like a refrigerator door closing, and a naked woman came outside, stood on the terrace, and sipped from a glass of orange juice.

Chip was transfixed and a moment passed before he got the camera up and pressed the button. Then a man joined the woman, as naked as she. He put his hands under her arms, lifted her off her feet and set her down on a tabletop. By the time Chip got his camera up again, the man's head was buried between her legs. She set the orange juice down and grabbed his hair with both hands.

Chip got three more shots, then the two went back into the kitchen. He checked the display and reviewed his pictures: They were good, but her face was obscured by the glass when she drank her juice, and, of course, his face couldn't be seen when it was between her legs.

He sat down on the ground and waited, hoping they would come outside again, but they didn't. He worked his way around to the other side of the house but could see nothing. He waited for more than an hour for another opportunity, then he heard the clatter of a garage door opening, and a Mercedes station wagon drove away from the house with two people inside.

He thought about going into the house, but if this guy had flashing security lights outside, he sure as shit had an armed security system for the house. He went home and e-mailed the photographs to Pat Bolton.

Almost immediately, he got an answer: "Great stuff, but no ID. Keep trying! I'm past deadline for next week, but there's always the week after!"

Chip heard his mother calling him to breakfast, and he went downstairs for some eggs and bacon.

"Did you sleep well?" she asked as she served him.

"I woke up early," he said, "and never got back to sleep."

"Are you going to look for a job today?"

"Yeah, Mom, sure."

"What kind of job?"

"I'll go check with the *New Mexican* and see if they've got an opening yet."

"How many times have you done that?"

"I don't know, half a dozen maybe."

"You should try somewhere else."

He wanted to show her the pictures he had shot, just to prove he was trying to earn money, but he could imagine what her reaction would be.

L AURENCE AND THERESA followed the directions they had been given to the Eagle house, in the hills above Tesuque. A large stone eagle greeted them at the gate, wings outspread, and the house was of a contemporary style, but inviting.

Ed Eagle greeted them and played bartender, and Stone and Gala arrived soon after. They sat down with their drinks.

"We had an incident last night," Laurence said.

"What sort of incident?" Ed asked.

Laurence told them about the new flash security lights.

"That sounds like a good idea," Stone said. "But what happened last night?"

"Yes," Theresa said, "I'd like to hear about that, too."

"I thought I'd keep it until we were here, then I wouldn't have to repeat myself."

"Well, go ahead."

"We were getting ready for bed. Theresa was in the shower, and one of the lights went off outside. I ran downstairs," he said, skipping the part about the gun, which neither Theresa nor Stone knew about, "and out into the piñons. I rousted somebody, apparently, and I could hear footsteps running and him brushing against the trees. He got to the road and ran for a short distance, then I heard a car start and got a glimpse of it as it reversed around a bend in the road. Then its lights came on and I heard it drive away in a hurry."

"Did you see the man?" Ed asked.

"Only his back. He was smallish."

"Did you see the car?" Stone asked.

"For a second or two. It was something small, like a Mini, I think."

"That sounds like the car I saw parked near your gate the night we came over," Stone said. "Must be the same guy."

"And he's not behaving like a burglar," Ed said. "A burglar would be in the house as soon as you left."

"We didn't leave last night, and our new security system is up and running."

Theresa spoke up. "I had the feeling—just a feeling—that there was someone in the trees outside the kitchen when we went down for breakfast." She thought about that. "I hope I was wrong, because neither of us was wearing much."

"Neither of us was wearing anything at all," Laurence pointed out, and everyone laughed.

"They wouldn't publish that . . ." Theresa began.

"They almost certainly would," Stone said.

"Oops."

"Maybe I should just invite them to the house," Laurence said. "Although I wouldn't know whom to invite."

"Just get a copy of everything at the supermarket checkout and call the editors," Susannah said. "If you want to go down that road."

"The other night you said I should ignore them."

"Two ways to go, mutually exclusive."

"Once they took some pictures and asked some questions, wouldn't they go away?" Laurence asked.

"That's a toss-up," Susannah said. "Could go either way. They might leave you alone, but I wouldn't count on it."

"Perhaps you should hire a publicist," Stone said.

"What for?"

"If you want to get your picture in the papers, you hire a publicist," Susannah said. "If you want to keep your picture *out* of the papers, you hire a publicist."

"That doesn't make any sense," Laurence said.

"I'm afraid it does," Stone interjected. "A publicist becomes a buffer between you and the media. He or she will know the bad ones and the fairly good ones, and can play them off against each other. They'll know that their best chance of cooperation is through a professional, which is what they think of themselves."

"I don't know any publicists, and I don't know how to find one."

"There are, basically, two kinds," Stone said. "L.A. and New York.

You don't really need both unless you're a married movie star who is sleeping with the nanny. There's a woman in New York, Faith Mackey. I can introduce you to her."

"What does someone like that cost?"

"You can afford it," Stone said. "If it doesn't work out, you can fire her."

"Maybe that's what I should do, hire her," Laurence said. "Theresa, what do you think?"

"I think it can't hurt, and it might help."

"All right."

"I'll have Faith call you tomorrow," Stone said. "I warn you, she can suck all the oxygen out of a room, but she's very good at what she does."

"I'll look forward to speaking with her," Laurence said.

THE FOLLOWING DAY Laurence and Theresa were having lunch on the terrace when Laurence's cell phone rang. A glance told him the call was a 917 area code, New York. "Hello?"

"Laurence? This is Faith Mackey."

"How do you do?"

"I do very well, thank you. I'm on the road from Albuquerque, about half an hour south of Santa Fe. What's your address?"

"One seventy-eight Tano Norte."

"Just a sec. Got you on Google Maps. Be there in forty-two minutes." She hung up.

"Who was that?" Theresa asked.

"Faith Mackey, Stone's publicist lady."

"Why did she hang up?"

"She's south of here, says she'll be here in forty-two minutes."

"What's she doing in Santa Fe?"

"I have no idea."

FAITH MACKEY was small and wiry, with short blond hair, somewhere in the mid-range between forty and sixty; she'd had some work done. When Laurence answered the door she shook his hand and talked quickly. He introduced her to Theresa. "Okay, L-a-u-r-e-n-c-e, am I spelling it right?"

"Yes."

"I pretty much know your story, but tell it to me in your own words in three minutes, so I can fill in the chinks."

"Chinks?"

"The empty places in your story." She beckoned with both hands. "Let's have it, we're short of time."

Laurence started from the beginning and talked as fast as he could.

"Great, stop. Got it. Have you got booze in the house?"

"Of course, would you like a drink?"

"No, you're giving a little cocktail party at five o'clock, maybe a dozen, fifteen people."

"Do I make canapés?" Theresa asked.

"Yeah, it's not enough people for a caterer. Cheese and crackers are okay, anything else you've got on hand." She looked around. "That's a relief."

"What's a relief?" Laurence asked.

"It's nice—I won't have to stage it. Maybe I'll move a couple things around. Dress casual, a little on the Western side, if you've got it."

"I have a fringed skirt and some boots I bought yesterday," Theresa said.

"Perfect."

"Everything I've got is Ralph Lauren," Laurence said.

"Ah, yes, courtesy of Miss Theresa, your personal shopper."

"Former personal shopper," Theresa said. "I resigned yesterday."

"I'm a former English schoolmaster," Laurence said. "I resigned, too."

"I don't blame you. You won, what? Six hundred million?"

"And change. Would you like some lunch?"

"I've got a sandwich in my purse. Where can I eat?"

28

FAITH MACKEY ATE with one hand and phoned with the other, never stopping either, while Laurence and Theresa watched from the kitchen. Finally, she finished her sandwich, drank her water, and beckoned them outside.

"Okay," she said, looking at her notes on a steno pad. "Laurence, I've got somebody coming over with some clothes for you and some hair."

"Hair?"

"There's a previous photograph of you with longer hair and a beard. We want to keep you looking the same—you'll be less likely to be hassled in public."

"Okay."

"Who plays the grand piano?"

"I do," Laurence said.

"Can you do standard cocktail stuff?"

"Yes."

"Then I want you playing when your guests arrive. It'll give you a chance to look them over, and they'll think you're the hired help until I introduce you. Now, when did you buy the house?"

"Four days ago."

"And moved in the same day?"

"Right."

"They'll already know that. Whose name is the house in?"

"Theresa's."

"You're going to want to get that changed to a corporate name or a trust."

"How would anybody know anything about the house?"

"Real estate agents are notorious gossips, and some of them string for the tabloids and worse, like the Drudge Report."

"What's the Drudge Report?"

"If you don't know, you don't need to. Some of the media may have already seen the sales contract. Have you closed?"

"No, tomorrow."

"You can do the name change at that time. Ask your attorney to create a new corporation in your home state. Where is that?"

"Florida."

"Good, call him today. Theresa?"

"Yes?"

"You're going to be my daughter today. Have you and Laurence been photographed together since you arrived?"

"Not to my knowledge. Well, there was one moment when I thought . . ." She explained her feelings about the morning before.

"Okay, if that happened, he was your boyfriend who left to go to New York this morning. Don't give them a name. Laurence, you're my houseguest here, and you're going back to California tomorrow. In fact, this cocktail party is taking place in California, part of the ground rules."

"Whatever you say."

Laurence told her about the incident with the intruder a couple of nights before.

"So, he's smallish and drives a Mini, or some such?"

"Right."

"He'll probably be here. Let's pick him out right away and be careful of him. Theresa, you will decline to be photographed. Laurence, I will place you against that wall over there to be photographed. The picture could be anywhere, not Santa Fe. After you are photographed, excuse yourself and go upstairs—tell them you have to pack for an early flight, don't say where."

"All right."

The doorbell rang.

"Theresa, please get that. If it's a lady with a makeup case, let her in. If not, call me."

Theresa went to the door and came back with a lady with two cases.

"Laurence, Theresa, this is Betty Simmons, ace makeup artist and dresser. Laurence, try on the clothes Betty brought."

Laurence took the case into the kitchen, put on the clothes, and returned.

"Excellent, a little on the scruffy side. When we get your makeup done you will be Laurence of old. They'll have no idea what new Laurence looks like."

"Are we going to answer questions?" Laurence asked.

"You are. They won't care about Theresa because she's my daughter and nothing to do with you."

"What sort of answers do you want me to give?"

"Truthful ones, but avoid answers that give hints as to where you live or can be found or what your intentions are for the future."

"They'll already know about the New York apartment and the Palm Beach house," he said.

"Nothing we can do about New York, unless you want to sell it."

"No."

"Okay, you've already sold the Palm Beach house and removed your belongings, closing in a few days. Let's get that one off your map, along with Santa Fe. They'll know about the Fairleigh, but you have hotel staff there to run them off."

"Right."

"Theresa, I'll explain you as my daughter. Stick to that story, deflect questions to me or Laurence. You're a civilian, and you don't want to talk about your personal life, got it? Keep it polite, but cool."

"Suits me fine," Theresa said. "Where do I live?"

"New Jersey. The New York media don't like going to New Jersey, and the L.A. media don't know where it is, except that Tony Soprano lives there." She checked her watch. "Okay, Theresa, you'd better scatter the food around where they can find it. Don't serve them. Put a selection of booze on the bar with an ice bucket and some mixers and a bottle of white wine. Let them do the pouring, you can disinfect later."

Theresa went to do Faith's bidding and Laurence was taken by Betty to the dining room table, where she opened her makeup case. "You had longer hair before, right?"

"A little longer. I had it cut nearly a month ago and not since."

"I'll put in a few extensions and trim them, then I'll give you a new haircut before I leave."

"Okay."

She took a fulsome beard from her case and painted some adhesive on his face.

"My beard wasn't nearly this long."

"Don't worry, I'll mow it back until you like it."

"Is all this going to look real?"

"It will when I'm done. You could do movie close-ups and nobody would know." She glued the beard firmly in place, then she spread a barber's cloth over him and inserted the hair extensions, combed and trimmed them. Most of the beard ended up in Laurence's lap.

"Now," Betty said, "I'm going to make you look older and dissolute. We want a lot of contrast between old Laurence and new Laurence." She painted a liquid under his eyes and on the end of his nose. "Scrunch up your eyes." He did so, and she dried it with a hair dryer.

When she was done, she brushed off the excess hair and took the cloth outside to shake it out.

Faith came and had a close look. "Betty," she said, "this is fucking wonderful. I imagine something, and you make it happen!"

Laurence had a close look at himself in the dining room mirror. "I look ten years older," he said.

"Then tell them that's so," Faith replied, looking at her watch. "Five minutes to go." She walked around the living room, moving a lamp here or a pot there. "Betty, you'd better wait in the kitchen. Anybody asks, you're a friend of Theresa's and you don't have anything to say. Hide your cases." Betty packed up and moved to the kitchen, while Faith flicked a few hairs off the dining room table. "Okay, Laurence, you're on the piano, until I call you over. Anybody asks, you don't take requests."

"What would you like to hear?"

"Rodgers and Hart, Irving Berlin, like that. It will bore these people rigid. Nothing up-tempo."

Laurence sat down and began playing "Blue Skies."

"Perfect!" Faith sang out as the doorbell rang, and she went to answer it.

LAURENCE WATCHED FROM THE PIANO, only occasionally glancing at his hands. They were a motley lot; quite young to sixtyish. He spotted the one from two nights ago instantly; no more than nineteen, dressed like the adolescent he was, unkempt hair, a camera with a long lens slung around his neck.

———

"ALL RIGHT, ladies and gentlemen, gather 'round," Faith called out, beckoning them toward her. Theresa came in with a tray. "I'm Faith Mackey, you all know who I am. That's my daughter, Theresa, from a much earlier, very brief marriage. This is my house. Theresa and her boyfriend picked it out for me, and I bought it sight unseen a few days ago. Her boyfriend left this morning for New Jersey. Laurence Hayward will join us shortly, and he will answer your questions, within reason. He's a nice guy, but he doesn't suffer fools gladly, so don't make a fool of yourself. For your information, we are all at this moment somewhere in the state of California, and that is where you are reporting from, though you won't be specific. Got that?" The crowd responded with a murmur. "NO MAKING STUFF UP! You'll get honest answers to respectful questions, and you'll stick with them and our location story for your reporting. If you stray, you won't be invited to another of these, ever, on either coast or in between. The fact that I bought this house is on deep background—not even the real estate agent knows I'm the buyer, and I want to keep it that way. I'm a publicist for others, not myself, so my vacation home will be our little secret. Blow it at your peril.

"Now, the bar is open, so help yourselves, but first sign the agreement forms stacked there, and with your real names, addresses, phone numbers, and e-mail addresses, plus the name of the medium you represent and the name of the person you report to. If you do not complete those forms, our little soiree will, for you, be a lot shorter than planned."

The group went to the bar, made themselves drinks, then filled out and signed the agreements, which Faith collected and scrutinized.

"Musician, give us a little fanfare!" Faith commanded, and Laurence did so. "May I present Laurence Hayward!"

Laurence got up and walked toward the group, grinning inanely.

LAURENCE TOOK A DEEP BREATH and remembered to be British. "Good afternoon, ladies and gentlemen. Have you any questions for me?"

"Yeah," a sixty-year-old woman said, "what's this horseshit about your being a schoolmaster at some upper-crust school in the U.K.?"

"Assistant schoolmaster, at Eton College, and the crust doesn't get any more upper than that. I resigned yesterday, when your British counterparts made it impossible for me to return to a quiet academic life."

"You blame the press?"

"Oh, yes, for everything. Always." That got a laugh.

"What did you teach?"

"English literature and art history."

"Why?"

"Because those are my subjects, just as maths and sciences might be another master's."

Someone else took over. "Where'd you go to college?"

"Magdalen College, Oxford."

"Which one, Maudlin or Oxford University?"

"They are collocated."

"What does that mean?"

"In the same place, one inside the other."

"I don't understand."

"Google it. Next question?"

"Why did you buy this house?" She motioned at her surroundings.

"What? This house?"

"Yes."

"I think Faith told you whose house this is. My only residence is in New York. I sold my Palm Beach house yesterday."

"I thought that was your father's place."

"Until his death, four months ago."

"Did he leave you any money?"

"He left me his house."

"Now that you're a billionaire, what are you going to do with it?"

"I'm a great deal less than a billionaire. Do your homework."

"How are you going to spend it?"

"I think I'll put about half of it into charitable trusts and piss away the rest."

"Piss it away on what?"

"Anything I like."

"Don't you have a house in England?"

"My family does."

"Who are your family?"

"People who don't like to read about themselves in newspapers."

The kid intruder spoke up. "Don't you have an elaborate security system around this house?"

"You'll have to ask Faith, it's her house."

"I have no idea!" Faith shouted. "I haven't read the instructions yet."

"Do you own a gun?" the kid asked.

"I'm an Englishman. We don't own guns, except to kill birds and game."

"How about a handgun?"

"We don't own handguns. They're for shooting people—our police frown on that."

"Aren't you an American, not a Brit?"

"I was born here, raised there."

"So you're a half-breed?"

"Sounds about right."

"What's your middle initial, B, stand for?"

"Bastard." Another laugh.

"Are you related to Laurence Olivier?"

"No, not even when he was alive."

"Then why is your name spelled like his?"

"It's a mystery. Perhaps my mother was frightened by his Hamlet."

"What Hamlet was that?"

"Stage or film, take your pick. Anybody got a real question?"

"What do you think of American women?"

"They terrify me."

"Why?"

"Look at Faith—isn't she terrifying?" Faith howled.

"Where are you going from here?"

"I'm already in California, so it's an easy choice."

"What do you like about California?"

"More places to get lost."

"Why do you want to get lost?"

"So I won't have to answer questions like this."

"Where will home be?"

"Like the song says, 'Any place I hang my hat.' Except I don't own a hat."

"Oh, come on, you've got to go somewhere."

"No, I plan to just dematerialize, as if I were on *Star Trek*. No one will ever see or hear from me again. I mean, what's money for, if not to buy complete isolation."

"How can a person live in complete isolation?"

"I'll send out for pizza and Chinese."

"Come on, pick a town or city."

"Wherever they deliver pizza and Chinese."

"Why pizza and Chinese?"

"My needs are simple—pizza, Chinese, and a bottle of Chateau Lafite, '29, and I'm happy anywhere."

"What was that wine again?"

"It's a jug wine—I never buy wine that doesn't have a screw top."

"What are your hobbies?"

"Playing bad piano and killing salmon."

"Where do you kill salmon?"

"Waist-deep in an icy Scottish river."

"Is that fun?"

"I don't know, I can't feel a thing when I'm waist-deep in an icy Scottish river."

"What's so great about that?"

"The media won't follow me there. They don't enjoy being wet and freezing. I may take up yachting for the same reason."

"Do you have a yacht?"

"Not yet."

"If you buy one, will it be a super yacht?"

"Why would I buy a yacht, if it weren't super?"

"What's something you can't buy with all your money?"

"My own country—at least, not one I'd want to live in."

"Do you have a girl?"

"Whenever possible."

"Do you prefer blondes or brunettes?"

"It hardly matters, they can change in an hour."

From a young woman: "Do you like a Brazilian?"

"I've never met one, but I'm told they're charming people."

"That wasn't what I meant."

"Wasn't it?"

Faith stepped in. "Thank you, folks, now for pictures. Right over here, Laurence." She stood him against a wall, as if for a firing squad, and the group gathered around, most with cell phones. Laurence gave them both profiles and dead ahead, as if in a mug shot. He smiled, laughed, and frowned, but resisted one cross-eyed, because he knew it would haunt him for the rest of his life.

"Thank you, ladies and gentlemen," Faith said. "This way out, don't forget to leave your bar glasses." She stood next to the bar and collected every one as they passed.

The kid reporter stopped to ask Laurence another question, but Faith got him by the collar and moved him toward the door on his tiptoes. "You'd better watch your ass, Chip Arnold," she said. "One of my security guys nearly plugged you last night." She closed the door firmly behind him and followed Laurence into the living room. "Great job, kiddo. I wish all my clients could handle them that way. That should get them off your back for a while."

"Do I have to go to California," Laurence asked, "or can I stay here in your house?"

"Sweetie, you're welcome in this house anytime. Make yourself at home. Now, is there anything else I can do for you?"

"What's my next move?"

"Get a haircut and a shave from Betty and be returned to your former glory. I've got an eight o'clock flight to New York, and my car's waiting."

"Did you come all the way out here for this?" he asked.

"Of course. Stone called me last night, and I was on a plane at daybreak." She shrugged. "It's what I do."

"And you do it very well," Laurence said, giving her a hug, then he went and submitted himself to the tender ministrations of the estimable Betty.

And shortly, he was himself again.

BUTCH HAD JUST taken Theresa's boxes to the Fairleigh and left them with the concierge, when the doorbell rang.

Curly stood there, his bulk filling the door frame. "Hi, Butch. You moved and didn't mention it to me."

"Theresa is out of town for a few days and offered me the place. I'd ask you in, but I promised her I wouldn't have visitors."

Curly brushed him aside, as if he were a pesky insect, and entered the apartment. "I see she took a lot of her stuff with her. Where'd she go for a few days?"

"Out of town. What do you want, Curly?"

"I need some money, not much—a few grand."

"You got a hundred and fifty grand out of our caper, just like me. In fact, I paid our expenses, so you did better."

"Well, I had a little run-in with some ponies."

"You've been going to the track? You don't know anything about the horses."

"You don't have to go to the track—there's a telephone service available, called a bookie."

"Oh, shit. How much did you lose?"

"How much did I have?"

"Not the whole hundred and fifty grand!"

"A little more than that. That's why I need the twenty-five grand."

"You lost . . ." Butch's mind boggled.

"The bookie also has a pickup service, where he sends a couple of guys over for the money you owe him. That's why I can't go to my apartment, and I have to bunk with you until I pay him."

"Another twenty-five grand, from me?"

"Actually, better make it thirty-five grand, what with the vigorish, and all."

"You expect me to give you thirty-five thousand dollars?" Butch asked incredulously.

"Not give, loan. I'm good for it."

"And just how are you good for it?"

Curly shrugged. "You know, I get ideas."

"You must be out of your fucking mind."

Curly took him by the lapels and lifted him to his tiptoes. "That's not a very nice thing to say to a person, Butch. Now, apologize."

"I'm sorry, I apologize."

Curly lowered him onto his heels. He went to the liquor cabinet and found it bare. "Where's that great scotch?"

"She took it with her. I can't afford to stock up."

Curly found a Yellow Pages and flipped through. "There you are—a liquor store that delivers, and it's just around the corner. Order some of that Talisker, the single malt."

"I don't have enough cash to do that."

"Butch, I know you well enough to know that you have a credit card. I mean, you're a career guy, now, aren't you?"

Curly made himself comfortable in an armchair. "Tell you what, give me forty grand right now, and you'll never hear from me again."

"Now it's forty grand?"

"I think that's a bargain, considering how much trouble I can be when I don't get what I want."

"Look, I spent a lot of mine, too. I had to fill out my wardrobe, for a start. I have to look good in my work."

"Okay with me, but I know you've squirreled away at least the fifty grand I need. Get it up."

"What I've got left is invested. You think I keep it in a shoe box around the house?"

"I don't care if it's in a shoe box or, more likely, in a safe-deposit box, which is where I'd keep it. Let's go to your bank right now."

"The bank closed at five o'clock."

"But that's where the cash is, right?"

"Curly, I'm not giving you any money. Now get out right now."

"Or what? You're going to kill me? You don't have the guts. Beat me up? You don't have the muscle. Call the cops? You'd go to jail, too. Are you beginning to get the picture?"

Butch was beginning to get the picture. "Listen, I can give you ten grand—that's all I've got, I swear. I'll give you a check right now, and you can take it to the bank tomorrow morning."

"Give me the check."

Butch found his checkbook and wrote it out.

Curly looked at it. "If this bounces, I'm going to come back here and beat the shit out of you. You won't be able to work for a few weeks, you understand me?"

"It's not necessary to threaten me, Curly."

"I think maybe it is. I think you know I'll do what I say, too."

Butch knew he'd do it; he'd seen him do it under the bleachers in the prison yard. Curly had forty pounds on him, all muscle, and nothing short of a shotgun to the head would stop him when he was mad. And he was looking mad.

Butch walked him to the door. "And I want the key to the Fairleigh apartment," he said.

"I'll mail it to you," Curly said, "and I'll see you tomorrow at the store, if the check bounces. I think your coworkers might enjoy seeing what I do to you."

Curly walked away, and Butch locked the door behind him. He was sweating profusely, something that always happened when he was scared.

LATER, he was putting his things into a dresser drawer when he came across something of Theresa's. It was a very small .25 caliber semiautomatic pistol, the proverbial "ladies' gun." And, on closer examination, he found it loaded, four in the magazine, one in the chamber. He remembered it vaguely as having belonged to their father. He shoved it to the back of the drawer and stacked underwear in front of it. He'd give it back to her later.

31

STONE LEFT SANTA FE without resuming his sexual relationship with Gala. Something had gone out of it for him, he realized, and she seemed to feel it, too.

He took off for Los Angeles and landed an hour and a quarter later at Santa Monica, where a car from the Arrington awaited.

It was a hot day, and as soon as he had been dropped off at his house on the property, he stripped off his clothes, grabbed a towel, and headed for the pool. He tossed the towel aside, then, naked, swam a few laps, then pushed off underwater and started toward the other end. To his surprise, someone dove in from the far end of the pool, and, as the bubbles cleared, he saw that it was a woman and that she was naked, too. Then she saw him, and they both rose to the surface.

"Good morning," he said.

"Good morning," she replied uncertainly, sweeping a lot of dark hair back from her forehead. "I wasn't aware that the Arrington was a haven for naturists."

"And yet you appear au naturel," he said.

"Not having any way to deny that, I confess," she said.

"And this is not, strictly speaking, one of the hotel pools. It belongs to my house, which is just there." He nodded.

"Well, that means that one of us should leave, and that it should be me. I apologize for the intrusion."

"Oh, you're not an intrusion, just a surprise. My name is Stone Barrington."

"How do you do?"

"Very well, thank you. And now I believe the quaint American custom requires you to tell me your name."

"I'm not sure I want you to know it," she replied. "I'm afraid you already know too much about me."

"From what I've observed so far, you possess the same equipment as other women, except that it may be delineated and arranged more artfully than usual. Your name is currently the only secret."

"Jinx," she replied. "Jinx Jameson."

"Is Jinx a family name?"

"A childhood nickname, because of my tendency as a toddler to break things. I was born Jennifer, but when people call me that, I tend to think they're talking to someone else."

"What would you like to do now, Jinx?"

"Well, I'd like to swim for a bit, since I'm already here."

"Would you be more comfortable if I got you a swimsuit?"

She thought about it. "In the circumstances, that seems a retrograde notion. If it's all right, I'll just swim a few laps, and then, while you avert your gaze, I'll flee the premises."

"I have a better idea—I'll give you a robe when you emerge, and then we can have some lunch at poolside."

"A kind invitation, thank you." She began swimming again, while Stone got out of the pool, found some robes, and ordered lunch.

AFTER THE WAITER had departed she swam to the ladder; Stone held up a robe between them, and she slipped into it and toweled her hair.

"Hungry?"

"Ravenous," she replied, slipping into the chair he held for her. "I just got off a plane from New York. What have we for lunch?"

"A lobster salad and a very nice Chardonnay by Far Niente, which also has the advantage of having the most beautiful of labels."

She sipped the wine and examined the bottle. "Right on both counts. Have you just come from somewhere?"

"Also from New York, by way of Santa Fe, where I spent a few days with friends."

"You don't have a home in Santa Fe? How disappointing. I always wanted to meet a man with a Santa Fe house."

"I'm sorry to disappoint you, but my friends make me so comfortable that I'm loath to invest in real estate."

"You're not penurious, are you? I despise that in a man."

"No one has ever accused me of such."

"I'm relieved to hear it."

"I'm happy to relieve you. So we're both New Yorkers?"

"I'm not a native, but a Southerner, from a small town in Georgia, called Delano. I came to New York after studying theater design at the Yale Drama School, nearly fifteen years ago."

"That's enough to make you a neo-native."

She laughed. "That's a new word. It describes me well. Are you a native?"

"Born and bred."

"And how do you occupy yourself in the Apple?"

"I'm an attorney, sort of."

"Sort of?"

"Well, my interests have broadened over the years, so I'm only a part-time attorney these days."

"What other interests do you have?"

"This hotel, among other things, and a growing list of others of the same name. And you design theater sets?"

"I do."

"And what brings you to Los Angeles? Film work?"

"No, I came to supervise the installation of a set that I originally designed for New York. After L.A., they'll take it on the road for a national tour, and the hell with them—they can install it themselves."

"What play?"

"*Native Daughter.*"

"I saw it a few months ago, and I enjoyed it, but of course I particularly admired the set."

She laughed. "Hardly anybody ever says that, unless they know I'm the designer."

"I admired it before I knew you were the designer. I especially liked your very effective use of the scrim."

"Careful, you'll make me blush with such language. What brings you to L.A.?"

"A meeting of the Arrington board, upon which I sit."

"Is it painful, talking company business while sitting on a board?"

"The board is well-cushioned, and the company good."

"You said that's your house?" she asked, nodding at it.

"I did."

"On the grounds of a hotel?"

"The hotel is named for my late wife, Arrington, and the house was built for her on this property, which belonged first to her previous husband, then after his death, to her."

"And now to you?"

"And now to the hotel, which bought it."

"It's becoming clear, as through a scrim. The actor Vance Calder once owned the land, didn't he?"

"He was her previous husband."

"Such a history!"

"Indeed."

She stretched. "That was a delicious lunch, but I feel a nap coming on."

"Shall we continue this conversation over dinner?"

"What a good idea." She stood up, shed the robe, and draped it over her chair, then she walked slowly away.

Stone appreciated the view for a few seconds before calling, "Seven o'clock? My house?"

She waved a hand in assent, then stepped through a small opening in the hedge that separated Stone's house from the cottage next door and disappeared from view.

32

THE BOARD OF DIRECTORS OF the Arrington Hotels Group convened at five PM that afternoon, and Stone, refreshed by his swim and renewed by his new acquaintance, attended.

His friend Marcel duBois chaired and began with an announcement. "Ladies and gentlemen, at around noon today a maintenance crewman watched a bellman unload a hotel van carrying half a dozen guests, and after they had claimed their luggage, a single suitcase remained. Our maintenance man immediately obtained what we call, with apologies to Linus, of 'Peanuts' fame, a security blanket, and covered the case. These blankets are woven of a metallic cloth that stops cell phone and Wi-Fi transmissions. The Los Angeles bomb squad was called to the scene immediately and arrived in unmarked cars, while our security people checked Stone Canyon Road and found a single individual in a car, attempting to make a cell call. They held him for arrest by the police. The case was taken to a safe distance by the bomb squad and was found to contain a homemade explosive device which was capable of killing anyone within fifty feet, and the cell phone confiscated from the arrestee was found to contain the number of a cell device attached to the bomb." There was a murmur of alarm from the board, but Marcel held up a hand for silence.

"Our security people immediately contacted their counterparts at the other three Arringtons—in Paris, Rome, and the south of England—who discovered similar devices at each location and suppressed them with security blankets until bomb squads arrived. One person was arrested, in England. I need hardly tell you that the quick work of our security people has undoubtedly saved lives today."

That got a round of applause from the board members present.

"These events have caused a question to arise which we must answer. To wit—should a public announcement be made regarding these events, and if so, in what detail? The floor is open."

A woman member raised her hand.

"Karen?"

"Thank you, Marcel. I believe we should make an immediate announcement about this, primarily because other hotels will wish to take precautions."

"I'm sorry, I should have told you that the police, employing an established protocol, have already contacted every hotel in the city and alerted them to the threat. Also, the police have searched the home of the arrestee and found a small-scale bomb factory in his garage. From the lack of further explosive materials found, and from questioning the arrestee, they are convinced that it was a one-man operation and that there were no accomplices. The same appears to be true at the other locations. However, that fact does not rule out the possibility that the arrestee was aided and abetted by some organization, and the police are making that a point of their investigations. Federal authorities are involved, as well."

Stone raised his hand. "Do the police know how the bag containing the device got into our van?"

"They believe it happened at Los Angeles International Airport, where the van was briefly unattended while awaiting passengers."

"The same at the other locations?"

"We have not had word yet about that. Stone, you are an attorney, is it your belief that, if we do not make a public announcement and an explosion should occur elsewhere in the city, we could be held liable by victims in a court of law?"

"I think not. I believe that whether or not to make a public announcement is for the police to decide. They may feel that an announcement might do more harm than good, not to mention the possible effect on the business and tourist trades. We cannot be blamed for leaving the decision to them."

"And certainly," said Karen, "keeping it quiet will make our own lives easier."

"That should be the least of our concerns," Stone said. "We must put our guests first. Still, I don't see how leaving the announcement decision to the police violates that principle. Certainly, our guests might be frightened to know that a bomber came so close, and we don't want them unnecessarily frightened. I do think that, in light of what has happened, we have an obligation to review our security practices, to see that there is no recurrence of this activity."

"That has already been done," Marcel said, "and although our security was sufficient to prevent an explosion in this case, patrols of the hotel grounds and the roads around us are being increased in frequency, and it will now be standard practice that any driver leaving his vehicle, for however short a time, will lock it."

"That said," Stone observed, "it appears that we have met our legal, moral, and ethical obligations to our guests and staff."

"Is that the sense of you all?" Marcel asked.

There was a murmur of assent, and the chairman moved on down the agenda.

33

JINX JAMESON APPEARED on Stone's doorstep, fashionably after seven PM, clad in white trousers and a thin white blouse that gave him a glimpse of her breasts through the gauzy material.

Stone greeted her with a light kiss on the cheek and showed her into the house. The butler took their drink orders, hers a single-malt scotch, his a Knob Creek Rye.

The desert air outside had cooled and made a fire in the study a cheerful sight. Jinx tossed the wrap she had brought onto a nearby chair and accepted a seat on the sofa next to Stone before the fireplace. "How was your board meeting?" she asked.

"Interesting. Forgive me if I don't supply details—those are confidential."

"I assume the bomb was discussed."

That brought Stone up short. "I beg your pardon?" he said, because he couldn't think of anything else to say.

"You are not the only board member with whom I am acquainted."

"I assume you're referring to Karen Miles," he said, guessing wildly.

"That's very astute of you."

"And very foolish of her to mention it."

"Confidentiality among women is sometimes defined more loosely than among men."

"Then it was *very* loose of her. May I suggest that you not pass that information on to anyone else of any gender?"

"You may."

"Consider it suggested."

She took a deep draught of her scotch. "She scared the shit out of me. At first I thought the bomb might have been near my cottage."

"It was not, and it was quickly discovered, disarmed, and removed. The person responsible was arrested nearby."

"Karen didn't bother to tell me all that."

"I should have thought that, having breached the board's rule of confidentiality, she would have been kind enough to put your mind at rest."

"You would think that, wouldn't you?"

"I suggest that, in the future, you not reveal anything to Ms. Miles that you would not like to see at the supermarket checkout counter."

"Has she a history of that sort of indiscretion?"

"I don't know, but I'd like to find out. How well do you know her?"

"I met her at lunch with friends in New York a couple of months ago. I've seen her twice since, in similar settings."

"It would be interesting to know if, after those three occasions, anything discussed there ended up in the tabloids."

"Funny you should mention that. One of my friends at the last lunch, a well-known actress, confessed to me that she had decided to divorce her husband, a well-known actor. While that comment was not addressed to Karen, she was certainly within earshot. I heard from my friend the next day that she had gone grocery shopping and had seen her face on the cover of a tabloid. She accused her husband of the leak, and he denied it vehemently. Perhaps he was innocent."

"Husbands are occasionally innocent," Stone replied.

Jinx laughed. "I suppose they are."

"How did you spend your afternoon?"

"Napping."

"And are you now feeling refreshed?"

"I am."

"So am I. I've felt that way since we met."

"Perhaps the circumstances may have something to do with that feeling?"

"More than perhaps," Stone said. "And your blouse reinforces the effect."

She smiled. "I suppose that, when choosing my clothes for the evening, I thought that I had nothing more to hide from you."

"A pleasant thought."

"Or you to hide from me."

"Touché."

The butler brought canapés and set them on the coffee table in front of them.

"I suppose you'll be working tomorrow?"

"Yes," she said. "It's my intention to supervise the erecting of my set by lunchtime, then spend the remainder of the day dressing it, then I'll fly back to New York the following day. What are your plans?"

"I plan to visit my son, who is a film director based at Centurion Studios, and see how he's doing."

"Ah, that must be Peter Barrington."

"It is."

"I had been told he was the son of Vance Calder."

"Stepson. His mother and I had a relationship before she and Vance were married."

Her eyes widened slightly. "And she married him, knowing that she was carrying your child?"

"A few weeks passed before she knew."

"And what did she do then?"

"Nothing, as far as I know."

"She didn't tell either of you?"

"No, though she thought that Vance came to suspect later on. Still, he and Peter had a good relationship."

"And when did the two of you have that opportunity?"

"A few years ago. It worked out very well in the end."

The butler refreshed their drinks.

"I'm sorry to be digging into your personal life."

"I don't mind. I'd like you to know me better, as I would like to know you."

"What a nice thought."

"And since you so immediately satisfied my curiosity, I'm happy to satisfy yours."

"That was a mutual satisfaction, if you recall."

"I'm happy you think of it that way. Oh, and I hope you like beef."

"One of my favorite things."

"Good. I've ordered chateaubriand for us. They do it very well here."

"Oh, *that* kind of beef. Well, I like that, too."

Stone laughed aloud.

The butler called them to dinner, at a table for two set in the study. Stone tasted the wine and pronounced it satisfactory.

"And what are we drinking tonight?" she asked.

"A Château Mouton Rothschild 1978."

"My goodness!"

"Drinking better wines was something I started to do when I began to prosper."

"What a good idea! When I began to prosper I began drinking wines with corks, instead of screw tops."

"A good move up. By the way, since we're both returning to New York the same day, may I give you a lift?"

"A lift in what?"

"I'm here in my own airplane."

"What sort of an airplane?"

"A jet."

"Well, I seem to be moving up in all sorts of ways."

34

AN ARRINGTON HOTEL CAR drove Stone to Centurion Studios the following morning, and his board of directors' pass got him through the gate. Peter's offices were housed in what had been Vance Calder's cottage on the lot, and he had expanded into another building next door.

Billy Barnett was waiting for him in a rocking chair on the front porch. Billy had begun life as Teddy Fay and had been a career CIA officer, working in and eventually directing their office of special services, which equipped agents with all sorts of things, from weapons to communications equipment and even more exotic items. Upon his retirement Teddy had started a personal war against certain politicians, and for some years he had been an elusive fugitive from justice, until Stone had used his friendship with the former president, Will Lee, to get him pardoned and his identity wiped clean from the government's computers. "Billy Barnett" was now an upstanding citizen.

They shook hands warmly. "Peter has another half an hour's work to do in the editing suite," Billy said. "He asked me to take you down to the studio commissary and get a table, and he'll join us for lunch."

Billy escorted Stone to a golf cart, and they drove down the New York Street—the largest and most used standing set at the studio—and thence to the commissary, where a table awaited them.

"I hear you had a brush with terrorism at the Arrington yesterday," Billy said.

Stone was astonished. "How the hell did you hear about that?"

"Hollywood is a small town within Los Angeles. Word gets around quickly."

"I've seen just two people since the board meeting, where the bombing attempt was discussed in the strictest confidence, and both of them knew about it."

Billy smiled and spread his hands. "What can I tell you?"

They ordered a cold soup and had finished that before Peter showed up. He and Stone embraced. "I'm glad you were safe from the bomb," he said.

"There, that's three for three."

"What?" Peter asked.

"No one is supposed to know about that, but everyone, including you, seems to."

"It's a small town," Peter said, and sat down.

Stone regaled him with questions about his work and got fulsome answers. He was proud of his son, and he enjoyed hearing about his career. "And how's our Ben Bacchetti doing in his new job?" Ben was Dino Bacchetti's son and Peter's production partner, but he had recently been elevated to the studio's head of production, the youngest in Hollywood since Irving Thalberg in the twenties.

"Ben is thriving. I think he actually enjoys being overworked."

"But he's still producing your work?"

"He is, and his new job means we have one less level to get approvals from. Only Leo Goldman stands between us and a production order, and he usually is thrilled to sign them."

"Funny how profits turn a CEO's head. How is Leo?" Goldman was fighting cancer but still at work.

"He's undergoing a new treatment that seems to be working wonders. He looks great."

"I'm glad to hear it."

"By the way, Stone," Billy said, "I don't know if you've heard this, but the man who was arrested trying to detonate your bomb yesterday was a Centurion employee."

"Good God!"

"I'm afraid so—young fellow in his twenties who was a technician in our armory." The Centurion armory supplied weapons and blank ammunition for the studio's movies. "There's some speculation that he might have built the bomb here."

"Are you aware that there were three other bombs?"

Billy and Peter shook their heads. "I guess it's not as small a town as I had thought," Billy said.

"No, the other bombs were at our hotels in Rome, Paris, and next door to my house in England. The plan was for all three to go off simultaneously. Fortunately, our security people here got the word out and all the plots were foiled. They captured one man in England, the Rome and Paris bombers got away."

"Have you heard anything about who the London guy was?"

"No, perhaps I should ask you two."

"I guess we're not as plugged in with England," Peter said. "None of the bombs went off?"

"No. We've got a new piece of equipment called a security blanket. If a bomb is discovered the blanket is thrown over it, and it blocks radio and cell phone transmissions that might detonate it."

"What a great idea!" Peter said. "I can use that in a movie. It sounds like your security people are really on the ball."

"That's true. With each of our hotels, we've had opposition from either terrorists or criminals—either the Italian Mafia or, even worse, the Russians."

"Have they been quiet lately?"

"I think they've found us too costly to deal with. The Italian godfather is in prison, and most of the Russian opposition is dead." He didn't mention that Billy had been instrumental in their demise; Peter still didn't know that Billy had saved their lives when he and Ben had been driving across the country to start their production company at Centurion.

"So, Dad, who are you seeing these days? I heard that the affair with the screenwriter cooled down."

"I guess you could put it that way. I've met someone interesting since I've been here, though—a theatrical set designer named Jinx Jameson."

"I know the name," Peter said. "They're doing one of her productions at the Ahmanson Theatre."

"That's why she's in town. I'm giving her a lift home to New York tomorrow."

"Well, if that doesn't impress her, nothing will. On the other hand, does she know you're the pilot?"

"I don't believe I mentioned that," Stone said.

"She's probably expecting something like the Centurion Gulfstream 650."

"I certainly hope not."

"You say 'private jet' and people think you're flying something that will carry thirty passengers, instead of six."

"You could have a point. Well, it will teach her not to anticipate too much."

"The world would be a simpler place if people didn't over-anticipate," Billy said.

"Perhaps I'd better drop a hint at dinner tonight."

"I wouldn't," Peter said. "She might back out, and you wouldn't want that, would you?"

"No," Stone replied, "I wouldn't. I'll keep my mouth shut."

STONE WAITED UNTIL they were in bed that night, on their second occasion, to mention casually that he was flying his own air-plane to New York.

"Really? What airplane?"

"A Citation CJ 3 Plus."

"How much total time do you have?"

"Around four thousand hours in half a dozen airplanes."

"How much time in type?"

"A couple of hundred hours. I owned two other light jets before, so I've got around twelve hundred hours in jets. You sound very famil-iar with airplanes."

"My father was a professional pilot, flew everything. The two questions he wanted to ask anyone who was flying him were total time and time in type."

"So, I passed the test?"

"Not until I've experienced my first takeoff and landing with you. I have a private license that I don't use very often, so I'll know what to look for. Can I fly right seat?"

"Sure. Speaking of landing, a client of mine and his girlfriend have invited us to overnight in Santa Fe on the way home. Do you have time for that?"

"I'll make time. I've never been to Santa Fe. Just one night?"

"Perhaps we'll add another, if we're invited."

"Who's the client?"

"A young man named Laurence Hayward."

"Why does that sound familiar?"

Stone sighed. "He won the Powerball lottery last month."

"Oh, yes, I've read about him in the papers. What sort of legal work do you do for him?"

"Pretty much everything. A fellow who's suddenly come into more than half a billion dollars needs all kinds of advice and services. I happened to be well positioned to put him into the right hands for legal, financial, real estate, and other services."

"What other services?"

"Whatever he needs."

"What has he needed so far?"

"All of the above, plus aviation advice and help with publicity. He bought the same airplane I fly and has ordered the new Citation Latitude for delivery next year. Right now, he's building time."

"Lucky young man."

"We'll see. Lottery stories seem to end badly for too many people."

"Do you think he'll crash and burn?"

"Not if I have anything to say about it. Right now, he's in the first rush of knowing he can buy virtually anything he wants. He's bought a New York apartment, and he bought the Santa Fe house at first sight. Luckily, he seems to have very good taste and judgment in just about everything. He also did something very nice for his mother and stepfather—he bought their city and country houses in England and gave them lifetime occupancy, so they can retire in great comfort with a lot of cash."

"That was sweet of him."

"Yes, it was."

"Enough of this chitchat," she said. "Make love to me again."

"No more chitchat," Stone said, turning his attentions to her.

THEY TOOK OFF from Santa Monica at mid-morning the following day, with Jinx in the copilot's seat, handling the radios. She also started to learn the Garmin 3000 avionics.

"I've flown a Cirrus with the Garmin 1000 panel," she said, "so it's not entirely foreign to me." By the time they landed in Santa Fe she had the rudiments down.

They took a rental car and drove out to Tano Norte. "I've been out here for dinner once," Stone said, "and it's a beautiful house, built by a woman with the reputation of being Santa Fe's top designer/builder." Fifteen minutes later they arrived and were greeted by Laurence and Theresa and shown into the guesthouse.

"The air is wonderful," Jinx said, inhaling deeply.

"It's also very thin. We're at seven thousand feet here, so don't overexert or drink too much until you've acclimated."

"And how long does that take?"

"A day or two, for most people. Don't go jogging."

"I suppose I have to give up sex until then."

"Certainly not. Sex is always good for you, no matter what the elevation."

They had a nap, then turned up in the main house at six, for a tour and cocktails.

"It looks like you've lived here for a long time," Jinx commented to Theresa.

"That's the fault of our builder, Sharon Woods. She furnished the place, right down to the bedding and towels."

They visited the bar for drinks, went into the living room, then Theresa took Jinx into the kitchen to get some canapés.

Stone and Laurence sat down on the living room sofa, and Laurence took out his iPhone. "There's something I want to show you," he said, switching on the phone. "Thanks to you I now have a hotshot security system both here and in New York. Mike Freeman's people called me early this morning to tell me I had had an intruder at the Fairleigh in the wee hours. They put together a little video to show me."

He went to a website and started the video, for which images from different cameras had been pieced together. It began just inside the front door of the apartment: the front door opened and a large man stepped inside and looked around, his face in the shadows. Then lights came on, and the image froze momentarily.

"Do you know him?" Stone asked.

"I do not, but he looks like that guy from the Three Stooges."

"Curly."

"Yes, but meaner-looking."

"You're right about that."

The video continued as the man moved from room to room. He was searching Marge's office, when something spooked him, and he ran for the door. Moments after he left, two hotel security men entered the apartment, and the video stopped.

"That's it," Laurence said. "He was in the apartment for less than two minutes."

"Didn't the alarm go off as soon as he entered?"

"No, the alarm is silent, ringing only at Strategic Services. I didn't want to alarm the neighbors with sirens. The silent alarm didn't go off until a minute after he entered, to give time for the code to be entered in the command module before it activated."

"Have the police seen this?"

"Yes, and they've identified him as one Marvin Jones, who had already been into the apartment once before—they identified him at that time by a fingerprint. The police have been looking for him ever since."

"He didn't appear to steal anything."

"I think he was looking for my checkbook again, but since his first visit, and after the checks he wrote, Marge has had a safe installed in her office and everything financial is kept in there."

"He was looking very interested in that safe when he was rousted," Stone said. "Don't worry, they'll haul him in eventually."

The women came back with the canapés, and Laurence whispered to Stone, "Theresa doesn't know about this, so don't mention it. I don't want to frighten her."

Stone nodded and accepted a canapé. "Laurence, Theresa, I've just had a thought: You don't know a lot of people in New York, do you?"

"I don't," Laurence replied. "Theresa, do you?"

"Mostly women I went to Mount Holyoke with."

"Every year, Strategic Services throws a party for its key staff and a couple of dozen of their best clients. This year, it's to be at my house, but my living room isn't really big enough. I wonder if you'd consider hosting it at your apartment? At no cost to you, of course."

The two young people exchanged a glance. "Of course. When is it?"

"In a couple of weeks. The invitations will go out in a couple of days."

"We'll be back by then," Laurence said. "Just let me know what time and how many. I'll hire waiters."

"Mike Freeman, the CEO, will take care of that. All you'll have to do is come to the party. Oh, and it will be black tie, so, Theresa, you'll have an excuse to buy a new dress."

"I can't complain about that," she said.

THE FOLLOWING MORNING, Stone called Mike Freeman and discussed the new venue. "His living room is enormous, and it will
be better for the guests than my house."

"Sounds good. I'd like to meet Laurence."

"And there's a grand piano and room for some musicians."

"I'll send our catering manager over to have a look at it."

"I'll ask Laurence to tell the concierge to let her in."

"When are you due back in town?"

"A couple of days. My companion hasn't seen Santa Fe yet."

THE FOUR OF THEM piled into Laurence's station wagon, since he and
Theresa hadn't seen much of the area, either. Stone drove, since he
knew the territory.

A couple of miles up Tano Road, Stone saw a car in his rearview mirror. He had a couple of turns to make to get into the center of the city, and the car turned with him, though keeping well back. "Laurence," he said, "remember the night I had a look at a car across the road from your house?"

"I do. Was it a silver Mini?"

"It was and is. It's been following us since Tano Road."

"It's a local kid who's a stringer for the *National Inquisitor.* It's not the first time he's made a bother of himself—he sneaked up on the house right after the security system was installed, and I nearly took a shot at him."

"With what?"

"I bought a pistol."

"I see."

"He came to the press event that Faith Mackey set up, and I thought I'd seen the back of him, but I guess not."

"Do you think he might be dangerous?"

"No, he's just a skinny kid trying to make a few quid—excuse me, bucks."

Stone turned onto Paseo de Peralta, which made a grand circle through some of the more interesting areas in town, then he turned onto Upper Canyon Road.

"Canyon Road? Isn't this where the art galleries are?"

"That part is down the hill, I just want to get a closer look at our tail."

Stone drove past houses that became less frequent as they climbed the mountain. At the very top of the road there was a turnaround, and momentarily, the Mini passed him on the way up and made the turn, too. Stone stopped the station wagon and turned to block the road, then he got out. "Stay here, please," he said to the others.

The Mini had stopped, and the young man stared owlishly at him through black-rimmed glasses as he approached. Stone rapped on the window glass with a knuckle; the kid thought about it for a minute, then the glass slid down. "What's on your mind?" Stone asked.

"Nothing, not a thing."

"Don't you know you can get into trouble doing this sort of thing?"

"What sort of thing?"

"Annoying people who want privacy. That's what you get paid for by the *Inquisitor*, isn't it?"

"I don't know what you're talking about."

"How about if I call Pat Bolton and tell him you're lousy at your job?"

"Who's that?"

"The guy you used to work for."

"Used to?"

"Not after our conversation. You've been Mr. Hayward's guest once, and that was supposed to be it. Pat agreed, along with the other editors, that Mr. Hayward wouldn't be bothered again."

"Who are you?"

"I'm Mr. Hayward's attorney. How do you like the Mini?"

"It's okay, why?"

"Because if I have to haul you into court, you won't be driving it much longer. You do get to keep making the payments, though." Stone handed him his business card. "Give that to your lawyer, and tell him he'll be hearing from me if I see you in my rearview mirror again, or anywhere near Mr. Hayward."

The kid stared stonily at him, then Stone went back to the Mercedes and drove away. The Mini sat in the road behind him, unmoving, then Stone turned onto Alameda and didn't see it again.

"You must have had an effective conversation," Laurence said, looking back.

"He seemed to get the picture," Stone said. "Would you like to see some galleries?"

"I'd like that very much," Laurence replied.

Stone turned into Canyon Road and parked. "Let's walk up one side and down the other. We can grab some lunch at Geronimo's."

AN HOUR AND A HALF LATER they had reached the top of Canyon Road and were seated at a table on the veranda, when the Mini drove by, and the driver took a snapshot as he passed.

"I guess I didn't make myself clear," Stone said.

"What can we do about it?"

"I know the guy he works for. He's been a problem in the past, but I thought we'd worked things out. I guess I was wrong. Do you have a guest list for the press event?"

"I believe I still have it."

"Let me know what the kid's name is."

"I'll do that."

AFTER THEY HAD had a good lunch, they walked back down the road, cruising the galleries. At the bottom they got back into the car and drove up the road, picking up Laurence's purchases along the way. They arrived back at the house with a dozen paintings and sculptures in the luggage compartment; the larger pieces would be delivered. They spent the rest of the afternoon hanging his purchases and taking delivery of a few others.

Later in the day they sat down for a drink. "You said you bought a gun," Stone said.

"I know, I know, you told me not to. Actually, I think you may have been right—I nearly shot at the kid stringer."

"Laurence," Stone said, in his sternest Dutch uncle voice, "do not, under any circumstances, bring the gun to New York. The city has very strict laws regarding the possession of weapons, even in one's own home, and the penalties are severe."

"Can I get a permit?"

"Permits are available but in very short supply. If you're not carrying satchels of currency around on a daily basis, or in the jewelry trade, you will almost certainly be denied a carry permit."

"How about a permit to keep it in my apartment?"

"Those are slightly less restrictive, but don't bring a gun into your home until you have the permit in hand."

"Okay," Laurence replied.

STONE AND JINX arrived at Teterboro, where they were met by Fred in the Bentley.

At home, Stone introduced Jinx to Joan, and Bob made a fool of himself over her. Stone gave Jinx the tour, then dispatched her to her own apartment downtown after asking her to dinner. She had promptly agreed. "Fred will come for you at seven o'clock," he had said, giving her a kiss.

Stone went into his office and called Dino.

"You made it back?" Dino asked. "I was beginning to doubt your return."

"We spent a couple of days with Laurence and his girl, Theresa."

"How is our young billionaire?"

"Half a billionaire—he started out with more, but after a few real estate investments and many pieces of art, his net worth is down a hundred million or so."

"That's gotta be tough on the kid."

"Well, yeah."

"I dreamed I came into that much money the other night, and I couldn't think of anything to spend it on."

"Sure you could, and if you couldn't, Viv would take up the slack."

"Good point."

"Dinner at Patroon, seven-thirty? I'll introduce you to a new *jeune fille*."

"See you there." They hung up.

Stone went through the mail and signed a stack of checks, while Fred unpacked for him. Joan sat down, handing him things to sign. "How's our boy billionaire?" she asked.

"Half a billionaire," Stone said. "There's a difference."

"What can a billionaire buy that a half billionaire can't?"

"An office building, his own country, like that."

"Ah."

"By the way, the annual Strategic Services event is going to be held at Laurence's apartment, instead of here. When the invite comes, accept."

"Will do. Helene will be enormously relieved."

"Why? She wouldn't have had to do anything. The caterers would have handled it."

"Yes, but she'd feel the responsibility to supervise them and count the silver when they'd gone."

———

STONE WALKED DOWN to Patroon, while Fred went to pick up Jinx; he got there first and found Dino and Viv waiting for him. A waiter brought him a Knob Creek.

"You promised us a new girl," Viv said. "Where is she?"

"She lives downtown—in an artist's loft, I think. Fred will deliver her."

"How convenient," Viv replied.

"Dino," Stone said, "if Laurence Hayward calls you to get your help with a gun permit, please turn him down."

"I nearly always turn down people who make that request," Dino said.

"Good." He looked up to see Jinx enter the restaurant and stood up to make the introductions. Once Jinx had settled into their booth, Viv pounced, grilling her for a good ten minutes about her work, her apartment, and anything else she could think of.

"I'm sorry about that," Stone said. "Viv is very protective of me."

"Jinx has reassured me," Viv said. "He's all yours, Jinx."

"I doubt it," Jinx said.

"No kidding, he's between flames."

"I'm delighted to hear it," Jinx said. "That reminds me, I arrived home to find the place full of scaffolding. I hired some painters weeks ago, and they picked now as the best time to come."

"You can bunk with me for the duration," Stone said.

"I presumed to bring a couple of bags. Fred is dealing with them."

"He can probably guess where to put them," Viv said.

"I like Fred. He seems a very competent person."

"You have no idea," Stone said. "He's an ex–Royal Marine commando, tough as nails."

"Yet charming."

"He is that, when he's not intimidating someone twice his size."

"How does he do that?"

"I don't entirely understand it. He can do a lot with a dead-eyed stare."

They ordered and dined. After dinner, Stone and Jinx walked slowly home.

"It's like a different city up here," Jinx said as they turned into Stone's Turtle Bay street.

"That's the way I feel in your neighborhood," Stone said. "I get a nosebleed if I go below Forty-second Street." They climbed the stairs to the front door, and Stone reached for his key. To his surprise the door was slightly ajar.

"Did you leave it that way?" Jinx asked.

"I did not," Stone said. "Will you wait here while I have a look around?"

"I'd rather come with you," she said.

"All right, but stay close behind me. I'm often armed, but not tonight." He put a finger to his lips and stepped inside and closed the door silently.

The living room was dark; he imagined that Joan had turned off the lights using an app on her iPhone. Stone stood and listened hard. He heard a tiny sound from below his feet, then beckoned Jinx to follow. They got into the elevator, the shaft of which was heavily insulated for sound, and rode down to the lower level. As the door opened, light from the car dimly illuminated his office. There was the scuffling sound of footsteps, and he heard the outside door near Joan's office open and close. He hit a light switch, then ran down the hall, opened the door, and stepped outside. He heard the sound of running feet going down the block toward Second Avenue, but by the time he made the sidewalk, whoever it had been was gone. He walked back into his office.

"See anyone?" Jinx asked. She had made herself at home on his leather sofa.

"Heard, didn't see. Somebody young, I think. He really sprinted down the block."

"Don't you have a security system?"

"Yes, but I didn't arm it when I left."

"Any cameras?"

Stone flinched, thinking of his advice to Laurence. "Sadly, no."

"How about the front door?"

"That locks when you close it. Whoever got in probably picked the lock, then went downstairs. I suppose that whatever he wanted would be more likely to be found down here than upstairs." He walked around his desk, opened and closed some drawers, had a look at the safe. "Everything seems in about as good an order as it gets. The safe is still locked, so I guess the intruder was no yegg."

"Yegg? Is that some sort of omelet?"

"An old-fashioned word for a safecracker. Or maybe he just didn't have time for that before we showed up. Let me check Joan's office."

He had a look in there and found it in good order, then returned to his office. "We may as well go upstairs," he said. "Nothing more to do here."

They got into the elevator and rode up to the top floor, then went down the hall to the master suite. "Your dressing room is there," Stone said, pointing.

Jinx had a look. "The service is pretty good around here," she said when she came back. "Fred even put away my thongs."

"He probably turned that duty over to Joan. I don't think he would be so bold."

She snaked an arm around his neck. "I hope you're feeling bold."

He was, and he proved it to her.

STONE CALLED Mike Freeman at Strategic Services the following morning. "I'm afraid I need some security cameras," he said, then told him of the previous evening's intruder.

"I suggested that a long time ago, but you had Bob Cantor install a system anyway. Not that Bob doesn't do good work, but you probably got all cheap on him."

Stone ignored that. "I want them cleverly concealed," he said.

"Hang on." There was a click, and Stone was in the hold void, listening to, of all things, country music.

Mike came back. "I'll have somebody over there in an hour to do an assessment."

"Great. Since when did you start listening to country music?"

"I don't."

"Well, your customers do, while on hold."

"Are you serious? Maybe it's your own phone system."

"Mine is mostly Mozart, occasionally some Oscar Peterson."

"I'll look into it," Mike said, then hung up.

AN HOUR LATER, Joan buzzed him. "Mike Freeman's security person is here."

"Okay, send him in."

"Take a deep breath," Joan said, then hung up.

There was a rap at his door, which was ajar, and a blond head appeared, followed by a tall, willowy body in a tight black business suit. "Mr. Barrington?"

Stone stood. "Stone. Please come in."

They shook hands. "My name is Heavenly Peace," she said. He motioned her to a chair, and she crossed her legs fetchingly.

"I'm sorry," Stone said, "I feel as though I've just stepped into a Bond film."

"That's very good. Amazingly, I haven't heard that one."

"May I ask, how did you come by your name?"

"My father's surname was Peace, and my mother was a religious fanatic."

"You must get asked about that a lot."

"Every day of my life—often, several times a day."

"Ever get tired of it?"

"A very long time ago."

"Still, you haven't changed it."

223

"Well, nobody has ever forgotten it. And everyone wants my business card."

"That's handy."

"I've always found it so." She recrossed her legs. "Now, what may I do to improve your day?"

Stone searched for a quip, then gave up. "Security cameras."

"Ah. For what purpose—home movies? Narcissism? Pornography, perhaps?"

"Security."

She smiled, revealing very white teeth against her fire-engine-red lipstick. "I'm sorry, my attention wandered for a moment. And how do you envision using these cameras?"

"Well, if I should come home and find my front door ajar and hear someone in this office, as I did last night, I would like to have images of that person or persons to remember him or her by."

"Do you wish this person or persons to know that they are being photographed?"

"I do not. And I would like for the cameras to have the highest resolution available and to operate well in low lighting conditions. So often when I see security recordings, the people in them tend to be unidentifiable."

"I know exactly what you mean. Do you presently have a security system of any sort?"

"I have one that does just about everything but employ cameras. It is my fond hope that you can install a camera system that is compatible with my present installation, rather than ripping it all out and starting over."

She stood. "Let's see what we can do. Where shall we start?"

"Well, since we're already in my office, what about right here?"

"May I borrow a legal pad?" she asked. "I left my handbag in the car."

Stone stood, produced one, and offered her a pen.

"You may remain seated," she said, "while I do a little survey."

Stone sat down.

She paced the room in every direction, taking notes all the while and occasionally adding a diagram. "Now," she said, "we will presume that you want the exterior door covered, along with the elevator and— What is that door?" She pointed.

"It leads to the garage."

"Ah." She made a note. "Now, shall we drift upward?"

Stone pressed the button for the elevator and allowed her to precede him into the car, while appreciating the view from that angle. They emerged in the entrance hall, where she began by inspecting the front door lock. "We'll want to replace that," she said. "Apparently it was picked last night. The Israelis make something more formidable." She made a note, then proceeded into the living room, making a diagram and marking camera locations on it. "Why do I feel there is a study?"

"Because you are gifted that way," Stone replied, pointing.

She reached for the doorknob. "May I?"

"You may." She opened the door and entered. "Such a nice room," she said, "and so you."

"Thank you."

"Now, if you would escort me to the top floor of the house, I think we can skip what's in between and save you some money, which Mike Freeman says is dear to your heart."

"Mike exaggerates." He led her back to the elevator and out onto the fourth-floor landing and into the master suite.

"Another very nice room. And is that a dumbwaiter?" She pointed.

"It is. Does it concern you?"

"Makes a nice ride up for a burglar, doesn't it?"

"Touché."

She opened a door. "Dressing room?" Then quickly closed it. "A lady's."

"From time to time."

"I don't think you'd look well in a thong."

"That one is mine. Do you think it's a target for a burglar?"

"Own any watches or other jewelry?"

"Touché again."

She finished the room. "What's on the ground floor rear?"

"The kitchen—opens to a common garden."

"Better have a look."

After her look at the rear of the house, she handed him a card. "Before you ask."

"When will I hear from you?"

"Normally, that's *my* line, but figure a couple of days to see a plan and some equipment. If you want to see an example of our work, visit Laurence Hayward's apartment."

"Good idea. I'll look forward to hearing from you."

"I'm glad," she said, then departed.

Stone mopped his brow; that had been a near thing.

BUTCH CRANE was working on a display in the Purple Label room when he looked up to see Curly walk in. There were half a dozen people, clients and sales associates, in the room. He strode across the room. "May I help you, sir?" he asked with a stone face.

"Yeah, sure. Where's the cash register?"

"The men's room is on the lower level. Take the elevator," Butch said, smiling. Then, sotto voce, "In the park, Fifth and Seventy-second, half an hour."

"Thanks, pal," Curly said, then left.

Butch went back to his work.

"Who the hell was that?" an associate asked.

"He was in the wrong store."

"He sure was. He looked like that guy with the Three Stooges."

"I didn't notice."

BUTCH TOOK HIS LUNCH HOUR and ambled over to the Central Park entrance at Fifth and Seventy-second, as if he were taking lunch in the park. He saw Curly on a park bench, just across the street; he crossed and sat down at the other end of the bench, taking the *Times* from his pocket and opening it. "What the hell do you mean, coming into the store?" he asked without turning his head.

"I go where the fuck I like," Curly replied. "Last night I was in Stone Barrington's house."

"Hayward's lawyer? Are you nuts? The guy's an ex-cop and best friends with the police commissioner. Theresa told me about him."

"And I had to read about him in a tabloid piece about Hayward. I couldn't count on my old buddy Butch to clue me in."

"Clue you in about what?"

"The guy's rich—not as rich as Hayward, but he's got a house full of stuff. I found myself a fence who knows the high-end market, so I'm branching out."

A police car pulled up across the road, and Butch and Curly both fell silent.

"Relax," Curly said, "they're just eating their donuts."

Butch said nothing; he found the Arts section of the paper and folded it to show the crossword puzzle, then started to work on it. "Curly," he said, trying not to move his lips, "listen to me. I'm done with you—no more money, no robberies or burglaries, no anything. If I hear from you again for any reason, I'll kill you."

"Kill *me*, you little piece of shit?"

"It's a promise," Butch said, "a guarantee." He heard a car door slam.

"Oh, shit," Curly said, then he got up and sprinted away from the bench.

Butch looked up from the crossword in time to see a cop chasing him, while the other started the police car and drove farther into the park. Butch went back to the crossword.

FIVE MINUTES LATER two cops walked up to him, both of them sweating and panting a little. "Excuse me, sir," one of them said, "do you know the man who was sitting next to you?"

Butch looked at the empty bench. "What man?"

"The one who was sitting there until we started chasing him."

Butch shook his head. "There was somebody there when I sat down, but I didn't really take any notice of him."

"What brings you to the park today?"

"Lunch hour," Butch replied. "I work over at Ralph Lauren, on Madison."

"Do you have an employer's ID?"

"Sure." Butch fished out the card from his pocket and handed it to him. "Who was the guy you were chasing?"

"Somebody on the wanted list." The cop returned his card. "Sorry to trouble you, Mr. Crane."

"Not a problem," Butch said, then went back to his crossword. He waited five minutes, then took a cab home. He let himself into the apartment and went to the kitchen drawer where Theresa's little .25 automatic lived. He unloaded it, field-stripped it, and wiped every surface with an oily rag, then reassembled it, wiped every round clean, reloaded the magazine, shoved it home, and put it into his pocket after wiping the exterior.

He left the apartment with a new feeling of confidence, rimmed with anxiety. He'd shoot the bastard if he saw him again, he swore to himself.

He was back in the Purple Label room in time to serve a customer who bought two suits, then was coaxed by Butch into a third. This day would end better than it started, he thought, as he took fitting notes from the tailor, then rang up the client's purchases, which came to nearly $10,000.

LAURENCE AND THERESA were met at Teterboro by Oliver, his driver, who put their luggage and Theresa's Santa Fe purchases into the Bentley.

"Laurence," Theresa said, "do you think we could invite my brother, Butch, to the Strategic Services party? I'd like you to get to know him better."

"Well, since it's at our apartment, I'm sure that would be all right. I'll mention it to Mike Freeman when I get the chance."

THEY LET THEMSELVES into the apartment, and Marge was there to greet them. "Welcome home," she said. "I've missed you."

"I've missed you, too, Marge," Laurence replied. "Any significant mail or calls?"

"Both are mostly begging letters and calls, but one from the police commissioner." She handed him a slip with the number.

Laurence tucked it into his pocket. "I'll call him later."

"Call him now," Theresa said, "and I'll unpack for you. Who knows your dressing room better than I?"

"Okay." Laurence went into the study, picked up the phone and called Dino.

"Commissioner's office," a crisp, female voice said.

"Laurence Hayward, returning the commissioner's call."

"One moment."

Dino came on the line. "Welcome home, Laurence."

"Thank you, Dino. It's good to hear from you."

"I hear on the grapevine that you bought a place in Santa Fe."

"You pick your grapes well."

"Have you met Ed Eagle and his wife, Susannah?"

"We traded dinners. Your grapevine was there, too, with a very fetching woman."

"Met her last night, and you're right. Listen, I've had some news of the intruder in your apartment."

"Wonderful. What news?"

"Two of my uniformed park patrol spotted him sitting on a bench at the Seventy-second Street entrance earlier today."

"Did they grab him?"

"It turned into a footrace, and the guy, big as he is, got the better of them. The good news is, they made him from your security camera shots, so there'll be other opportunities."

"I'm glad to hear that," Laurence said. "I'd better let you get back to keeping the city safe."

"I'll be in touch," Dino said, and they both hung up.

40

SOFIA BUCKSTEIN got off a train at Grand Central and made her way toward the main hall, towing her carry-on suitcase that contained four days' of clothing, all of it with the labels removed, in case she had to abandon it. Her shoes were good for sprinting, if necessary, and the big bag slung over her shoulder contained the stuff of her work: cash, credit cards, and wristwatches she had taken off marks; three wallets, each stuffed with a different passport, a driver's license, a couple of credit cards, and some useful fluff like insurance cards. Her iPhone was tucked into a silk holster, clipped to a bra that supported her ample breasts. She didn't carry a gun, but there was a very sharp little switchblade tucked into a garter. She had had to use it only once, but it was always there. Then she looked up and saw the guy.

He was clearly rough trade, and she liked that. He was heavy, in a muscular way, had a shaved head tucked under a tweed cap—very different from the men in handmade suits on the train that she could think of only as marks.

She walked straight up to him. "Where can a girl get a drink around here?" she asked him, straight-out. "And are you buying?"

He gazed down at her. She was only five-three, but very well built. "Right this way, sweetheart," he said, taking the handle of her roll-on and starting down the platform. "You gotta name?"

"One for every occasion," she said. "Let's start with Maria."

"That's classy, I like it. I'm Curly, for obvious reasons," he said, lifting his cap. He led her into a restaurant in the station, parked her case in the cloakroom, and steered her to a bar stool.

"So," she said, "how's business?"

"Slow," he replied, "but not too slow." He beckoned a bartender. "What'll you have, Maria?"

"Macallan 12 will do me."

"Two of those," he said to the bartender, and laid a fifty down, "and make them doubles."

"You work the platforms regular, Curly?"

"When I don't have anything better to do."

"What's your pitch?"

"A judo chop to the back of the neck," he said. "If you do it just right, you can catch them before they hit the pavement."

"How do you get away with that in a place like this?"

"I start yelling for somebody to call nine-one-one, and I give the bum chest compressions while I pick his pocket. Then I get somebody to spell me and I disappear. Anybody stops me, I tell 'em I'm going for a cop."

"Well, it's simple, I'll give you that, and you save a lot of time not having to work the guy."

"That's me, simple and direct. Charm has never been my strong suit."

"I like that in a man. You ever get picked up for that dodge?"

"I have another talent—I run like a deer, and nobody, but *nobody*, catches me."

"Where'd you get in such good shape?" She poked him in the belly. "Hard as a rock."

"In a prison gym. There wasn't anything else to do. How 'bout you, babe? What's your game?"

"Whatever works. I like trains, 'cause you can always get off before somebody tumbles and misses his stuff. I've done it on the run a couple of times and walked a few miles to get another ride. Mostly, though, I leave 'em on the platform, having made a dinner date—one I never keep. By dinnertime, he's changed his pants and missed his wallet."

"Where are you based?"

"Down South, where the sun always shines."

"And where do you lay your head, here in the Apple?"

"Is that an offer?"

"Could be. Are you always so hot to trot, Maria?"

"Could be. What'd you have in mind?"

"You name it, I love it."

"A man after my own heart. You got a place in town?"

"I do. It's a fifteen-minute cab ride this time of day."

She tossed off her scotch. "What're we waiting for?"

He knocked back his own drink, left another ten on the bar, grabbed her case, and led her to a cab. She gave him half a blow job on the way uptown. Best not to wear him out too soon, leave him wanting more.

SOFIA/MARIA EASED OUT of the bed and used the john, then she grabbed a robe off a hook, rolled up the sleeves, and had a look around. A one-bedroom with a king-sized bed, a kitchenette, a sleeper sofa with a biggish TV across the room—the basics, but not bad. Curly was pretty much in that category, too; she had only to test his stamina. This place was good for three or four days before she dumped him and took a train somewhere. She hadn't done a Chicago run for a while, and she usually had good luck going west. A hundred in the pocket of a conductor kept him sweet and dumb, when the cops questioned him. She watched the evening news and read the *Daily News,* which was on the coffee table, then she went back to the bedroom, dropped the robe, got into bed, and took his balls in her hand.

Curly stirred. "What's that I feel?" he mumbled.

"Your balls in my hand," she said. "You up for another run?"

"You read my mind," he said.

"Oh, are these where you keep your mind?" She gave them a little squeeze and got the correct response.

He rolled over on her. "Put it wherever you like," he said.

And she did.

CURLY MADE A GOOD BREAKFAST, the mark of a man alone. He made soft, scrambled eggs, microwave bacon, an English muffin, fresh orange juice, and very strong coffee. "Getcha anything else?"

"Anything else, and I'd explode," she said. "You mind a strictly professional observation?"

"As long as it doesn't hurt too much."

"Why do you work so hard looking like an ex-con?"

"'Cause that's who I am."

"Then try being somebody else for a while, you'll do better, make more money."

"Be specific."

"You've got a full head of hair hidden in your skull—grow some of it, and get it cut nice."

"It's a lot of trouble."

"Looking good already is. And get a couple of suits made."

"Too expensive."

"If you read something besides the tabloids you'd see ads for tailors. They ain't Savile Row, but they'd look a lot better on you than that low-end mall stuff you wear. They'd fit, for one thing."

"It's a thought."

"Something else—you keep your weight up to intimidate people."

"It's a good thing when you want their money."

"Lose thirty pounds and talk 'em out of it. If you keep hitting people in the back of the neck you're going to paralyze somebody or worse, kill 'em."

"So what?"

"So the cops want you a lot worse when it's a serious crime. I mean, a guy gets rolled in a train station, a cop can dust him off and send him home with a few words of friendly advice, but when the cop has to ride in the ambulance with him to the ER and watch some intern try to bring him around and fail, and his wife and kids show up and scream, that makes the cop want to put you away, or worse, shoot you."

"You have a point."

"And that tattoo on your neck really sets you up for a lineup in a precinct, you know?"

"It's permanent."

"It's a couple of hours in a doc's office and a grand out of pocket. Ditch it, grow some hair, get some clothes."

"Then I'd look like everybody else."

"That's kind of the point, Curly. That's how you stay out of lineups. Nine out of ten people the cops question are going to say you looked like the guy on the Three Stooges, don't you know that?"

"I always kind of liked it."

"It's fine in prison, not so good on the street. Do you have a real name?"

"Marvin Jones."

"Well, Marv, that's nice and anonymous. A girl could like a name like that."

"Okay," Curly said, "my hair is already growing, I'll skip lunch, and you can pick out a tailor for me and walk me through the experience."

"And when I get back in a week or two, you can take me to a nice restaurant and buy me a steak."

"Back from where?"

"A girl's gotta keep moving, if she wants to make any money."

HEAVENLY PEACE SHOWED UP with two men carrying toolboxes; she was dressed in a nicely tailored boiler suit with a Strategic Services emblem embroidered above her left breast and carrying a small suitcase. "May I leave my case here somewhere, Stone? It's got my civvies in it, for later."

"Of course," Stone said, "just leave it in my closet over there." He pointed across his office.

"Now, you've seen the plans, can we start in here? We'll make as little noise as possible, then we'll drift upstairs."

"As you wish," Stone said. "I've got to read some documents. I'll take them up to my study while you work in here."

"See you later," she said, tossing her long blond hair out of her way, then quickly pinning it up.

Stone took his briefcase upstairs and settled into a comfortable chair. His phone rang. "Yes?"

"Dino on one," Joan said.

Stone punched the button. "Morning."

"Yeah, and a nice one, too. I hear you have an unusual security tech wandering around your house. Quite a dish, huh?"

"Yeah, I think this is Mike Freeman's idea of a joke."

"You're taking it all wrong—he's heard you're lonely, and he just wants to make you feel better."

"Nah, he just wants me to walk around the house with a bulge in my trousers all day."

Dino laughed loudly. "First step in feeling better."

"I thought Jinx was the first step in feeling better."

"She's nice, but she heads off downtown every day to her studio, and you only see her at night."

"What's wrong with that?"

"Nothing, but she's a professional woman with a lot of work on her hands, so she can't devote herself fully to you."

"That describes just about every woman I've met since Arrington died, even Heavenly Peace."

"Nice name, huh? It's how you'll feel when she's through with you. And she's not the type to take her work to bed with her."

"You have a point. Jinx has a bad habit of sketching ideas while I'm trying to get to sleep. Her painters are supposed to be out of her place today, though, so I should be able to get some rest."

"Tell you what, if she abandons you, bring Hev to dinner."

"Where'd you have in mind?"

"How about Rotisserie Georgette, on Sixtieth? I'll book."

"Let's see how the day goes."

"Talk to you later."

There was a knock on the study door, and Jinx came in. "Joan said you were up here."

"I've got workmen in my office installing security cameras, the result of our little incident the other night. What brings you uptown this time of day?"

"I came to get my stuff."

"Abandoning me?"

"Not entirely, but I've got a show opening in Philadelphia in a couple of days that needs some fine-tuning, and maybe even a new set, so I'm out of town for a week, at least."

"I'll miss you."

"Not so much. We've had some nice times, but I think I'm too much of a working girl for you."

"Call me when you get back?"

"Would you like to come to Philadelphia for a couple of days?"

"Probably not—too much going on here."

"Okay, see you when I see you." She came over, pecked him on the forehead, and left the room.

Stone went back to work. An hour later, Hev stuck her head in. "My guys have got your office in hand, I think. Mind if I start on the master suite?"

"Go right ahead."

"Is the coast clear up there?"

"Clear, and likely to remain so."

She smiled. "Oh, well."

"Hev, would you like to join some friends and me for dinner to-night?"

She cocked her head and smiled at him. "What a nice idea. I'll check my bag and see if I have something suitable."

"I'll bet you do. You can shower and change upstairs when you're done with work."

"Where are we going?"

"Rotisserie Georgette on Sixtieth."

"Then put me down for a yes." She left, closing the door behind her.

Stone called Dino. "You're on for dinner."

"I've already booked for three—Viv is in Miami for a couple of days. Seven-thirty."

"We'll see you there."

STONE WENT UPSTAIRS at the end of the day, expecting to find Hev still working, but when he walked into the master suite, he heard her shower running. He considered calling on her there, but resisted the temptation. Then, while he was resisting, the door opened, and she appeared wearing only a bath towel.

"Oops," she said, retreating behind the door.

"Quite all right. You look very nice in a towel."

"Why don't you relax, and I'll be with you in a few minutes."

"Good idea." He stretched out on the bed and dozed.

STONE WAS STILL DOZING when he felt the bed move and opened an eye. Hev was sitting there, still wearing the towel, but her hair was dry and her makeup applied.

"What time is dinner?" she asked.

"Seven-thirty."

"Then we have nearly an hour, don't we?"

"We do."

"How would you like to spend it?"

"Without the bath towel," he replied.

She whipped it off and tossed it in the direction of the guest bath. "There, is that better?"

"Much better." He reached for her, but she shied away.

"I'm not getting into bed with a fully clothed man," she said. "I have my standards."

Stone quickly fixed that, and she crawled across the bed and sank into his arms.

"Is this all part of the Strategic Services home security program?" he asked. "Mike Freeman didn't mention it."

"Apparently," she said, "Mr. Freeman is a mischief maker." She stroked his lower belly. "Such nice abs," she said, "for a man of your age."

"Thanks, I think."

She poked at his belly. "How do you maintain them?"

"Painfully."

"Oh, and they're not all that's nice." She stroked him.

"It likes you, too," he said.

She kissed him on a nipple and that brought him fully to attention.

"All we need is a lubricant," he said, starting to reach for a bedside drawer.

She pulled him back. "No, we don't," she replied, and she was right.

SHE SHOOK HIM AWAKE at six-thirty. "We don't want to be late meeting your friends."

Stone sat up on one elbow. "Actually, it's only one friend. His wife is out of town. You may know her—Vivian Bacchetti?"

"We all know Viv," she said. "So we're having dinner with Dino?"

"We are. Dino and I have had more dinners without Viv than with. She's always traveling on business. I'd better get into a shower."

"While you're doing that, I'll freshen up and get some clothes on."

"But you look so nice as you are."

"I'm delighted you think so, but we don't want to cause a scandal at Georgette's, do we?" She repaired to the bathroom.

He showered and put on fresh clothes. Fred awaited them downstairs, and they arrived at the restaurant on time. Dino was already at the table with a drink in front of him. "Yours is on the way, Stone, and this must be Hev?"

"HOW DO YOU DO, Dino?" she asked, offering her hand.

"Not as well as you do," he replied.

"I'd like a vodka gimlet, straight up," she said, and Dino spoke to their waiter.

Two hours passed and a large roast chicken was reduced to a pile of bones before them.

"Is your installation complete?" Dino asked.

"Tomorrow," Hev replied.

"That's very fast."

"It's a wireless installation, the latest thing." She dug an iPhone from her bag, fired it up, and opened an app. "Here's the view of your office, Stone."

Stone took the phone from her. "It looks like a movie set," he said, "photographed from half a dozen angles."

"Pick one and tap on it."

He did so, and a shot of his desktop filled the screen. "Wow."

"It's even more impressive on an iPad," she said. She took him through the other angles, then zoomed in and out. "Now the master suite."

"Oops," Stone said, "I forgot to make the bed this morning."

"Stone," Dino said, "you never lift a finger in that house, and it's never less than neat for more than five minutes."

"Oh, shut up, Dino," Stone said, while Hev giggled. "Look, there's Bob," she said. The dog trotted into the room and promptly hopped onto the unmade bed and curled up.

"Can I yell at him?" Stone asked.

"I can look into adding that feature, but usually our clients would rather be phoning the police instead of yelling at intruders."

"It could be a very good dog-training device," Stone said, "and maybe even a good marketing pitch for wronged husbands."

"Give me your iPhone," she said, "and I'll download the app and set it up for you."

Stone gave her his phone and continued to fiddle with hers. "Uh-oh," he said suddenly. "We have company."

She took her phone and gazed at the image. A large man was wandering around his office, wearing gloves and a woolen cap and opening drawers. The shot was from above, and the cap shielded his face.

"How the hell did he get in?" Stone asked.

"The same way he did last time," Hev said. "I'll bet you didn't arm the alarm system."

Dino pressed a speed-dial button on his phone. "This is Bacchetti. I want a squad car in Turtle Bay immediately." He gave his office the address. "The front door should be open."

"Don't rub it in," Stone said. Hev handed him back his phone, fully operational. "The guy is going through every drawer and cabinet."

"He's quite neat," Hev said. "I don't think he wants you to know he's been there. Hang on! He's heard something, and he's getting out."

The culprit ran toward the back of the office and disappeared through a door.

"He's headed for the kitchen," Hev said, "and we haven't got set up there yet."

"No, he's headed through the kitchen and out the back door into our common garden," Stone said. "Dino, can you get a car to cover the exit from the garden to Second Avenue?"

Dino got out his phone and gave the order, checking his watch. "They'll be there in two minutes."

"Hev, I think covering my house is going to be a bigger order than you planned," Stone said.

"Mike Freeman will love that," she replied. "What else do you want done?"

"Certainly the kitchen and a view of the garden from upstairs. And you need to adjust your cameras so that an intruder's face won't be shielded by a hat or a hoodie."

"Consider it done," she said, tapping notes into her phone.

"And you still have to change the outer door locks," he said. "That's twice this guy has picked the lock."

"We had to order the new Israeli locks. They'll be in tomorrow."

"Aw, shit!" Dino said, listening on his phone.

"What?"

"They missed the guy on Second Avenue. He's flown the coop."

"That's bad news," Stone said.

"The news isn't all bad," Dino said. "I recognize your intruder."

"Who is he?"

"His name is Marvin Jones, just out of the joint."

"But we couldn't see his face."

"I still recognized him."

"From where?"

"From tapes of the cameras in Laurence Hayward's apartment. Trust me, it's the same guy."

STONE SLID OUT OF BED, trying not to wake Hev. They had been at it until the wee hours, and he was still tired, not to mention sore.

He got into the shower and dumped some shampoo on his head, which got into his eyes, momentarily blinding him. Then a body rubbed against him. "Now who could that be?"

"How soon you forget," Hev said, taking him in her hand.

"I'm a little sore down there," he said.

"Awww. And I was so looking forward."

"It will soon be restored to health, if we give it a little rest."

She stepped out of the shower and appropriated his towel. He followed her, wet, and found another bath sheet in his linen cupboard.

By the time he got back to the bedroom she was dressed in her Strategic Services jumpsuit.

"Having been rebuffed, I'm off to work," she said.

"That wasn't a rebuff, just a momentary retreat."

"I'll forgive you this time."

"Oh, thank you. I feel so much better now."

His bedside phone rang, and he picked it up. "Yes?"

"A package was hand-delivered from Strategic Services," Joan said.

"I'll be down shortly." He hung up. "Hev, there's a package from your office."

"That will be your new door locks," she said.

"Do me a favor, go out the front door, then ring my office bell from the outside."

"We're deceiving Joan, are we?"

"We hope to, but I won't count on it. Look surprised about the package."

"I'll try." She kissed him and left.

Stone sat down on the bed and called Laurence Hayward.

"Good morning, Stone, how are you?"

"Very well, thank you, and welcome back."

"Thank you."

"Laurence, it seems we have a mutual problem."

"And what is that?"

"Do you know a man named Marvin Jones?"

"Well, we haven't been properly introduced, but I have security footage of him in my apartment."

"Funny, so do I. In my house."

"Dino told me his name."

"Same here."

"I don't get it," Laurence said, "what's the connection between you, me, and Mr. Jones?"

"I don't get it either. I'm baffled."

"A very good word for my condition."

"Run your tapes for the time you were gone, and see if he pops up."

"I certainly will, and right away."

They hung up, and Stone got dressed. As he was about to go downstairs, Laurence called back.

"I've viewed my tapes, and Mr. Jones does not make an appearance."

"I'm still baffled," Stone said.

"So am I. Will you call Dino, or shall I?"

"I'll speak to him," Stone said, then hung up. Then it occurred to him that he had nothing to tell Dino, who had already seen the video from his house. He went downstairs and found Joan at her desk. "You said I had a package?"

"Never mind, Ms. Peace arrived from somewhere or other and relieved me of it, said it contained our new locks. What's wrong with our old locks?"

"They've been picked twice," Stone said, then explained the situation.

"But what's the connection between this Jones, you, and Mr. Hayward?"

"We are both baffled."

"Dino, too?"

"We are all baffled."

"Add me to the list." She took her Colt .45 from her desk drawer, popped the magazine, ejected a round, looked it over, then reloaded it, worked the action, and returned it to the drawer. "Okay, I'm ready for him."

"Please, please, don't shoot the man. It was so messy last time, what with the carpet and all."

"Should I offer him coffee and Danish?"

"You may hold him at gunpoint while calling nine-one-one."

"Not Dino?"

"Dino doesn't really like taking nine-one-one calls. He'd rather hear about it later."

"And who can blame him?" She gave Stone his mail and went back to work.

Stone sat down at his desk and reviewed the mail, sorting the real stuff into one pile and the catalogs and begging letters into another. The pile of real mail was much the smaller of the two, and he gave it to Joan to handle.

Bob came in and lobbied for a cookie, and Stone, against his better judgment, gave him one. "I know this isn't your first of the day," he said to the dog.

Bob requested another.

"Not I, pal. Try Joan."

Bob padded into Joan's office and didn't come back.

"You're a pushover!" he called out to her.

"Look who's talking!" she called back.

A LITTLE LATER, Dino called.

"Good morning."

"You sound tired," Dino said.

"Don't start with me."

"I'll bet Ms. Heavenly Peace isn't a bit tired."

"I said, don't start."

"Girls like that never wear out, they just keep going, like that rabbit in the commercials."

"Dino, I'm too tired to handle this."

"I thought so."

"What do you want?"

"There's news on the Marvin Jones front."

"Tell me."

"We're canvassing all the locksmiths on the East Side, down to Fourteenth Street."

"Oh, good. Why?"

"Before he went to prison for financial no-no's, Mr. Jones worked for three years for a locksmith."

"Surely the terms of his parole would prevent him from working for another locksmith. No locksmith could hire him."

"He's not on parole—not anymore, anyway."

"Has he been out that long?"

"No, I guess you haven't heard about the overcrowding in the prison population?"

"I did see something about that in the papers. Did he get sprung?"

"Yes, him and a lot of others."

"Then there must have been overcrowding among those released at the parole offices."

"Exactly. He and others, with no record of violent crimes, were discharged from parole, an unintended consequence of which is that Mr. Jones, not being on parole, but a free man, can work for a locksmith again. He can even apply for a license, having served an apprenticeship before the law caught up with his financial indiscretions."

"So, you're canvassing all the locksmiths on the East Side?"

"Down to Fourteenth Street."

Stone sighed. "Call me when that hen lays an egg." He hung up.

SOFIA/MARIA GOT OFF the train and grabbed a cab to Marv's apartment. He was surprised to see her. "I thought you'd be gone for a week."

"I got lucky and made a good score."

"How good?"

"Good enough for it to be dangerous to keep on. They were looking for me. I changed trains and came back."

"I'm glad you had a good score, because I'm scraping bottom," he said.

She produced a wad of bills and handed it to him. "There's five grand. Now you can take me out to dinner."

SHE CHOSE an elegant Italian place on the East Side, Caravaggio, where they knew her and gave her an excellent table. Menus were brought and drinks ordered. "Try the osso buco," she said.

"What's that?"

"A calf's shank, cooked a long time, served with risotto." ·

"Okay."

AN HOUR LATER they ordered brandy. "Okay," she said, "why are you running on empty?"

"I had the Barrington place set up to get cleaned out. The pictures alone are worth a couple of hundred grand, at least."

"What happened?"

"A lot of security equipment suddenly appeared. The cops were all over me both times."

"You went there *twice?* You must be nuts."

"I was getting desperate for money."

"Do you know if you got made?"

"I was talking to Butch in Central Park, and two cops rumbled me. I outran them, but I think they must know what I look like."

"If they know what you look like, they know who you are. Who's Butch?"

"A guy I knew in the joint. He put me on to the place at the Fairleigh."

"What's the Fairleigh?"

He told her the story.

"Sounds like they've got cameras there, too."

"I guess."

"What did you hope to find there?"

"Butch and I stole some checks and cleared three hundred grand with them."

"And now you're skint? What happened to the money?"

Curly looked sheepish. "The ponies took it from me."

"You're starting to look like a bad risk, Marv. I think you'd better get out of town—for a long time."

"Got any ideas?"

"You say Barrington's place has a lot of art? How do you know it's worth anything?"

"I read a lot in prison. I recognized some of the artists, particularly Matilda Stone."

"Who's that?"

"An American painter. He's got maybe a dozen of her paintings."

"And how do you get rid of stuff like that?"

"I know a fence who deals in high-quality stuff. He'll take them off me. I reckon my end would be a hundred grand, maybe more."

"Tell me about the cameras."

"Nothing to tell—they're invisible, at least to me."

"Then how do you know they're there?"

"Because the cops were all over me. I came in through the front door, picked the lock both times. There's a security box in a front hall closet, but the system wasn't armed either time. Still, I heard the cops coming after I'd been in the house maybe three minutes. They even tried to cut off my escape route through the common garden. They had to know I was there, so I figure cameras."

"Makes sense," she said. "Do you know where the pictures are?"

"Four of them are in the living room, another four in the study."

"You said there were a dozen."

"I'm guessing. I did some research at the library and Matilda Stone is Barrington's mother, and he owns at least a dozen of her works. She's got stuff in the Metropolitan Museum. I figure the others are in the bedroom."

"And this fence is ready to take them off your hands?"

"Cash on delivery, ten grand a picture."

"So the eight you're sure about are worth eighty grand to you?"

"Right."

"Marv, it sounds to me like you'd enjoy a spell in Florida. I know how to make you comfortable there."

"That's where you live?"

"It is. And it's warm all winter. Have you ever spent a winter in a warm place?"

"No, and I think I'd like that."

"You bet your sweet ass you would. Now all I have to do is to think of a way to crack the Barrington place."

"You do that," Curly said.

"Leave it to me. How about the Fairleigh place? He got any pictures?"

"Now that you mention it, yes—more than Barrington, maybe. There's four Milton Averys."

"Who's Milton Averys?"

"Avery—another American painter."

"You're sounding like quite the art expert."

"I told you, I was always reading when I was in prison."

"Time well spent."

"The Averys are only worth five grand apiece from the fence."

"Still."

"Yeah, still."

"You know anything about alarm systems?"

"Yeah, I do."

"Well, Marv, what if we cut the power to the system?"

"They've got battery backups."

"Ah. When are the alarm systems not armed?"

"When the people are there."

"Or when they go out and forget to arm them, right? That worked twice for you."

"Yeah, but Barrington has two systems—one for the motion detectors and the door and window sensors, the other for the cameras."

"The cameras are no good unless somebody's watching, right?"

"Yeah, I hadn't thought of that. They record when nobody's watching, though."

"We don't care if they record, if they can't identify us. In fact, they've already identified you, so it doesn't matter if they make you again."

"It matters when they show the tapes at my trial."

"Well," she said, "there is that."

45

C URLY PUT TOGETHER his gym clothes in a bag.

"Going somewhere?" Sofia/Maria asked, looking up from the *Times* crossword.

"To the Y," Curly replied.

"What for?"

"Work out, do some weights, have a swim."

"You do that a lot?"

"A couple times a week—more, if I'm bored."

"You bored?"

He laughed. "Around you? Never!"

"Good answer. Is there some other reason you go to the Y? Besides working out?"

"Sometimes I see some of the guys from the joint."

"You got somebody in mind?"

"Maybe."

"Whozzat?"

"I'll tell you later, maybe."

"Getting all secret on me, huh?"

"You don't need to know everything."

"That's where you're wrong—everything is exactly what I need to know."

"Well, you're just going to have to sit on it, aren't you? Get your nails done or something."

She examined her nails. "That's not the worst idea you've ever had. There's a nail salon down the block."

"I'll be back late this afternoon." He let himself out.

At the Y, Curly rented a locker, changed, and went to the weight room. He had been there half an hour when the guy came in. They exchanged a glance but didn't speak at first. Finally, when they were both satisfied they could talk without being overheard, they sat on a bench together.

"How's it going, Irv?" Curly asked.

"Could be worse," Irv replied.

"Could you use a gig?"

Irv shook his head. "I don't want to go back to prison," he said.

"All I need is for you to give a place the once-over, tell me how to deal with the security. You don't have to go in."

Irv shook his head. "I don't know."

"There's ten grand in it for you."

"Yeah? Up front?"

"I have to collect from the fence before I can pay you. I can give you a grand up front, though, if that'll help."

"That'll help. Tell me about the place."

"There's two systems—a regular alarm system, then a later, camera installation. I need to make them both go out for half an hour, and maybe you can tell me how to do that."

"And I don't have to go inside?"

"Up to you. I just need enough peace and quiet to get some goods out of the place. It's a town house in Turtle Bay."

"That the place with the common garden out back?"

"Right."

"I did two places there, couple years ago, before I went inside."

"You got caught?"

"Not for Turtle Bay. A bitch snitched me out for another job. I got three to five, but then that early-release thing came along. When do you need this?"

"Soon, next day or two."

"Can I do it at night? I like working when the people are out."

"Suit yourself." Curly handed him a piece of paper with the address and his cell number. "Don't get caught with this on you—memorize it."

Irv looked at the paper for a little while, then handed it back. "Got it. I'll need the grand."

Curly produced the wad of bills from a pocket. "Don't be too long."

"Maybe I'll take a look tonight."

"Call me." Curly went back to his lifts.

———

THEY HAD JUST come home from a neighborhood restaurant when Curly's cell rang.

"Who's that?" Maria asked.

"Friend of mine. Be real quiet." He picked up the phone. "Yeah?"

"It's me. I had a look."

"And?"

"There's the two systems, like you said. They've also got the Israeli door locks."

"The hell they do—I went in there twice, and I can't pick an Israeli lock."

"I can. Did, in fact. I can get you in and shut down the systems, but here's my thing—I want twenty-five grand, and I get the hell out of there as soon as you're in."

"How long am I good for?"

"Maybe half an hour, more like twenty minutes, to be safe. The system's monitored by radio. When it goes down they'll try to fix it first, then they'll call the cops. I reckon you'll have twenty minutes before you're rumbled. Do you know exactly what you want and where it is?"

"Pretty much."

"Then it shouldn't be a problem, should it? Oh, and I want fifteen grand up front, the rest when your fence pays. Forty-eight hours to wrap it up?"

"That can be done. Let me talk to my partner."

"I'll call you back in half an hour. I'll need an answer then." Irv hung up.

Maria was staring at him. "Israeli locks? What's that about?"

"Let me tell you about Irv," Curly said, and he brought her up to date, pretty much.

"And he's going to want fifteen grand up front?"

"That's right. Have you got it?"

"Maybe."

"Don't fuck around with me, Maria. Are you in or out?"

"I get half of the take, after paying Irv, and I don't go anywhere near the house."

"That works for me."

"When do you want to do it?"

"Maybe tomorrow."

"I'll have to visit a bank for the money."

"Whatever you say."

"You get everything set up—Irv, the fence, everything. There's no reason this shouldn't go smoothly. One thing—how are you going to get the paintings out?"

"I'll put them in bags I've already got and bring them out on a folding hand truck to Second Avenue, where you'll be waiting in a rented van."

"Me?"

"Unless you want to bring in another partner. The more people, the less money, and the riskier."

"Oh, hell, all right. Where we going to take the goods?"

"Here, then we return the van. The fence will come here with the money."

"I want all twelve pictures," she said.

"Well, me too, but we're not exactly sure where the other four are."

"I like your theory about the bedroom."

"I'll try it, but I can't promise."

"Christ, they've got to be *somewhere* in that house."

"I'll only have twenty minutes."

"Then you'd better move your ass, hadn't you?"

46

STONE LAY ON HIS BACK and took deep breaths. Sweat poured off him, and his crotch was on fire.

"Are you up for another?" Hev asked.

"You were sent here to kill me, weren't you?"

She laughed. "Killing you softly."

"I don't know where you get so much energy."

"You inspire me, babe."

"Hev, do you want to go to the big Strategic Services party tomorrow night?"

"Oh, I know about that."

"Yes, but would you like to go with me?"

"Look, sweetie, that's for management and big-time clients. I'm a worker bee, I don't float in that pond. If Mike Freeman saw us there together he'd think we were both crazy."

"I'm sorry, that never crossed my mind."

"It's flattering that you didn't consider it, but take somebody else."

"Okay." He had no idea whom to take. He was in one of those dry spells between women.

Hev got dressed. "I'm finishing up today. I'll show Joan how to arm the system, if you aren't around."

"Good idea. She'll understand it the first time, and then she can explain it to me."

Bob trotted in and hopped onto the bed.

"Oh, no you don't," Stone said to him. "I know you've already had breakfast and your cookie."

Bob denied everything.

"You lyin' dog," Stone muttered, and headed for the bathroom. He was relieved that Hev didn't follow him into the shower; he needed a rest.

He shaved, and as he left the bedroom his phone rang. "Hello?"

"It's Holly," she said. Holly was an old friend—formerly army, then CIA, and now the President's national security advisor.

"I seem to have a distant memory of someone by that name," he said. They had agreed that she would make the calls, since she was usually too busy at the White House to take them.

"I've got a free chopper ride to New York tomorrow. You got a free evening?"

"Better than that, I've got a great party to go to. Bring a killer dress, it's black tie."

"That sounds like my kind of party. I should be in around midday."

"Come straight to the house, and make yourself at home."

"Yes, sir, I'll do that, sir." She hung up. Holly never wasted a moment on the phone; she had been national security advisor to the President for nearly two years, and every moment counted.

Stone got dressed, then checked the guest bathroom and dressing room for signs of the previous woman. He found a lipstick and put it in his pocket.

Downstairs, Joan was occupied with her security lesson from Hev. He worked for a couple of hours, then Hev came into his office.

"I'm outta here," she said, "and I won't be back unless the equipment malfunctions, and I mean the security equipment, nothing personal."

"You're very kind," Stone said, slipping the lipstick into her cleavage.

"Cleaning up after me, huh?"

"A friend called and is coming in from out of town."

"Then you need a blank page to work on." She kissed him lightly. "It's been fun," she said, "but we both know it's over."

"I'm sorry to hear it."

"Law of the jungle—stay in your own tree. I learned that a long time ago."

"That's good advice, I guess."

"Joan knows the equipment as well as I do," she said.

"The security equipment, you mean."

"That's what I mean. Let me give you an overview—both your systems are now interconnected, and the cameras and the alarm share all the keypads. You can arm or disarm the system from any keypad. Arming it from upstairs in your bedroom turns on the whole house, but on the top floor not the motion detectors. Bob would have a field day with those, and you wouldn't get any sleep. Everything is monitored by our East Side tech office, where the rent is cheaper than at headquarters. There's always at least one guy sitting at a console, gazing at a bank of monitors, and if he gets an alarm, his system switches to the premises involved. He'll call the house to see if it's a false alarm. If he doesn't get ahold of somebody with the cancellation code, he'll call the cops. I suggest you change your security and cancellation codes. Your house number and your date of birth are too obvious. Joan knows how to do it."

"I'll see if I can think of another code I can remember."

"What would you do without Joan?" she asked.

"Perish."

"Right. Okay, sweetie, I'll see you when I see you, if I see you at all." She kissed him again, grabbed her toolbox, and fled the premises.

Joan came in. "Okay, you ready for some training?"

"No, I am not. I have to be in the mood for that sort of thing if I want to remember it."

"Then let's leave the codes as they are for the moment, otherwise you'll light up this place like a Christmas tree the first time you try to arm the system."

"Agreed. Oh, you'd better call Bob Cantor and tell him Strategic Services are running the thing now."

"Already done. He was hurt a little, I think."

"Can't be helped. We can't have strange people roaming the house at will, even if we are photographing them while they're doing it."

"When are they going to invent a camera that shoots intruders with something more serious than a lens?" Joan asked.

"They probably already have, but that would rob you of the pleasure of killing strangers and messing up the rugs."

"Oh, well, it was fun while it lasted."

"By the way, Holly Barker is choppering in tomorrow around midday. If I'm not here, please see that she gets settled and that Helene gives her lunch."

"I keep hoping she'll come and stay," Joan sighed.

"Not while she can pretend she's President of the United States. I can't compete with that kind of fun."

"I guess not. Still, I worry about her working too hard."

"You can mention that to her when she gets in, but don't expect her to take you seriously. She thrives on overwork."

"I've never understood people like that," Joan said.

"Who does? They're a breed unto themselves. Still, I'd rather have Holly keeping an unblinking eye on the world more than anybody else I know."

"Me too."

47

HOLLY BREEZED INTO the house in time for lunch, and they had it on a little table in Stone's study. "So," he said, "how goes the nation?"

"Steady as she goes," Holly replied. "With women in charge, did you expect anything less?"

"Certainly not, and I haven't noticed any stray nukes going off."

"Nor will you on our watch."

"Are you really enjoying yourself, Holly?"

"I simply can't tell you how much. It's like playing with the world's largest chess set, and I get to make all the moves. Well, many of them. Well, I get to suggest which moves are to be made, and sometimes my advice is taken."

ᶜₗ

"Does Kate Lee really need a national security advisor?" he asked mischievously.

"She certainly does, and me in particular. Seriously, there are so many cards on the President's table, so many hands being played all at once, that she, like any president, needs somebody to remember it all and help out with the decisions. It never ceases to amaze me how many Republican businessmen there are who think they can waltz into the White House, rearrange the foreign policy furniture, and expect everything to keep running smoothly. It's more than a full-time job, it's a way of life, and you can't just turn it off for a round of golf. Things go right on happening, and you'd better be on top of them the way Kate—and I—are."

"The nation is fortunate in your service."

"The nation better believe it. Now, enough about how I'm running the world. What are you doing with yourself?"

"Lately, I've been much involved with a new client—a young man who won six hundred million dollars in the lottery and is spending it as fast as he can."

"Too fast?"

"Not yet, and he spends it on worthwhile things like houses and estates."

"Rather like another young man I know, so he must be something of a sage."

"I hope he will grow into one, once the fog of great wealth burns off and lets the sun shine on him."

"Is great wealth such a burden?"

"You bet your sweet ass it is. Dealing with it is a full-time job."

"And yet you always seem to have so much free time, running off to England and to the West Coast and to Maine."

"My genius lies in choosing the right people to deal with it and staying out of their way, until I want some money to spend on another house."

"Are you going to buy any more houses?"

"Pray God, no. I've a property glut as it is, although I did sell the Connecticut house."

"Such a nice house, too. I'll miss it."

"I hardly ever went there."

"You hardly ever go to Maine, either."

"That's too true, but a fellow needs a place on the water."

"Though I haven't seen it yet, I've heard the English estate is on the water."

"True, but that's water over there, not over here. No, ma'am, I'm not buying any more houses."

Joan buzzed him, and he picked up the phone. "Yes?"

"Ed Eagle for you on line one."

Stone pressed the button. "Ed, how are you?"

"Better than you would believe. You're very well, too."

"How can you tell?"

"Because something wonderful is about to happen to you."

"I'm delighted to hear it! Am I allowed to know what?"

"Gala is moving back to L.A. full-time and is selling her Santa Fe house, and she'd like to sell it to you."

Stone was caught completely off guard. "No, I can't."

"Of course you can."

Stone closed his eyes and images of the place flooded his brain—the large, airy rooms, the tall trees on the lot, the sunsets, the pool and hot tub. "Ed, really, I have too many houses already, and I don't have time to decorate it."

"You won't have to, she'll sell it completely furnished, except for a few pictures she wants to take with her, and you'll have a wonderful time combing the Canyon Road galleries for replacements. And you can have it cheap, if you take it before she hires a real estate agent."

"How much?"

"She's going to ask three million nine for it, but with no agent involved she'll sell it to you for three million, intact, immediate closing."

Stone felt himself slipping back into the water, after clawing his way up the beach to real estate safely. "Oh, God."

"That's wonderful, Stone. It'll be great having you for a neighbor! Susannah is already excited to have you in town. We'll throw a housewarming for you, so you can meet some people, and I'll use my influence to get you season tickets to the Santa Fe Opera."

The last chink fell into place for Stone. "All right, to whom do I make the check?"

"Put Joan back on, and I'll sort it all out with her. We'll be ready to close immediately—Gala is already ensconced in L.A., so you can have possession tomorrow, if you like. Now put Joan on before you change your mind."

Stone buzzed Joan. "Ed Eagle wants to speak to you. Make him happy."

"You bought another house, didn't you?"

"Oh, shut up." He hung up and turned back to his lunch.

Holly peered at him. "Did I just hear you make another real estate transaction?"

"A house in Santa Fe," Stone said sheepishly.

"So much for good intentions," she said.

"And they were the best of intentions, too. Wait until you see the place—it's perfect."

"I would expect no less."

"Holly, can you take a week off from running the world and come out there with me? We can leave tomorrow."

Holly looked sheepish herself. "Funny you should mention that—when I left this morning, the boss ordered me not to come back for at least two weeks. I haven't even had time to figure out what to do with myself."

"Let me figure that out for you."

"I place myself in your hands. I'll have to make some phone calls now and then, though."

"If I know Kate, she probably told you to leave your phone behind."

"Well, she did say she would order the White House switchboard not to take my calls. I think she may have even been serious."

"If you try that, I'll tell on you, and you'll be in big trouble."

Holly put down her fork. "I'd better call her and break the news." She went to Stone's desk, picked up the phone, and dialed a number.

"The President, please. It's Holly Barker calling." She listened for a moment, and her face fell. She hung up. "The White House operator has orders from the President not to put any of my calls through. I can't believe she would do such a thing."

Stone laughed. "Now you're officially on vacation. And I'm not going to let you watch the news, either!"

STONE EXPERTLY TIED his black bow tie, slipped into his dinner jacket, and stuffed a white silk pocket square into the breast pocket, then he stepped out of his dressing room and found Holly, all five feet ten inches of her, sans heels, in an emerald silk dress that set off her red hair and skin color.

"You're actually ready?"

"I don't believe in futzing around for an hour while the gent taps his foot and looks at his watch."

"Bless you. Let's get out of here." They took the elevator to the ground floor and exited the front door to find Fred waiting beside the Bentley. A moment later they were under way.

"Damn it," Stone muttered under his breath, "I forgot to arm the security system."

"Don't worry, sir," Fred said, "I'll do it when I return to the house."

"Thank you, Fred."

They were set down at the garage entrance to the Fairleigh and took the elevator to the top floor. A uniformed butler let them into the penthouse apartment, and Laurence came over to greet them.

Stone introduced Holly. "I see you've hired a butler."

"Mike Freeman provided him, just for the evening. Come, I want you to meet my mother and stepfather. They arrived yesterday from England." He took them to an elegant-looking couple who were occupying a sofa before the fireplace.

"Stone, these are Derek Fallowfield and my mother, Dorothy. Stone Barrington and his law firm are my principal advisors."

Hands were shaken.

"I hope you had a good flight," Stone said.

"We're still a little jet-lagged, but Laurence has made us very comfortable in the flat downstairs," Dorothy said.

"Yes, I had that done up for them," Laurence said. "Excuse me, I have other guests to greet."

While Dorothy and Holly chatted, Derek pulled Stone aside. "Look here, Barrington," he said quietly, "I'm very concerned about all the money Laurence is spending. My calculations put his recent spending at more than a hundred million dollars. Did he really win enough to be all right for that?"

"He's quite able to handle it," Stone said. "You have nothing to worry about."

"I'm relieved to hear it," Derek said, snagging another glass of champagne from a passing waiter. "This really is quite an establishment, isn't it?"

"It certainly is. When Laurence bought it, it was the finest property on the market."

"The boy has turned out to be smarter than I thought," Derek said. "I thought he was going to spend his life teaching English and art history to schoolboys and playing jazz piano."

"He has many interests," Stone said.

"He's taking us to Santa Fe to see his new house there," Derek said. "Where in God's name is Santa Fe?"

"New Mexico."

"Is that in Mexico?"

"No, it's an American state, just south of Colorado."

"Ah, yes, Colorado."

"As it happens, I've just bought a property there myself, so perhaps we'll see you while you're in town."

"We'd be delighted. Who is the young woman you're with? She's a stunner in that dress."

"She's the national security advisor to the President of the United States."

"Good God! Do all your civil servants look like that?"

"Hardly any of them," Stone said. "Holly is the exception. Before her current job she was a deputy director of the CIA."

"I'm slightly acquainted with the head of our MI6," Derek said, "and I think she's attractive, but not like Miss Barker."

"Dame Felicity Devonshire?"

"You know her?"

"We're neighbors down in Hampshire. She's just across the Beaulieu River from me."

"I belong to a yacht club down there, on the Isle of Wight—the Royal Yacht Squadron."

"So do I."

"My word, Barrington, you do get around!"

"So does your stepson."

"Yes, that's quite a girl he's got. We're very impressed with her."

"He stole her from Ralph Lauren," Stone said.

IRV HAD WATCHED from across the street as the Bentley drove away. He got out his cell phone and dialed Curly. "They've left the house, and he was wearing a tuxedo, so they're out for the evening. Now's the time."

"We're just around the corner. Be there in a minute."

Shortly, a gray van drove up, and Curly got out and got into Irv's car. "How do you want to do this?"

"I think we'll go in through the downstairs street entrance. It's more sheltered than the front stoop."

"You're sure you can handle the lock?"

"Don't worry, it'll take a couple of minutes, but I've cracked these Israeli jobs before."

"I'll give you a head start while I get my handcart out of the van."

Irv approached the house while Curly went back to the van.

"I want to get away from here," Sofia/Maria said.

"Chill, Maria, we're good to go. Barrington has left the house wearing a tuxedo. Now make three right turns and pull over as near to the southwest corner as you can get." He set the folding cart on the pavement, and she drove away. Curly crossed the street, looking around for cops, and found Irv crouched at the bottom of the little flight of stairs that led to Barrington's office.

"How's it going, Irv?"

"It's going. Keep quiet, I need to concentrate."

Curly sat down next to him and watched him manipulate his lock picks. Suddenly, the door was open.

"Come on," Irv said. "We've got about thirty seconds before the alarm blows, maybe a minute."

"I know where the box is," Curly said. "Follow me."

TEN BLOCKS AWAY, a bored security technician named Sid manned a bank of monitors in the basement of a small office building. He had been at work for half an hour and had ordered a pizza for his dinner and had changed into his Strategic Services coveralls, dumping the contents of his pockets on his desk. He usually worked with a partner, but the man had called in sick.

He sat down and checked the condition of the systems he was monitoring. Suddenly, an alarm began to beep. He switched his monitors to an apartment a few blocks away but saw nothing. He looked up the phone number and called.

"Hello?" a woman's voice said.

"This is Sid, at Strategic Services. I have an alarm at your place. Is everything all right? Do you need the police?"

"It's my fault, I entered my old code before I thought about it."

"What is your cancellation code, please?"

"Black Cat."

"Thank you, ma'am. I'll cancel your alarm. Let us know if we can be of service."

His phone rang. "This is Sid."

"This is Domino's. Our guy is at the service door with your pizza."

"I'll be right there." He grabbed some money from his desk and trotted down the hall to the door. He opened it and leaned against it while he paid the pizza guy. It was heavily sprung and took an effort to keep open. Then his foot slipped; he pitched forward, and the heavy door slammed behind him. He went to his pocket for the keys, then remembered that they were on his desk with the contents of his pockets.

"Oh, shit," he said to himself.

49

THE TWO BURGLARS ran into Barrington's office and got the door to the security panel open.

"Piece of cake," Irv said, flipping switches. A piercing alarm siren beat against their eardrums, then Irv found the right switch, and it stopped. "That's enough to alert the security company," Irv said. "You'd better get your ass in gear."

Curly ran up the stairs carrying his handcart.

SID TRIED THE FRONT DOOR of the little office building: locked tight, and there was no watchman. He was going to have to call for help, and he dreaded doing so. He felt his pocket for his cell phone, then remembered it was on his desk with the rest of the contents of his pockets. He glanced at the deli across the street and remembered it had a pay phone. He groped in his pockets: no quarters, no coins at all. He found the three dollar bills the pizza guy had given him for change and walked across the street to the deli. The place was deserted, only the counterman there.

"Hi," Sid said, "I'm from across the street, and I locked my cell phone in my office." He placed a one on the counter. "Can you give me four quarters, please?"

The counterman pointed at a sign. NO CHANGE FOR PHONE, it read. "Tell you what, give me one quarter for a buck."

"What's that in your hand?" the counterman asked, nodding at the Domino's box.

"It's a pizza."

"We sell pizza," the man said accusingly.

"Domino's puts more stuff on theirs than you do on yours. C'mon, Mac, give me a quarter for a buck."

The man ignored him and wiped something imaginary off his counter.

"All right," Sid said, placing another dollar on the counter, "two bucks for a quarter."

"The boss would fire me."

Sid came up with his last dollar. "It's all I've got. Be a human being."

The man opened the cash register and started removing bills.

"You've got quarters staring you in the face," Sid said.

The man ignored him.

"That's it," Sid said. "I'm never ordering a sandwich here again."

"When did you ever?" the man said.

"Go fuck yourself."

"At least I'll know I'm doing it with somebody who loves me."

Sid walked out and hailed the first cab he saw. "I'll give you three bucks for a quarter," he said to the driver through his ever-open window.

"What's wrong with the ones?" the driver asked.

"Not a thing. I just need to make a call, and I don't have any change."

The driver popped a quarter out of his change holder and grabbed the three bills, then drove away.

Sid looked up and down the block. Where the hell was another pay phone? He sighed and went back to the deli, where he found a CLOSED sign on the door, which was locked. The counterman was pushing a mop around the place.

FRED FLICKER had just pulled into the garage in the Bentley when the alarm siren wailed for a moment, then turned off. Had the garage door opener set off the system? he asked himself. That shouldn't happen. He got out of the car, unbuttoned his jacket, and unholstered his little .380 automatic, which was big enough to frighten or wound, but not big enough to bring a man down, except with a shot to the heart or the head. He walked over to the door and let himself quietly into the house.

He walked stealthily into Stone's office and saw the door to the security panel open. Uh-oh, he thought. He heard a noise to his left and wheeled, the gun in front of him. The figure of a man was running toward the kitchen. Fred screamed, "Please! Stop or I'll shoot!" The "please" was intended to sound like "police." The man kept moving; Fred lowered his aim and squeezed off a round. He was surprised at how much noise the small gun made in the enclosed space. The man made the kitchen door and kept running. A moment later, Fred heard the back door slam. The man had made the garden.

UPSTAIRS, Curly had four pictures on his cart when he heard the gunshot. He ran toward the back stairs to the kitchen, down them, and out into the garden, passing Irv, who was running with a big limp.

"Don't you leave me here, you son of a bitch!" Irv yelled.

Curly made the gate to Second Avenue and looked for the van. Shit, she had parked across the street, and traffic was heavy. Irv caught up with him just as the light changed, and they both made it into the van. "Let's get out of here!" he yelled at Maria, and she floored the vehicle.

FRED CHECKED UPSTAIRS and found the cart with the four pictures on it, then he looked into the kitchen before he called. Nobody there. He called Stone's cell number and got an answer after four rings.

"What?" Stone demanded.

"We've had an intrusion," Fred said calmly. "I put a bullet into one of them, but he kept running. They both made it out of the house. They were after your mother's pictures, had four of them on a cart, but they left everything behind. Shall I call nine-one-one?"

"No, but the police will be there soon. Get your story straight before they come." Stone hung up.

"Yes, sir!" Fred said into the dead phone.

SID FINALLY FOUND a pay phone in a candy store two blocks away and made the call, then he waited at the service door to his building, and four minutes later a Strategic Services van pulled up, and a man got out.

"I'm locked out," Sid said.

"So I hear. I've got a master key." He unlocked the door and Sid ran for his monitoring room. A light was flashing that told him an alarm had gone off at the Barrington residence. He tapped in the code and brought up the cameras at the scene. A small man was sitting at Barrington's office desk; he appeared to be checking his e-mail on his iPhone. He called the number and got an answer.

"You're a little late, aren't you?"

"Technical difficulties," Sid replied. "Do you require assistance?"

"Negative," Fred said, then hung up.

STONE FOUND DINO talking to a beautiful actress, who was a guest at the party. Viv was across the room talking to somebody else. He beckoned to Dino.

"What's up?" Dino asked.

"Two intruders at my house. Fred winged one of them, but they both got away."

Dino sighed and pulled out his cell phone. "That's the last time I'll ever see that gorgeous woman." He pressed a cell phone button. "This is Bacchetti. I need a pair of uniforms and a team of detectives in Turtle Bay." He gave them the address. "They'll find a Fred Flicker there. He belongs, so tell them not to give him a hard time." He hung up. The actress was across the room, talking to two other men. "Shit."

MIKE FREEMAN came over to where Stone and Dino stood. "You two look a little tense," he said.

"We've had a pair of intruders at my house," Stone replied. "They were after pictures, but Fred Flicker disturbed them and put a bullet into one of them before they made their escape into the back garden."

Dino's cell rang. "Bacchetti. Yeah, well, alert all the emergency rooms on the East Side. If a man comes in with a bullet wound, tell 'em to call us." He hung up. "My people are at your place, listening to Fred's story. They appear to like it."

"Well, then," Mike said, "you can both return to being guests, instead of looking like the Mod Squad."

"Right," Dino said. "We're not going to hear anything more, unless some guy turns up in an ER with a gunshot wound. Excuse me, there's somebody I want to talk to." He went in search of the actress.

SOFIA/MARIA DROVE CAREFULLY. "All right, Irv, I'm dropping you at the ER entrance of Lenox Hill Hospital. In the meantime, try not to bleed on the seat. I'll have to clean it up before I return the van."

"You mean it's not stolen?" Irv asked.

"Thank your lucky stars—it means the police aren't looking for it."

"I haven't been paid," Irv said.

"That's because the alarm went off," Curly pointed out. "It was your job to make that not happen, and you blew it."

"Give me the money, Marv," she said, stopping at a traffic light. She took the envelope, gave Irv a thousand for the hospital bill, and dropped the rest into her bag. "Irv, whatever you do, don't let a doctor admit you. The police will get around to checking the hospitals, and you don't want to be there when they arrive. Get some stitches, a bandage, and an antibiotic, and get the hell out of there."

"Shit," Irv said.

"Well, yeah," Maria replied. She drew to a halt. "That's the door, there, in the middle of the block. Tell the ER nurse that you were working late at a machine shop, and you fell onto a running drill."

"Oh, yeah," Irv said, "that's plausible."

"Then write your own script, but don't let the words 'gunshot wound' pass your lips. Got it?"

Irv got out and slammed the door, then began limping toward the door. Maria put the van in gear and departed. She drove Curly back to his apartment and stopped out front. "Did you bring the cart with you?"

"No, but I wiped it clean before, so it won't have any prints."

"Where did you buy it?"

"At a hardware store uptown."

"Get out of the car, Marv."

"Yeah, see you later."

Sofia drove away, "Sure, the hell you will." Her packed bag was in the rear of the van. She drove the vehicle to New Jersey, out toward Newark Airport, and stopped at an all-night, self-service car wash, where she used the pressure washer where Irv had bled on the rear seat, then hosed down the rubber mats and the carpet. She drove to the airport, noted the mileage and time on the rental receipt, and handed it in to Hertz. "This wasn't supposed to be a drop-off," she told the man in charge. "It just worked out that way. Charge me, if you have to." She paid him in cash, took the shuttle to the terminal, and looked for a Fort Lauderdale flight. She had to wait only forty minutes before it boarded.

"Well, fuck you permanently, Marv, for bungling the job," she said aloud to herself. "At least I only lost a thousand bucks."

DINO HUNG UP HIS PHONE. "My detectives missed the guy by ten minutes at Lenox Hill. He'd been shot in the ass and told the ER nurse he fell onto a drill. Can you believe she bought that?"

"Yes," Stone said. "She was probably at the end of her shift and didn't want to do the paperwork for a gunshot wound."

"You guys lead interesting lives," the beautiful actress said. "Are you married?"

"He is," Stone said, pointing at Dino. "And she's standing over there by the piano. The redhead in the blue dress."

She took Stone's arm and pulled him toward the bar. "Let's get another drink, then you can tell me about yourself."

"Actually, I'm with the other redhead at the piano, the one Dino's wife is talking to."

She recovered her arm. "Big girl, isn't she?"

"Yes, and tough, too."

"Nice meeting you." She wandered off into the crowd.

Holly came over. "Who just dismissed who in that conversation?"

"It was mutual," Stone replied.

"I'm proud of you. What the hell is going on with you and Dino, anyway?"

"We had a break-in at the house. Fred winged one of them, but they got away. Dino's people nearly caught him at the ER, but missed him by minutes."

"Did you lose anything?"

"No. They wanted my mother's pictures, can you imagine that?"

"Well, yes, they're very fine pictures."

"But how would a burglar know I had them and, moreover, what they're worth? I find that extremely odd."

"Google yourself, and I'll bet you'll find a mention of the pictures and their value."

"God, it's that easy to plan a crime these days?"

Laurence came over with Theresa and another young man. "Stone, you know Theresa."

"Of course. Theresa, this is Holly Barker."

"And this is my brother, Butch Crane," Theresa said.

Stone shook the young man's hand. "Butch, good to meet you."

"Butch has pretty much replaced me at Ralph Lauren. He's doing very well there."

"Good for you, Butch."

"Thanks very much." Butch handed him a card. "Stop in and see me when you're in the store. I'll see you're well taken care of." He handed Holly a card, too. "And you, as well, Holly."

"I'll do that," Holly said, tucking the card into her bra.

"You throw a good party, Laurence," Stone said.

"No, Mike Freeman does. I only provided the stage for his performance."

Mike came over. "I talked to my people. They've got videotape of your break-in. One of them was the same guy who did it before, one Marvin Jones. The other is a fresh face, fresh out of the joint, named Irving Schwartz. Dino's people are looking for him."

"Excuse me," Butch said abruptly. "There's somebody I want to speak to." A moment later, he appeared beside the beautiful actress.

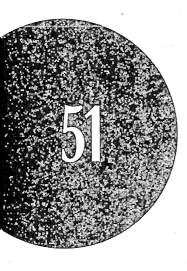

THERESA FOUND BUTCH talking to the actress and pulled him aside.
"Listen," he said, "I'm busy right now."

"Too busy to accept a gift?"

"I'm sorry, I didn't mean to sound huffy."

She took an envelope from her bag. "I'm proud of how well you're doing, little brother. Every time I see someone from the store I hear compliments."

"I'm delighted to hear it. I'm working hard and enjoying every day."

She handed him the envelope. "This is for doing well and making me proud."

Butch opened the envelope and found the documents transferring title of her apartment to him.

"Good God, sis, this is fantastic."

"It's paid for—no mortgage payments, just property taxes. It's all explained in the documents. Pay your bills on time and soon you'll have a credit rating. Every grown-up needs a good one."

Butch embraced her. "Thank you for taking such good care of me. It's a whole new world, and all because of you."

"Just keep making me proud. And by the way, Laurence paid off my mortgage. That's why I can give you the place. He would be embarrassed if you thanked him, but I wanted you to know." She was pulled away by another guest, leaving Butch alone.

Butch walked over to the fireplace and warmed his butt against the flames. He couldn't believe how well things were going, except for one thing: Curly. He had heard Dino mention Marvin Jones, and he knew who that was. He couldn't believe the guy had tried to burgle Stone's house.

His thoughts were interrupted by the actress, who handed him a drink. "Single malt, wasn't it?"

"You're the most beautiful bartender I've ever seen," he replied, sipping his drink. "Do you live in New York?"

"I live a couple of floors down in this building," she said.

"How convenient."

"Do you live here?"

"No, this is my sister's place, with her boyfriend."

"Ah, Laurence."

"Right. I have a place a little farther uptown."

"Who do you work for?"

"Ralph Lauren."

"Personally?"

"The company. I'm managing a couple of departments now," he lied, "but they tell me I'm destined for greater things."

"I'm sure you are. When this party wraps, why don't you stop by my place for a nightcap?"

"What a good idea."

She squeezed his hand. "I have a few more bases to touch. I'll see you a little later."

Laurence came over. "Having a good time, I see."

"The best evening of my life," Butch said. "I want to thank you for everything you're doing for Theresa."

"That reminds me," Laurence said. "I have to say a few words to the crowd, and I see that Mike is setting me up."

There was the tinkle of a knife on crystal, and the group fell quiet.

"Good evening, all," Mike said. "On behalf of Strategic Services, I want to welcome you to our party, held at the home of our client Laurence Hayward."

Applause.

"I just thought I'd mention that another client of ours, who, in line with our policy of client privacy, shall remain nameless, had intruders in his home earlier this evening, and they were caught on a camera system that we installed earlier this week, thus preventing the loss of some very valuable art."

More applause.

"And now, our cohost has a few words to say to you." He stepped aside and brought Laurence forward.

"Good evening," Laurence said, waving Theresa to his side. "I want to welcome you to our home. It's good for a new boy in town to make some friends. I also want to announce that Theresa Crane and I are going to be married quite soon, as soon as my accountant and attorney can agree on which state we should be in when the wedding occurs."

Applause and laughter.

"And, finally, I want to say that you are all welcome in our home at any time."

More applause.

Laurence and Theresa began accepting congratulations as people approached them.

Butch gave his sister a thumbs-up from across the room. The actress ambled over.

"Ready to get out of here?"

"All set."

He followed her to the door, and they took the elevator down two floors, where she let them into her apartment. It was smaller than Laurence's but beautifully done up. "Are you spending much time in New York?"

"I'm starting to shoot a new dramatic series for television here early next month," she said. "We have high hopes for it, so, with a little luck, I expect to be in the city for several years. That's why I bought and decorated this apartment."

"That's very good news," Butch said. "New York will be a better place for having you here."

She moved closer to him. "I feel like celebrating." She kissed him lightly.

"How can I help?"

"Follow me," she replied, taking his hand. "You haven't seen my bedroom yet."

"I can't wait."

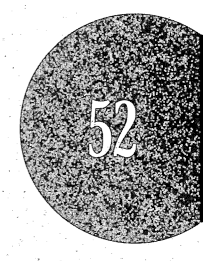

CURLY HAD FALLEN into bed still dressed after Maria had dropped
him off, and now he woke, vaguely disoriented. "Maria!" he
called. He wanted breakfast, and he had grown accustomed to her
making it. It was past ten o'clock, and he was hungry.

He looked around the apartment for her and noticed that her
suitcase was gone from the closet, and so were the clothes that had
been hanging there. It took a moment for him to realize that Maria
had decamped.

He didn't even know if Maria was her name; all he knew was that
she lived in Florida, and that was a big state. He had her cell number,
but it was a throwaway. He also knew that he was very close to flat
broke. He had been counting on the Barrington score to refresh his

cash flow, and that hadn't happened. His rent was due in a couple of days, and his electricity bill was already overdue. He picked up his phone and called Butch.

"Hello?"

"It's me. We need to talk."

There was a long silence before Butch spoke again. "It'll have to be late tonight. I have obligations until then."

"Right now will do nicely."

"One AM at the band shell in Central Park, near that bench we sat on. Take it or leave it."

"Okay, okay."

Butch hung up. Curly thought he was getting a little too big for his britches; tonight he would have to trim the boy's wick a little, teach him who was still boss.

THE ACTRESS'S NAME was Brooke Taylor, and Butch treated her to lunch at the new Ralph Lauren restaurant in the Fifty-fifth Street store. His bosses wouldn't complain about his spending time with a celebrity, who might become a major customer.

"What a beautiful room," she said, looking around.

"Would you like a glass of wine with lunch?"

"No, I have to watch my weight. I've no time to lose pounds before we begin production."

He ordered mineral water for them both.

"Last night was a lovely evening," he said, "particularly the very last part of it."

"I thought so, too."

"Once you start shooting, what will your schedule be like?"

"When we're shooting interiors I start at nine—it's in my contract—and I don't work after six, except for night exteriors. When we shoot morning exteriors, it's likely that I'll be speaking lines by seven AM. It's a thing about the light."

"I'm just figuring out how I can spend as much time as possible with you without exhausting you."

"If I'm in bed by ten—and asleep by midnight—I'll be fresh as a daisy when the car comes for me."

"Now that's a schedule I can live with."

"But not when we're doing morning exteriors. I have to be asleep early on those days."

"I can live with that."

"Good, because you'll have to. This is going to be a career-making series for me, and I'm not going to screw it up just to get laid."

"And I wouldn't allow you to, on my account. I want to see you happy at all times."

"And if the series goes the way I think it will, then I will be happy. The writing is outstanding, and the production values will be deluxe. My set apartment is almost as nice as the one I live in."

"Which is very nice indeed. I compliment you on your taste and style."

They ordered lunch and both made do with a salad.

"Where did you get your schooling?" she asked at one point.

"Groton and Yale," he replied truthfully, not mentioning his graduate course in being a convict. Then he reconsidered. "There's something you should know about me, and you'd better know it now."

"That sounds ominous."

"You may think so. A few years ago I was working at a brokerage house, and I got mixed up in a transaction that went wrong. I took responsibility for my share of it and pled guilty to financial fraud. I did three years of a five-to-seven-year term. I was released in a program to reduce the prison population by paroling nonviolent, first-time offenders, and I was discharged from parole shortly thereafter. The whole episode was a major lapse in judgment and a moral failure on my part. Neither of those things is going to happen again."

"Does the Lauren organization know about that?"

"Yes, I told them everything at my first interview, and they were very good about it. Now I'm a free man, very well employed, with a paid-for apartment and a good income. And my prospects are unlimited. I'm clean in every respect." Well, he thought, in every respect but one: the cash from the raid on Laurence Hayward's bank account, or, at least, what was left of it after Curly's incursion.

"Thank you for being frank with me," Brooke said. "I would have been shocked if I'd found out about it by other means."

"I wouldn't have wanted that. It's why I told you."

"I admire you for doing so."

"Nothing to worry about in the future," he said. "I'll check with you before I rob any banks."

She laughed. "You'd better!"

After lunch he walked her to her car, which was idling at the curb, and kissed her. "Dinner tomorrow night?"

"Not tonight?"

"There's some unfinished business I have to take care of tonight."

"With a woman?"

"There's no woman with a claim on my time, except for my sister."

"You have a good relationship?"

"We love each other—like sister and brother."

"I'll make you dinner tomorrow night, then. Come at seven."

"I'll look forward to it." He put her into the back of the town car and waved her off, then went back to work.

All afternoon he thought about his evening, how it had to go. He checked the movie schedules and made his plan based on that. He had to be very, very careful. His future looked bright, if he could pull this off. If he didn't, well . . .

That afternoon, he got two calls from Curly and ignored them both. He didn't want to talk to him, and he erased all evidence of having received his calls. Curly would be there; he would want the money.

Butch intended to see that he got what was coming to him.

53

S TONE WAS AWAKENED by the bell on the dumbwaiter, which meant that Helene was sending up breakfast and the paper. Last night had degenerated into a drunken jam session, sharing the piano with Laurence, who played better than he did. He and Holly had not gotten to bed until nearly three AM, and they had not gone immediately to sleep, being otherwise occupied.

He kissed Holly loudly on the ear. "Breakfast!"

"Ow!" she howled. "Now I'm deaf."

"You don't have to hear to eat."

He got up and brought the tray from the dumbwaiter to the bed. "Bacon and eggs!" he shouted, and that brought her fully conscious.

She found her remote control and sat her bed up. "That was quite an evening," she said.

"It certainly was."

"You were very good on the piano and even better on me."

"You're just sex-starved," he said.

"Right about that! Working late hours isn't good for your love life."

"You haven't forgotten how."

"It's like roller skating or swimming—once you learn . . ."

"I'm just a tiny bit hungover," he said.

"A tiny bit? Then you didn't drink enough."

"That's debatable, but I don't think I'm fit to fly this morning. Tomorrow would be better."

"Fine by me. I'm at least as hungover as you are."

"Again, debatable, but we'll get an early start tomorrow, and with the two-hour time difference, we'll be there by early afternoon."

"I'm looking forward to being a jet-setter. Will you teach me to fly the thing?"

"What sort of avionics do you have in your airplane?"

"Garmin 1000."

"Then you'll learn the 3000 easily. After that, you need only sixteen days of training to get your 525 type rating."

"Sixteen days? I could nearly achieve world peace in that time, and if I ever get that much time off again, I'm not going to spend it in a flight simulator."

"Then leave the flying to me. You can work the radios while I do the crossword."

"Deal."

After breakfast, they made love, then fell asleep again, until Joan buzzed.

Stone picked up the phone. "What time is it?"

"Ten-thirty. What's your excuse for not being up?"

"A late, liquid night. We're not leaving for Santa Fe until tomorrow."

"Good. Ed Eagle has e-mailed you the closing documents for your new house. You can sign online and return them to him the same way. They're waiting for you in your inbox."

"Got it. Now can I go back to sleep?"

"You've got a stack of documents messengered over by Herbie Fisher, and you have to review them before you leave."

Stone groaned.

"It's your own fault, you should have left this morning before they arrived."

"Herbie would have just sent them to Santa Fe."

"I know. They're waiting on your desk."

Stone struggled from bed and into a shower, leaving Holly to recover on her own.

HE SIGNED the closing documents for the house and returned them to Ed Eagle, then authorized the wire transfer of funds. After that he started on the work Herbie had sent. Joan buzzed: "Dino on one."

"Good morning," he said.

"You mean good afternoon, don't you? It's lunchtime."

"I overslept."

"Sleep is not all you had too much of last night. Everybody enjoyed the concert, especially with me on drums."

"Did I get drunk enough to admit to you that I bought a house in Santa Fe?"

"You're kidding! When do I get to go?"

"How about tomorrow morning? Gala has moved back to Los Angeles, and I closed on her house a few minutes ago."

"Let me call Viv, and I'll get back to you." He hung up.

Mike Freeman called and thanked him for the impromptu entertainment the evening before. "You both sounded great."

"Thanks, Mike. Listen, I closed on a house in Santa Fe this morning. Can you send somebody around to assess the security system and recommend any needed beefing up?"

"Certainly."

Stone gave him the address and directions.

"When will you be there?"

"Tomorrow afternoon. Anytime after that. Tell them to call my cell number to let me know when they're coming."

"Consider it done. Have a good trip."

"Oh, Mike, can you give Viv a few days off? I'd like the Bacchettis to come with us."

"Sure, she's got it coming."

TEN MINUTES LATER, Dino called back. "You're on."

"Meet us at Jet Aviation at nine AM."

"We can do that." He hung up.

Stone called Jet Aviation, ordered fuel, and asked them to have the airplane on line at eight-thirty AM.

Fred knocked on his door and was invited in.

"Tell me about last night," Stone said.

"After I dropped you at the Fairleigh I came back here, and as I pulled into the garage I heard the alarm go off, then immediately stop. I figured somebody was tampering with it, so I came in here with my gun in my hand and the safety off. There was one guy in this room, and he immediately ran for the back door. I got a single round off, aiming low. I figured I would cripple him, but he kept going. Then I heard somebody running upstairs, and I went up there."

"And what did you find?"

"I found him gone out the back way, too. I gave chase, but they were too far ahead of me. I saw them get into a gray van on Second Avenue, but they had a head start. I couldn't see the number plate, but I'm sure there was a smallish woman driving."

"It was probably stolen."

"Probably. The cops came, and they were curious about what had occurred but didn't give me a hard time. I figured the commissioner had already spoken to them. They did take my gun, so they could do ballistic tests on it."

Stone reached into a desk drawer, extracted his Colt Government .380, and handed it to Fred. "You can borrow this, until yours comes back."

"Thank you, sir."

"You handled yourself well, as always, shooting to wound."

"Things would have got a lot messier if I'd killed the bloke. Have the coppers ID'd him yet?"

"One Irving Schwartz, ex-con. They missed him by ten minutes at the Lenox Hill ER."

"Did they get the bullet?"

"Good question. I'll ask."

"I take it you're not leaving for Santa Fe today."

"Right, but we'd like to drive away at eight tomorrow morning."

"I'll have the car ready. Any other passengers, besides Ms. Barker?"

"No, the Bacchettis are coming, but the City of New York is providing them with transport."

"Righto. See you tomorrow, unless you need me tonight."

"I think we'll dine in."

"I rehung the pictures in the living room," he said.

"Thank you."

Fred excused himself and left.

54

CURLY WAS WATCHING an old movie on TV when the house phone rang, and he picked it up.

"Yeah?"

"Curly, it's Chico." Chico was the building superintendent.

"Yeah, Chico."

"You gave me a hundred to tell you if the cops visited."

"Yeah."

"They're on the way up, two detectives."

Curly's entire system went into flight mode. He grabbed a back-pack containing his passport, some money, and a couple of extra false IDs, stuffed his laptop into it, opened a window, and stepped out onto the fire escape, being careful to close the window behind him. As he started up the stairs, he heard banging on his door and shouting. He ran faster. It was only two flights to the roof, and he was already there when he heard the window in his apartment open. A man shouted, "Nothing out here."

"Head for the roof," another voice yelled, and Curly got a running start and made the eight-foot leap to the next building. He had already measured the distance during his planning for escape. He ducked behind the stairwell entrance to the next roof and pressed his body against the door. There was too much unobstructed distance to the next building to run for it without being seen.

"Go on," one of them shouted to the other, "go for it!"

"Are you out of your fucking mind? I'm not going to get myself killed just to bag some burglar. You do it."

"Aw, come on, we'll go next door and take the elevator."

Curly waited for a slow count of ten, then sprinted across the roof and jumped the parapet to the next building. He was three buildings down the street before he saw the two cops emerge onto the roof next to his own.

There was more shouting that he couldn't understand, then everything went quiet. He peeked from his hiding place and saw no one on any roof. He had to pick the lock on the structure housing the staircase, then he walked down to the top floor and took the elevator down. He took a cap and a scarf from his backpack to camouflage his closely cropped head (he had begun to grow his hair on Maria's advice). He looked down the street and saw what appeared to be an unmarked police car turning the corner. He walked to the nearest subway and rode downtown to the Y, where he rented a room. Then he changed and went down to the weight room. He was surprised to find Irv there, watching others work out.

"How you feeling, Irv?" Curly asked, sitting beside him on a bench.

"Not up to working out," Irv replied. "I can't do that with a sore ass."

"They give you antibiotics to take?"

"Yeah. They seem to be working, too."

"Remember to take them all. If you stop, the infection might come back."

"I got the news on that from the nurse in the ER."

"Good. I got rousted by a couple of detectives less than an hour ago."

"Well, you're still walking around, so I guess they didn't grab you."

"Only because I was ready, and the super warned me they were on the way up. That was a hundred well spent."

"Are you broke?"

"I had some mad money in my bag. That'll hold me for a while. I could use a score, though. You got anything on the back burner?"

"Maybe. What can you put in up front?"

"C'mon, Irv, I gave you fifteen Gs up front for the other job and another grand for the doctor."

"I have met my obligations on that job, and more, and I earned that money."

"I'm not saying you didn't, it's just that you're well heeled at the moment, and I'm not. We can do a score together, and I'll take the short side of a sixty-forty split."

"It'll have to be seventy-five/twenty-five."

"Okay, okay, what's the job?"

"I know a pawnshop with a nonworking alarm system. It's fat—all sorts of stuff, including guns, and there's a safe I can likely crack, where he keeps his cash."

"Well, I could use a gun."

"I thought you were opposed to them."

"Most of the time, yeah, but I think somebody's going to try to off me tonight."

"Well, I'm not packing heat, but I've got a snub-nosed .38 at home that I'll sell you for a grand."

"A grand for a hot pistol?"

"It's cold as ice, never been used in a crime. I found it in a desk drawer on a job."

"I'll give you five hundred out of my share of the take on our job."

"Oh, it's 'our' job, is it? Don't go getting any ideas about that. You're the help on this one, just like I was on the last one."

"Okay, okay, but I need the piece tonight, and six rounds, too."

"Okay, if we can do the job tonight."

"I've got a late date. What time?"

"Say, eleven. We'll be through by midnight, if the safe gives. If not, you'll have plenty of guns to choose from. You got a place to stay?"

"Yeah, I'm okay on a bed. When and where do you want to meet?"

"Pick me up at my place in a cab."

"You don't have wheels for the getaway?"

"I'm gonna take only what I can carry, in a duffel bag. I'll have one for you, too."

"You're gonna walk the street with hot goods?"

"I reckon it's better than driving a hot car."

"Maybe you've got a point."

"Okay, ten o'clock at my place?"

"Sure."

"Ring the bell twice and wait under the stoop. Don't get seen."

"Got it."

"It may take me a few minutes to get downstairs, so be patient."

"All right."

"And, Curly?"

"Yeah?"

"I'm gonna walk away from this one clean, and then I'm getting out of town. I'm not going back to my place."

"Okay."

"My point is, I'm not standing for a screwup on this job, and if you get in my way, or if you try to take something that's mine, I'll kill you. That's straight up."

Curly took a deep breath. "Understood." He got up and left the weight room and went upstairs and stretched out on the bed.

He knew exactly how Irv felt, because he felt the same way.

55

BUTCH SPENT HIS DAY thinking about his night. So much so that a couple of his coworkers mentioned his absentmindedness. He tried to concentrate on his customers, and that worked, to an extent. He checked the movie schedules for a third time.

For lunch, he ate a sandwich in the stockroom, still going over and over what he was going to do. He tried to think what could go wrong, but he was sure it would go right. The only thing to fear was the unexpected.

He brought home some hot food for dinner and saw his next-door neighbor, a middle-aged woman called Nan, as he entered his apartment; that was good luck. He turned on the TV and made it pretty loud; she had complained about it before. He watched a TV program until six-thirty, then got out of the building without encountering anyone and took a cab to the movie theater on Sixty-sixth Street near Second Avenue. He bought a ticket for the seven PM showing, and concentrated as hard as he could on the film and its plot. It helped that it was one he had been looking forward to seeing.

At the film's finish he walked around the block, then got in line and bought a ticket for the nine PM showing. Then he had a magnificent stroke of good luck: he met a woman who worked at the store who was also in line and had a brief chat with her. He went into the theater and sneaked out as soon as the feature began.

He got another cab home and waited across the street to be sure the lobby of his building was empty, then he went upstairs and let himself into his apartment. He undressed, put on pajamas and a robe, went next door and rang the bell.

"Who is it?" Nan asked through the door.

"It's Butch from next door."

She apparently took a moment to confirm that through the peephole, then opened the door. "Good evening, Butch."

"Hi, Nan. I was expecting a delivery this evening, and it didn't come. I thought they might have left it with you."

"No, I didn't have any callers this evening."

He managed a yawn. "Thanks, Nan. I'm sorry to disturb you. Guess I'll be off to bed. Oh, by the way, I saw a very good film tonight." He gave a brief account of the picture. "I think you might enjoy it."

"Thank you, Butch, perhaps I'll go." She closed the door.

He went back to the apartment, switched off all the lights, then he got dressed. He looked in his closet for something to wear and found an old plastic raincoat that he'd forgotten to throw away when he moved in. He set that on a chair within easy reach, then sat down on the living room sofa and went over it all again in his mind.

STONE TOOK HOLLY to Patroon for dinner, where she was treated as an old friend.

"I love this place," she said as they settled into a booth. "Is this your new Elaine's?"

"I'm afraid not. There is no Elaine's without Elaine, and she's gone. The restaurant was like her living room, where she welcomed friends to a party every night. That's how she stayed in business for forty-eight years. She liked you, and she didn't like all that many women."

"I liked her, too, and I'm flattered she liked me. How'd you meet her?"

"Back when I was walking a beat, I started stopping in there late for dinner, and we got along. I wasn't exactly one of her regulars, and I ate at the bar. After I'd been going in there for a couple of years, she'd give me a table, and after I made detective I could afford to go more often."

"Dino, too?"

"Yep, but he had his own list of favorite places, when pretty much all I had was Elaine's."

The owner, Ken Aretsky, stopped by their table. "No Dino and Viv tonight?"

"We're going to be spending a few days with them in Santa Fe, leaving tomorrow. I bought a house there."

"Another house? You'll be like Ted Turner soon. He has, what, ten places?"

"God save me from that fate," Stone said. "Joan can barely keep up with what I've got now. I did sell Connecticut, though."

"That was brave of you." Ken continued on his rounds.

Stone turned his attention back to Holly. "How long are you going to stay in your job?"

"Until Kate fires me."

"She'll never do that, but White House people tend to burn out after a couple of years. Hardly any of them seem to make it into their president's second term."

"I never got tired of working at the Agency," she said, "and I was there a lot longer than Kate's two terms will last, if she gets reelected."

"Are you concerned about whether she will?"

"No, she loves the job, and Will is in charge of keeping her political bridges intact. He's a big help with Congress, too; he has so many old friends there."

"I thought he was Babysitter in Chief these days."

"He likes people to think that, but he has two nannies to back him up, so he's either on the phone or consulting with Kate most of his days. He sometimes works in the study off the Oval Office, so she can pop in between appointments in the Oval and talk over the meeting she's just had. It's a great system for both of them. And every time I'm out of the office for a day, they ask if I've seen you, thinking I've come to New York."

"I'd like it if that could happen more often," he said.

"I'd like that, too, but there are few opportunities. Kate had to practically run me out of the White House to get me to come up here."

"I'm looking forward to having you with me in Santa Fe," he said.

318

"I'm looking forward to it, too, but I haven't gotten to the point where I can stop thinking about what's going on in the White House. When I get back, I'm going to need some pretty extensive briefings on what happened while I was gone. And I know Kate has walled me off, but it bothers the hell out of me that no one is calling for advice on how to handle some problem or other."

"They're ignoring you?"

"Yes, and it's really annoying that I'm not as indispensable as I thought."

"When we get to Santa Fe you'll discover a lot to keep your mind off Washington."

"What will I discover?"

"A whole new kind of town. It's nothing like anywhere else I've ever been."

"Well, I'll admit, that sounds intriguing."

"My worst nightmare is that you'll get there and immediately want to go back to Washington."

"I don't think that's an option. Kate would have the Secret Service turn me away at the gate. I wouldn't be surprised if she'd already canceled my White House pass."

56

S OFIA GOT UP EARLY on her first day home and went shopping for breakfast. She came home, scrambled some eggs, microwaved some bacon, toasted an English muffin, and poured herself some fresh-squeezed orange juice. She ate while her coffee brewed, and when she had finished eating, took her coffee into the living room and turned on the TV, switching to *Morning Joe*, her favorite political show, and opened *The New York Times*.

She couldn't concentrate. She felt bad about leaving Marv so abruptly; it wasn't what he would have come to expect of her. Finally, she picked up the phone and dialed his number. She got an immediate recorded announcement that she had dialed a number that was not in service. He had thrown away his throwaway phone.

She got out some stationery and wrote him a note:

I'm sorry I left so suddenly. I tried your phone, but it was no longer work-ing, but mine still is. Call me, and let's talk about your coming down here for a while. Marie.

She set it aside to mail later.

CURLY GOT UP and worked out for a while, then watched some TV in the lounge. Later he went to the pay phone and called Chico, the super.

"Hello?"

"It's Curly," he said. "Thanks for the call yesterday. I got out just in time."

"It's what you paid me for. I guess you got away."

"Have they been around again?"

"First thing this morning. I told them I hadn't seen you."

"I may come around later today and pick up some things," he said.

"They probably won't be back."

"If they do come back, put that flower pot in your kitchen window, and I'll stay away."

"Okay."

Curly watched some more TV, then took the subway uptown and walked down his block and past the building. Chico's kitchen win-dow opened onto the space below the stoop, and there was no flower pot there. He walked the block a couple of times, more to be sure there were no cops watching the place, then let himself into the building.

He took the elevator to the floor below his apartment, then walked up the stairs and listened at the hall door. He heard nothing, so he opened it and went to his apartment door. It hung slightly ajar, the doorjamb was splintered, where they had kicked it in. He listened again, then crept into the apartment.

It had been turned over, but nothing had been taken, as far as he could tell. He went into the kitchen and looked in the bucket under the sink, where he had hidden the paperwork he had used to raid Hayward's bank account. It was still there, and he took it into the living room and shredded it in the small machine under his desk. He unplugged his small desktop computer and dropped it into his shoulder bag, then went through the apartment, taking some clothes and making sure there was nothing else in the apartment that would tell the police anything about him. He didn't bother to wipe the place down for fingerprints, since they already knew who he was.

He left the apartment, leaving a fifty stuck in Chico's door, and walked away from the building. A couple of blocks away he came to a construction Dumpster. He bashed the computer against the side of it and tossed the remains into the Dumpster, then went on his way, wondering why the cops hadn't taken the computer. Maybe they just weren't that interested. He still had his laptop in his bag, and it was easier to use when traveling.

He stopped in a candy store and bought the cheapest throwaway phone they had. He thought about calling Butch at work but figured he wouldn't respond. He'd just have to keep their date. But he meant to be ready for it. Once Butch was out of the way, he'd head for Fort Lauderdale and start looking for Maria.

He'd been thinking about her a lot. He sat down on a bench at a bus stop and called her cell number. Probably, she's already tossed it, he thought. To his surprise, she answered.

"Hello."

"It's Marv."

"Oh, I'm so glad. I just tried to call you."

"I already tossed the phone."

"I'm sorry I walked out."

"It's okay, I understand. The cops came for me early in the morning, but I got a warning from the super and beat it out of there."

"Are you all right?"

"Yeah, I'm fine. I'm going to do a little business with Irv tonight to get some traveling money, and I thought I'd head south, if you still want me there."

"Of course I do." She gave him her address. "Come as soon as you can. Don't call this number again. I need to get rid of the phone."

"Got it. I'll be down there in a couple of days."

"Sounds good."

He gave her his new throwaway number. "In case you change your mind."

"I won't. I'll be glad to see you." They both hung up.

CURLY LEFT THE Y via the emergency exit and walked down the alley to the street, where he found a cab. It was raining lightly and was colder; he pulled his jacket more tightly around his neck. He got out at the corner and walked down the street to the building where Irv had a small apartment. As requested, he walked down the steps to the basement door and waited under the stoop.

Irv appeared a little after eleven and handed Curly a slip of paper. "Take a cab to this address and wait for me across the street from the shop. We don't want to be seen together."

"All right."

Irv handed him a brown paper bag with something heavy in it.

"This is what you wanted, and I'm taking five hundred out of your end to pay for it. There's six cartridges, too."

"Fine with me," Curly said, slipping the bag into his jacket pocket.

"Me first," Irv said. "Wait a couple of minutes then find a cab." He strode off as best he could, limping.

Curly checked the address, in the East Nineties, then headed for the corner and hailed a cab. Ten minutes later, with little traffic to slow him, he got out of the cab and checked the block. No person in sight. He crossed the street and found Irv waiting behind some trash cans.

"You watch for anyone, and I mean *anyone* coming," Irv said.

"Right," Curly replied, and turned toward the street while Irv went to work on the front door. Finally, he heard it open.

"Come on," Irv said.

"How do you know the alarm isn't working?" Curly asked.

"Inside information. Besides, do you hear an alarm?" He hustled Curly inside. And led the way to the rear of the store. Outside the small rear office was a large double-doored safe.

"Here's how it goes," Irv said. "You wait in the front, staying out of sight. If you see anything small enough to put in your pocket that might be worth real money, take it, but I'm pretty sure everything worth stealing is in this safe. This is probably going to take me half an hour, maybe longer. I managed to practice on a similar model, so it shouldn't be impossible."

"Then go to it," Curly said. He walked up front and looked around. Shades were drawn over the windows and door, so he didn't have to worry about being seen from the street. He took a taped flashlight from his pocket and had a look around with the narrowed beam. There was a tempting case of guns, but he was already heeled; everything else was musical instruments, stereo equipment, binoculars, and knickknacks. He took the .38 snub-nosed Smith & Wesson from its bag, scooped up the cartridges, and loaded them, then crumpled the bag and put it back in his pocket; he was leaving no trace.

He found a stool, had a seat, and waited.

When they had been inside nearly an hour, Irv sang out, "Got it!"

Curly got up and walked back to the safe and played his flashlight beam around the contents. Quite a lot of jewelry, but he wasn't taking anything that could tie him to the job. What interested him more was the steel box Irv was working on with a hammer and chisel. "Faster this way," he said. He hit the lock a couple of heavy blows, and it popped open, revealing stacks of cash, each secured by a rubber band. Irv stuffed the cash into a black bag he had apparently brought with him. "We'll count it at my place," he said, "but I reckon there's at least thirty grand here." He handed Curly the bag. "Let me lock up before we go."

Curly pulled the .38 from his pocket. "I'll pay you for the .38 now." He took a couple of steps back and fired at the back of Irv's head. The man sprayed blood and bone, then collapsed like a punctured balloon and lay still.

Curly tripped the front door lock and closed it firmly behind him. At the corner he turned down the avenue and glanced at his watch. Half an hour to get there; he would walk it.

BUTCH DRESSED IN THE DARK; he pulled on a black sweater, got into his plastic raincoat, and brought along a knitted cap. Finally, he went to a kitchen drawer and put on a pair of light gloves, then retrieved Theresa's little .25 automatic, which had been wiped clean of prints, inside and out. He put that into his raincoat pocket.

He closed his apartment door behind him, then took off his loafers and padded down the stairs to the lobby, encountering no one at this hour of the night. Once on the street, he walked rapidly the few blocks to the Fifth Avenue and Seventy-second Street entrance to Central Park and turned toward the band shell, three minutes' walk away. As he approached, he checked the time: 12:46 AM. He took a seat in the front row of the benches and waited.

In the few minutes remaining, he reviewed how he had come to this point in his life. During all his time in prison, he had avoided any violence but what was necessary to keep from being bullied, and after he had been discharged from parole he swore to himself that he would not ever do anything that might return him to prison. Curly had destroyed all that for him—first, with intimations of friendship, then by crude threats, then by the raid on Laurence's bank account. He admitted to himself that he had willingly cooperated with Curly, but he had rapidly grown sick of him. He had promised that if he ever saw the man again, he would kill him, and now he was at that point, and he wasn't sure he could go through with it.

Still, he had brought no money to give Curly, so unless he was allowed to walk away, he would have to take steps.

He heard no footsteps, but then suddenly, Curly sat down beside him.

"Evening," he said. "I've got something for you." He reached into a bag and pulled out a stack of hundreds, secured with a rubber band. "Here's the fifteen grand I took from you, maybe with a bit more for interest."

Butch was flabbergasted. He took the money and set it on the bench beside him. "Where'd you get it?"

"A friend and I made a score earlier tonight. This was my share."

"Well, shit, Curly," Butch said, "that's damned good of you. I hadn't ever expected to see it again."

"I'm hitting the road, and I've got more than enough to get me there," Curly said. "There's a girl, too. She lives in Florida, and that's where I'm headed. I think I've had it with New York and New York's had it with me."

"Well, Curly," Butch said, "I wish you and your girl every happiness." He took the .25 automatic from his pocket, pointed it at Curly's right temple, and fired.

Curly collapsed sideways onto the bench and lay very still. Butch picked up the black bag, stuffed the money Curly had given him into it, then looked into the other bag he had brought with him; he was sure that the computer contained information about their raid on Laurence's bank account. He found Curly's MacBook Air laptop and put that into the black bag with the money. He went through Curly's pockets and there was nothing of note except a snub-nosed pistol, which he dropped on the ground next to the body; then he got up, tucked the black bag under his arm, and walked out of the park.

He walked home, stopping at a garbage can to smash the laptop and hide it under the other trash, reckoning there might be some reference to him in the contents, then he walked home.

During the remainder of his walk, he unloaded and dismantled the small gun and dropped pieces of it and the remaining ammunition and his raincoat and gloves in trash cans along his route.

BACK AT HIS BUILDING he found the lobby empty and took the elevator to his floor. He then pressed the lobby button and let it descend back to the lobby. He let himself into his apartment, switched on the kitchen lights, and examined his clothing for blood spatter, but the raincoat and gloves had taken it all; he was clean.

He went into the living room and emptied the black bag onto the dining table. A quick count told him there was a little over fifty thousand dollars there. He would add that to his safe-deposit box tomorrow. He hid the bag in a kitchen drawer.

He was overwhelmed with relief at having removed the only obstacle to his success and happiness, and he fell into bed exhausted and slept soundly.

58

DINO FOLLOWED VIV into the rear seat of his city-owned SUV, and as his escorting policeman closed the door his cell phone rang. "Probably Stone to see if we're on time," he said, putting the phone to his ear. "Bacchetti." As he listened, his expression changed. "Be there shortly," he said.

Viv looked at him. "What?"

"We've got ourselves a double murder," Dino said. "Let's go into Central Park, Seventy-second Street entrance, then turn left to the band shell."

The car entered the park and left the road, driving down the broad sidewalk until he came to the yellow police tape. "I shouldn't be long," he said to Viv as he got out. Out of habit he clipped his badge to his jacket pocket, though every cop on the scene knew him by sight. "What've we got here?" he asked a detective.

"One stiff," the man replied. "It's somebody you're interested in."

Dino walked around the body on the bench and looked at the face. "That would appear to be one Marvin Jones," he said.

"His ID confirms that identity, plus a couple of others," the detective replied.

"I was told it was a double homicide," Dino said. "Where's the other one?"

"In a pawnshop in the Nineties."

"A murder-suicide?"

"The other stiff is Irving Schwartz, the guy Jones was with when they broke into the Barrington house, the one who turned up at Lenox Hill with a bullet wound to the ass."

"Ah." Dino pointed at the .38 lying on the ground near the bench. "Would that be the murder weapon?"

"It would appear to be of the same caliber as Schwartz's head wound."

Dino peered closely at the hole in Jones's temple. "I don't think that was made by a .38."

"That's the puzzle, Commissioner. The murder and the apparent suicide appear to have been accomplished with different weapons."

"So where's the smaller caliber one?"

"It probably left with the shooter."

"So he stages a suicide, then leaves the scene with the weapon? That's not very smart."

"Well, it does leave us with less to go on in solving this one, so it's not completely stupid of the guy."

"Any evidence left of the departing shooter?"

"Not a thing. There was some rain, but the area around the band shell is all paved, so no footprints."

Dino pointed. "What's in the bag?"

"Not much—nothing that would help us. Thing is, the owner of the pawnshop says a hundred and fifty grand was taken from his safe, but neither Schwartz nor Jones is in possession of it."

"Well, first of all, I can't see a pawnshop holding that kind of money. Thirty or forty, maybe, so that bit of testimony is probably meant for his insurance company."

"It gives us a robbery motive for this shooting, though."

"Was there a third guy involved in the robbery?"

"Not that we have found any evidence of. The only thing missing from the pawnshop safe was the cash. They left the jewelry."

"So why would the other two come to Central Park? They could have divvied up the cash on the spot."

"I think what we've got is two robberies and two murders," the detective said.

"So where does the third guy come in? I mean, he was certainly here, so he and Jones must have planned to meet, but why Central Park at what time?"

"ME says between midnight and two AM."

"I guess it's lonely enough." Dino looked around. "Well, I'm on my way out of town, so I don't have time to solve this for you."

The detective laughed. "I guess not."

"I'll be back in a few days. Try to have it wrapped up by then." He started to go then hesitated. "Check Jones's prison record. Find out who his buddies were—that might be a start."

"I'll do that, Commissioner. Thanks for the suggestion."

"Don't mention it. Have a good time." Dino walked back to the car and got in. "Teterboro, as originally planned," he said to his driver.

"What was it?" Viv asked.

"A guy named Marvin Jones, who was in Stone's house the night of the Strategic Services party. Also, the other guy who was there, but he's dead in a pawnshop uptown, and the two of them were shot with different weapons."

"That's weird."

"Yeah, but it's the kind of thing that makes police work interesting," Dino replied.

STONE WAS NEARLY FINISHED with his preflight inspection, with Holly looking over his shoulder, when Dino and Viv arrived.

"Good morning," Stone said.

"Good morning," Dino replied.

"You can put your luggage up front."

Dino did so. "Sorry we're a little late. As I was leaving the house, I got a call about a double homicide."

"Anybody we know?"

"As it happens, yes. The victims were the guys who attempted the burglary at your house, Marvin Jones and his buddy Irving Schwartz, late of the ER at Lenox Hill, where he presented with a gunshot wound to the ass."

"Who did us the favor?"

"It appears that Jones put a round into Schwartz at a pawnshop in the East Nineties, after Schwartz had cracked the safe. Jones then turned up at the band shell in Central Park, an apparent suicide."

"I get the motive for shooting Schwartz. What was his motive for offing himself?"

"I don't think he had one. His so-called suicide was effected with a small-caliber shot to the right temple, while Schwartz got it with a .38, ballistics pending. There was a motive—the cash was missing from both scenes."

Stone thought about that. "So Jones was murdered by a third party?"

"It would appear so, and he took the small-caliber with him, along with all the money."

"How much money?"

"The pawnbroker claims over a hundred grand, but that's just what he told his insurance company. I suspect it was a lot less."

"Any leads on the identity of the third party?"

"None."

"I'd check on his prison associates. These guys don't have a wide acquaintance among civilians when they get out."

"Already being done."

"Nothing to keep us here?"

"Zip."

"Then let's go to Santa Fe." Stone locked the forward luggage compartment, opened the cabin door, and ushered Dino and Viv aboard.

"You're flying right seat in the cockpit," he said to Holly.

"Gotcha," she said, climbing aboard and taking her seat.

Stone climbed in, secured the stairs, and entered the cockpit. He ran through his checklist, got a clearance from the tower, and taxied to the runway.

Ten minutes later, they left the ground and were given a vector to the west. Stone set his assigned altitude of 40,000 feet into the autopilot, switched it on, and allowed it to take over the flying.

"Could you hand me the *Times* crossword?" he asked Holly. "It's in my flight bag."

"Sure."

Stone switched on the satellite radio and tuned it to the classical channel. They climbed to altitude with Mozart in their headsets.

"We'll have the sun behind us all the way," Stone said.

AUTHOR'S NOTE

I am happy to hear from readers, but you should know that if you write to me in care of my publisher, three to six months will pass before I receive your letter, and when it finally arrives it will be one among many, and I will not be able to reply.

However, if you have access to the Internet, you may visit my website at www.stuartwoods.com, where there is a button for sending me e-mail. So far, I have been able to reply to all my e-mail, and I will continue to try to do so.

If you send me an e-mail and do not receive a reply, it is probably because you are among an alarming number of people who have entered their e-mail address incorrectly in their mail software. I have many of my replies returned as undeliverable.

Remember: e-mail, reply; snail mail, no reply.

When you e-mail, please do not send attachments, as I never

open these. They can take twenty minutes to download, and they often contain viruses.

Please do not place me on your mailing lists for funny stories, prayers, political causes, charitable fund-raising, petitions, or senti-mental claptrap. I get enough of that from people I already know. Generally speaking, when I get e-mail addressed to a large number of people, I immediately delete it without reading it.

Please do not send me your ideas for a book, as I have a policy of writing only what I myself invent. If you send me story ideas, I will immediately delete them without reading them. If you have a good idea for a book, write it yourself, but I will not be able to advise you on how to get it published. Buy a copy of *Writer's Market* at any book-store; that will tell you how.

Anyone with a request concerning events or appearances may e-mail it to me or send it to: Publicity Department, Penguin Random House LLC, 375 Hudson Street, New York, NY 10014.

Those ambitious folk who wish to buy film, dramatic, or television rights to my books should contact Matthew Snyder, Creative Artists Agency, 9830 Wilshire Boulevard, Beverly Hills, CA 98212-1825.

Those who wish to make offers for rights of a literary nature should contact Anne Sibbald, Janklow & Nesbit, 445 Park Avenue, New York, NY 10022. (Note: This is not an invitation for you to send her your manuscript or to solicit her to be your agent.)

If you want to know if I will be signing books in your city, please visit my website, www.stuartwoods.com, where the tour schedule will be published a month or so in advance. If you wish me to do a book signing in your locality, ask your favorite bookseller to contact his Penguin representative or the Penguin publicity department with the request.

If you find typographical or editorial errors in my book and feel an irresistible urge to tell someone, please write to Sara Minnich at Penguin's address above. Do not e-mail your discoveries to me, as I will already have learned about them from others.

A list of my published works appears in the front of this book and on my website. All the novels are still in print in paperback and can be found at or ordered from any bookstore. If you wish to obtain hardcover copies of earlier novels or of the two nonfiction books, a good used-book store or one of the online bookstores can help you find them. Otherwise, you will have to go to a great many garage sales.